SAULT

—WHAT COULD BE WORSE
THAN GREAT LAKES EROSION?

A NUMBER OF VERY WONDERFUL PEOPLE HELPED ME PREPARE THIS
BOOK FOR PUBLICATION. EACH CONTRIBUTED SIGNIFICANTLY. THANK
YOU EVIE, ANDY, STEVE, JOHN, EMALEE, CHARITY, GEORGE, AND GAY.

AS ALWAYS, A SPECIAL THANK YOU GOES TO LORA C. AND THE TAL-
ENTED MEMBERS OF GRAND VALLEY ARTISTS FOR THEIR HELP ON
COVER DESIGN.

SAULT

—WHAT COULD BE WORSE

THAN GREAT LAKES EROSION?

MICHAEL CARRIER

GREENWICH VILLAGE INK
AN IMPRINT OF ALISTAIR RAPIDS PUBLISHING
GRAND RAPIDS, MICHIGAN

SAULT

—WHAT COULD BE WORSE
THAN GREAT LAKES EROSION?

Published in 2020 by Greenwich Village Ink, an imprint of Alistair Rapids Publishing, Grand Rapids, MI.

Author can be emailed at michael.jon.carrier@gmail.com. You can follow Michael's tweets at @MikeCarrier999.

ISBN: 978-1-936092-08-6 (trade pbk)
Printed in the United States of America

Library of Congress Cataloging-in-Publication Data

Carrier, Michael.
    SAULT / by Michael Carrier. 1st ed.
ISBN: 978-1-936092-08-6 (trade pbk. : alk. paper)
1. Hard Boiled Thriller 2. Mystery 3. Thriller 4. Novel 5. Murder 6. Burglary 7. Lake Superior. 8. Michigan's Upper Peninsula. 9. Deadwood. Singapore.

DISCLAIMER: None of the books in either the "Getting to Know Jack" or "Jack's Justice" series represent true stories—they are all works of fiction. All characters, names, situations and occurrences are purely the product of the author's imagination. Any resemblance to actual events, or persons (living or dead) is totally coincidental.

What people are saying about the "Getting to Know Jack" series

I f you enjoy this book you should consider reading the other books in this series. And, I would appreciate a short review on Amazon. You can do this by going to this book's page on Amazon. It is not necessary to have purchased the book from Amazon, only to have an Amazon account. Thanks, Michael.

Top Shelf Murder Mystery—Riveting. Being a Murder-Mystery "JUNKIE" this book is definitely a keeper ... can't put it down ... read it again type of book... and it is very precise to the lifestyles in Upper Michigan. Very well researched. I am a resident of this area. His attention to detail is great. I have to rate this book in the same class or better than authors Michael Connelly, James Patterson, and Steve Hamilton. — Shelldrakeshores

Being a Michigan native, I was immediately drawn to this book. Michael Carrier is right in step with his contemporaries James Patterson and David Baldacci. I am anxious to read more of his work. I highly recommend this one! — J. Henningsen

A fast and interesting read. Michael ends each chapter with a hook that makes you want to keep reading. The relationship between father and daughter is compelling. Good book for those who like a quick moving detective story where the characters often break the "rules" for the greater good! I'm looking forward to reading the author's next book. — Flower Lady

Move over Patterson, I now have a new favorite author, Jack and his daughter make a great tag team, great intrigue, and diversions. I have a cabin on Sugar Island and enjoyed the references to the locations. I met the author at Joey's (the real live Joey) coffee shop up on the hill, great writer, good stuff. I don't usually finish a book in the course of a week, but read this one in two sittings so it definitely had my attention. I am looking forward to the next installment. Bravo. — Northland Press

My husband is not a reader— he probably hasn't read a book since his last elementary school book report was due. But ... he took my copy of *Murder on*

Sugar Island to deer camp and read the whole thing in two days. After he recommended the book to me, I read it— being the book snob that I am, I thought I had the whole plot figured out within the first few pages, but a few chapters later, I was mystified once again. After that surprise ending, we ordered the other two Getting to Know Jack books. — Erin W.

I enjoyed this book very much. It was very entertaining, and the story unfolded in a believable manner. Jack Handler is a likable character. But you would not like to be on his wrong side. Handler made that very clear in *Jack and the New York Death Mask*. This book (*Murder on Sugar Island*) was the first book in the Getting to Know Jack series that I read. After I read Death Mask, I discovered just how tough Jack Handler really was.

I heard that Carrier is about to come out with another Jack Handler book—a sequel to *Superior Peril*. I will read it the day it becomes available. And I will undoubtedly finish it before I go to bed. If he could write them faster, I would be happy. — Deborah M.

I thoroughly enjoyed this book. I could not turn the pages fast enough. I am not sure it was plausible but I love the characters. I highly recommend this book and look forward to reading more by Michael Carrier. — Amazon Reader

An intense thrill ride!! — Mario

Michael Carrier has knocked it out of the park. — John

Left on the edge of my seat after the last book, I could not wait for the next chapter to unfold and Michael Carrier did not disappoint! I truly feel I know his characters better with each novel and I especially like the can-do/will-do attitude of Jack. Keep up the fine work, Michael, and may your pen never run dry! — SW

The Handlers are at it again, with the action starting on Sugar Island, I am really starting to enjoy the way the father/daughter and now Red are working through the mind of Michael Carrier. The entire family, plus a few more, are becoming the reason for the new sheriff's increased body count and antacid intake. The twists and turns we have come to expect are all there and then some. I'm looking for the next installment already. — Northland Press

Finally, there is a new author who will challenge the likes of Michael Connelly and David Baldacci. — Island Books

If you like James Patterson and Michael Connelly, you'll love Michael Carrier. Carrier has proven that he can hang with the best of them. It has all of the great, edge-of-your-seat action and suspense that you'd expect in a good thriller, and it kept me guessing to the very end. Fantastic read with an awesome detective duo—I couldn't put it down! — Katie

Don't read Carrier at the beach or you are sure to get sunburned. I did. I loved the characters. It was so descriptive you feel like you know everyone. Lots of action—always something happening. I love the surprise twists. All my friends are reading it now because I wouldn't talk to them until I finished it so they knew it was good. Carrier is my new favorite author! — Sue

Thoroughly enjoyed this read — kept me turning page after page! Good character development and captivating plot. Had theories but couldn't quite solve the mystery without reading to the end. Highly recommended for readers of all ages. — Terry

* * *

Here are the Amazon links to my previous books in the Jack Handler Saga:

Getting to Know Jack Series

Jack and the New York Death Mask:	http://amzn.to/MVpAEd
Murder on Sugar Island:	http://amzn.to/1u66DBG
Superior Peril:	http://amzn.to/LAQnEU
Superior Intrigue:	http://amzn.to/1jvjNSi
Sugar Island Girl Missing in Paris:	http://amzn.to/1g5c66e
Wealthy Street Murders:	http://amzn.to/1mb6NQy
Murders in Strangmoor Bog:	http://amzn.to/1IEUPxX

Jack's Justice Series

Ghosts of Cherry Street:	http://amzn.to/2n3lrRf
Assault on Sugar Island:	http://amzn.to/2n3vcyL
Dogfight:	http://amzn.to/2F7OkoM
Murder at Whitefish Point:	http://amzn.to/2CxlAmC
Super Shoal:	https://amzn.to/3dTZE9o
Deadwood to Deep State:	https://amzn.to/3bSjwba
Sault:	

Jack Unleashed
(New Series Starting in the Fall of 2020, with "To China with Love" the first title.)

Sault is the Fourteenth Book in the Jack Handler Saga

Characters throughout the Jack Handler saga remain largely the same. Jack Handler, a retired Chicago Homicide detective who now works as a private security contractor and lives on Sugar Island in Michigan's Upper Peninsula, is always the main character. If you would like more information on the various characters, you can turn to the back of this book to find a section called: "Main Characters." It provides a brief description of all the main characters, including Jack himself.

A second character that appears in all the books is Jack's daughter, Kate Handler. She is a beautiful, single woman, who works as a homicide detective in New York City. She, through the course of the saga, has been promoted to the rank of lieutenant.

Red is also a main character starting in "Murder on Sugar Island." Red is a fourteen-year-old boy who has become a foster son in the Jack Handler household. Red is normal for his age, but is special in the respect that, due to a physical injury, cannot speak.

Red is joined by another fourteen-year-old boy (Robby) as a foster son to Jack in the third book of the saga: "Superior Peril." These two boys live, "work", do school, and share amazing adventures with Jack Handler throughout all the subsequent books in the saga.

But, those are not the only ones to be living at the Handler Sugar Island Resort. Before Red came into the picture, he had a wonderful golden retriever named Buddy. And Buddy moved in with Jack as well.

Chapter 1

Late August
At The Mouth of the Au Sable River

Because the prevailing Huron currents flow from north
to south, it seemed logical for Jack and Henry to begin
their search at the mouth of the Au Sable River as it
empties into Lake Huron.

The September air felt cold. A southeast wind was blowing
briskly at a fairly constant ten to fourteen mile-per-hour clip. But,
it was the unseasonable temperature that created the discomfort.
The thermometer at Jack Handler's rented motorhome registered
a chilly forty-two degrees.

"Damn," Jack mumbled to himself, "*it isn't even autumn yet.
This weather is more like something I'd expect to see in mid-Oc-
tober, or maybe even November.*"

With shoreline maps spread out before them on the galley
table in the thirty-three-foot Airstream, Jack and his good friend
Henry—AKA Chuchip Kalyesveh—were sketching out their plans
for the next four days, and beyond if necessary. The task at hand
for the two of them was to carry out an exhaustive "man search"
along the western shore of Lake Huron, from the mouth of the Au
Sable River, south along the shore, and then to some of the nearby
islands. Both men understood that if they were not successful on

the first day, they would move their operation south a notch and launch a similar effort on the next day, and then again on the following. They resolved that the only event that could put an end to their search was success.

The purpose driving their challenging efforts—they were searching for *anything* that might provide some clue as to the whereabouts of a group of young anglers, their leader, Jack's two fourteen-year-old foster boys—Red and Robby, and the Handlers' beloved quasi-human companion, their Golden Retriever named Buddy. While Red and Robby were not a regular part of the Boy Scout troop, Jack had given them permission to go fishing with the group while he and Henry engaged themselves in a very dangerous mission in New York City—one sanctioned by Secret Service Agent Roger Minsk.

The fishing trip, while not officially authorized by the Boy Scouts, was organized by Jack's friend Ted Klanoski—AKA *Legend*. Accompanying them on the one-week *End of Summer* camping/fishing trip out in Michigan's Huron National Park were Legend's five Boy Scouts. His plan was for them to go fly-fishing in the Au Sable during the day, and then to spend the nights in a large cabin that was owned by the parents of one of Legend's Boy Scouts. At least, that's how it all was supposed to go when Legend outlined his plans to Jack.

But, when Henry dropped the boys and Buddy off at the cabin, he learned that Legend was now thinking about taking the boys out to some of the neighboring islands, such as Charity Island, Little Charity Island, and Gull Island—all small islets located a few miles off the western shore of Lake Huron.

The Au Sable, which is a major tributary to Lake Huron, drains a north-south area that includes nearly two thousand square miles in north-central Lower Michigan. Running from Grayling to the big lake to the east, the basin is almost one hundred miles long and up to thirty miles wide. It encompasses parts of eight counties, and most of the Huron National Forest.

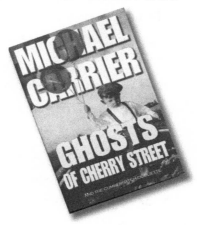

If you would like to learn more about "Legend," that character is developed in the Jack Handler thriller: Amazon Best Seller *Ghosts of Cherry Street*

Jack's plan dictated that he would walk the shore from the river—which empties into Lake Huron just south of Oscoda—southward to Whitestone Point. While Jack was searching the shore, Henry would start the day out by piloting a large Zodiac Rigid-Hull Navy Seal type Inflatable raiding craft out to the small islands mentioned by Legend.

Jack and Henry had earlier surveyed the area by air, searching from a distance of about a thousand feet for anything that might suggest the group was safe, or even still alive. They saw nothing that gave them hope.

The plan was for Henry to first search the largest of the three islands—Charity Island. He would be looking for any signs of life, or even anything that would suggest the group might have visited the island.

Once that phase was completed, Henry would then steer his boat out to Gull Island, which was shown by the map to be just off the southern tip of Charity Island. Unfortunately, when the men did the fly-over, due to the enormous surge of water, they were unable to find any visible group of rocks or trees at the coordinates listed for Gull Island.

"The surge totally ate up Gull Island!" Henry exclaimed at the time. "Little or nothing is showing where that island supposedly used to be."

Gull Island was the principal piece of real estate where Legend had suggested they might go to fish, as he had been there before with his uncle. Even though they had not spotted anything from the air, Jack thought again that Henry might find something helpful by a 'boots on the ground' search.

From Gull Island it was only a short distance to Little Charity Island. There Henry would perform the same search as he did on the other two islands.

If, at any point, either Jack or Henry were to find evidence suggesting that the group had been to any of the places they were searching, he would relay his findings to the other. Of course, each was equipped with a cell phone, but experience had taught them that a redundant means of communication was always desirable in an emergency. Plus, cell phones relied totally upon nearby towers, and they both knew that the accessibility of towers was not always a possibility. Unfortunately, the range of portable point-to-point radios was severely limited to under two miles.

The Zodiac rigid inflatable they rented was large enough to

transport nine fighting Navy Seals, plus a crew of three. While this amounted to a lot of boat for Henry to power around in by himself, they had made the decision that it would be better to have a boat large enough to accommodate the rescue of the whole group at the same time, were they to find the boys trapped in a distressing situation.

The plan also dictated that should Henry satisfy himself that he had thoroughly completed his search of the islands, and if he were to come up empty, he would return to aid Jack in the land search.

Buddy and the boys had now been missing for over one full day—ever since the monstrous early September freighter explosion took out the Poe Lock, and virtually decimated the northeastern section of Michigan's Upper Peninsula. While the blast was almost immediately deemed to have been nuclear, by virtue of its enormous force, those responsible for the horrendous explosion were not known. At least, as is the case with many horrific terrorist attacks, no one had as yet stepped forward to take credit for it.

While the identity of the evil ones responsible for all the devastation in the North Country weighed heavily on Jack's mind, he understood that for the "right now" he needed to concentrate all of his thoughts and energies on one single goal—locating and rescuing the group of missing friends and fishermen, and his two boys in particular. So that is exactly what he and Henry set about doing.

Largely due to their presumption that the blast was nuclear, the Federal Government initially had ordered the total evacuation for a distance of thirty miles from ground zero. That included the entirety of Sugar Island, as well as the northern section of Neebish

Island, south to Rudyard, and west to Dollar Settlement.

The Canadian Government did the same for areas north of the border. They immediately established and strictly enforced a ban on all travel to or from Island Lake, east to Echo Bay, and west to Lake Superior. Operating under the assumption that a nuke was involved, both Canada and the U.S. initially banned all human contact with the waters of Lake Huron, as well as that of Lakes Erie and Ontario. Given that essentially all municipal drinking water—from the site of the explosion to the point where the Saint Lawrence River empties into the Atlantic Ocean—was drawn from these huge lakes, the humanitarian challenge presented by the attack seemed virtually insurmountable.

The situation facing residents along southern Lake Michigan and Lake Superior was substantially less impossible to deal with. Almost all of Lake Superior was largely spared destruction by virtue of the fact that the surface of its water stood twenty-one feet above that of Lake Huron. So, when the locks were destroyed, the flow out of Lake Superior was dramatic, thus carrying virtually all of the pollution south, past Sugar, Neebish, St. Joseph and Drummond Islands, and then eventually south and east into Lake Huron.

Initially there was a considerable backflow into Lake Michigan. That prompted the United States Army Corps of Engineers (USACE) to order the opening of all dams and locks affecting lake levels between Lake Ontario and the Atlantic Ocean. They did this because they feared that the backflow might, if it were seriously polluted with radiation, immediately kill off millions of fish in Lake Michigan. While this act totally ended all ship traffic from the Great Lakes eastward, it did substantially reduce the backflow into the southern portions of Lake Michigan. This eased the immediate pressures on the water filtration facilities for large municipal populations of Chicago and Milwaukee, and, at least for the short term, prevented the infiltration of backflow waters into the Mississippi River. This was of considerable early concern for the USACE, as the Chicago River flows from southern Lake Michigan down into the Mississippi River Basin.

Within hours after the relevant locks and dams along the Saint Lawrence Seaway were opened, allowing the free flow of Great Lakes water eastward, the United Nations Security Council was convened at the request of Russia. The stated concern was that by opening the Seaway floodgates the United States was committing the "gross act of carelessly and unnecessarily releasing dangerous amounts of radioactive pollution into the Atlantic Ocean, an international body of water. Therefore, the United States must be required to cease its attempt to drain the Great Lakes via the opening of various gates and damns associated with that system."

The Security Council consists of fifteen member nations—five permanent (the United States, China, France, Great Britain and Russia), and ten elected members. The vote was fourteen to one—the U.S. being the only member voting against the demand to close the fifteen locks to slow the flow of pollution into international waters. As one of the permanent members of the Council, the United States was able to block the motion via its veto power.

So, the polluted waters continued to flow out to the Atlantic Ocean.

Chapter 2

For the days leading up to the blast, both Jack and Henry had been fully engaged in an operation geared to ferreting out those responsible for the recent attempted assassination of POTUS—the President of the United States. That was fortunate for Jack and Henry, as it meant that they were not near the locks at the time of the blast. The explosion was so catastrophic that it not only took out both the upper and lower gates of the two primary locks—the Poe and the McArthur—it virtually decimated the entire city of Sault Ste. Marie on both the American and Canadian sides. Not only did it catastrophically damage the city, but it also caused severe damage at the Handler resort on nearby Sugar Island. While numerous residents of the island were killed or severely injured, those physically able to escape were prevented from doing so because the enormous surge not only destroyed the ferry that serviced the island, but it rendered most smaller vessels useless.

For the first days following the blast, no one was permitted to venture onto the island because of the feared radiation pollution. Fly-overs and satellite imaging suggested that perhaps only about half of the million or so sugar maples on the island remained totally unscathed—much of the damage being caused by the numerous late season forest fires birthed by the blast.

In addition to the immense damage wreaked on Sugar Island by the explosion itself, the rapid release of the twenty-one-foot wall of water inundated the island's entire west shore—this included several of the river-front buildings at the Handler resort.

On the positive side, the surge of water struck so suddenly that it rapidly extinguished many of the flames caused by the bomb's curtain of fire. Of course, the flash flood on Sugar and Neebish Islands went unnoticed by human eyes, because anyone occupying space near the St. Mary's River at the time would have been immediately incapacitated by the incredible force of the initial shock wave.

The crater produced by the blast itself was enormous. While its depth was impossible to immediately determine in any precise way, it was estimated to have been between one hundred and two hundred feet deep. Given the fact that the composition of the matter that lies beneath the locks was known to be solid rock, the likelihood of the depth of destruction being much greater than two hundred feet was small—regardless of the strength or nature of the device. And besides, the early abundance of concern regarding the possibility that the device used was nuclear resulted in the hesitancy to rush the inspectors onto the scene.

Initially, Secret Service Agent Roger Minsk had told Jack that, on the basis of his inside information, the U.S. Department of Defense suspected that if the bomb used was some sort of nuclear device, it was likely of Russian origin, probably part of their stockpile that apparently went missing after the fall of the Soviet Union. However, Roger also explained to Jack that "nothing definitive was yet known concerning the nature of the blast, nor had anyone yet taken credit for it."

Roger had known Jack for decades, and had used him on many of the "special missions" to which he (Roger) had been assigned. Such had been the case regarding the mission that had just taken Jack and Henry to New York; and only weeks before that, on a very important top-secret mission overseas. In fact, Roger had deemed that earlier mission to be of such critical importance that he chose himself to accompany Jack on it—and in so doing, was severely injured.

The foreign mission that nearly proved fatal for Roger involved a trip to Singapore where the two of them labored to save POTUS from an assassination attempt by Deep State operatives. The mission had been ordered by former President Bob Fulbright, who had of late become the *de facto* leader of the so-called *Loyal Governmental Forces* (generally referred to as the LGF, or just the *Loyalists*) that were aligned against the *Deep State*.

"Deep State," a term that was originally coined to denote a virtually secretive governing apparatus in Turkey, has in recent years been applied to certain aspects of what is sometimes referred to as a *nefarious shadow government* here in the United States. It is thought to be composed of various members of leadership within the military, intelligence services, judiciary, and even possibly involving members of "organized crime."

While it was not generally thought that this North Country bombing was the work of the Deep State, some of Fulbright's closest allies were openly suggesting that members of the opposition had foreign connections that could readily have procured a nuclear weapon from subversive Russian operatives, and then engineered the delivery and detonation of the device themselves.

"Why would the Deep State even consider such a perverse

affront to the U.S. Government and our way of life?" Fulbright asked. "Because Deep State was so profoundly humiliated by its failed attempt to take out POTUS in Singapore," was the answer.

The fact remained that all theories relating to origins, at this point, were based on conjecture and not sound evidence. However, after experiencing the highly sophisticated—and nearly successful—assassination attempt on the life of the current President, no one could totally dissuade the Loyalists from at least considering this sort of thinking. For one thing, the complex type of weapon alone virtually eliminated the likelihood, if not even the very possibility, of the blast having been the work of Islamic terrorists—like those responsible for the 911 attacks.

All indications were, even at this early stage, that the bomb used was a nuclear device of some sort. Initial speculation reached that conclusion by virtue of two bits of evidence: First of all, its tremendous strength. The explosion was estimated to have been equal to about one-half that of the bomb that exploded over Hiroshima in 1945, the event effectively ending World War II. That bomb was determined to be equal to fifteen thousand tons of TNT—or 15 KT. The largest known conventional weapon in the U.S. arsenal was the bomb known as MOAB—the acronym for The GBU-43/B Massive Ordnance Air Blast explosive device. The bomb that acronym designated came to be "affectionately" known as the "Mother of All Bombs."

Two weeks after the explosion, one of Jack's neighbors on Sugar Island described it like this to Jack over coffee:

"It was close to midnight at the time the bomb was dropped. I was out back of my house convincing Burt, my two-year-old Husky, to make his before-bed contribution. And, since I had to be outside with him, I thought I'd drop my axe on a few pieces of firewood. I have to say, I felt the blast as much as I saw and heard it, you know. I figure my house is about ten miles from the locks. That's quite a ways. But, I still felt the heat of the blast on the side of my face. And the rumble. Never heard anything like that before in my whole life. And the ground shook beneath my feet. Burt ran inside—tail between his legs. I immediately made a beeline to a clearing so I could check around to see if I could figure out what was happening. I sensed that it was coming from the direction of the Soo Locks, but it sounded much too close for that. And then I saw the huge cloud. Even though it was dark, it shined like a light bulb. I just knew it was a nuclear explosion. But, I couldn't figure out for the life of me why anyone would drop an *atomic bomb* on the Sugar Island Ferry, or even on the Soo Locks, for that matter. Confused the hell outta me. … It *was* an atom bomb, you know. Don't let anyone tell you different. I was there. It was an atom bomb. And the damage. Have you gone over there to take a look? They got it cordoned off, of course, but I got through with a buddy of mine. I couldn't believe it. Every ore carrier, or boat of any decent size, they were all laying on their side—all the way from the International Bridge into Whitefish Bay. They're either setting on the bottom, or they're on their side. Millions and millions of dollars just wasting away. … And bodies. My friend told me that they're still finding bodies. Still! … Trust me, it was an atom bomb. Just like at Hiroshima."

Jack knew that it had not yet been determined whether or not it was a nuclear explosive device, but he was not about to debate his friend regarding it.

Each cylindrical device was physically huge. At nearly four feet in diameter, and over thirty feet in length, it was larger in size and weight than the combined physical dimensions of both nuclear devices exploded over Japan. Yet, a single MOAB generated only about .011 of a kiloton of TNT, while the smaller of the bombs used over Japan was estimated at around 15 kilotons of TNT. If a MOAB type device were used to blow up the Soo Locks, while one such bomb would take out the Poe Lock, it would not have produced such a devastatingly large crater, nor would it have destroyed the whole city of Sault Ste. Marie.

In addition to its strength, the second element that was suggesting its being nuclear was the fact that substantial evidence of radioactivity was detected throughout the area immediately after the blast.

Eventually, it was thought that forensics would likely be able to accurately determine the composition, type and origin of the device. However, for safety reasons, it would be some time before scientists would be permitted to examine the site up close.

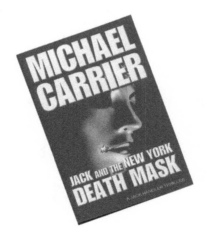

While I do not recommend that a reader start with *Jack and the New York Death Mask*, I do advocate that before you move on to my second series, that you check this book out. My first series (Getting to Know Jack) consists of seven books. The same is true of the second series (Jack's Justice). All fourteen books are available at better bookstores, and on Amazon.com.

Chapter 3

Another aspect of the scene that complicated the process of acquiring accurate evidence resulted from physical positioning of the device when it exploded. In order to exact maximum damage to the locks, those responsible for the attack placed the explosive device at the very bottom of the canal and adjacent to the concrete lock wall. This meant that when the bomb was detonated, it was beneath a fully loaded thousand-foot ore carrier, plus between twenty-five and forty feet of water, as the lock was in the process of dropping the water level to accommodate the east-bound freighter. While most of the water in the lock at the time of the explosion would have been instantly vaporized or displaced by the blast, as would the rock at the bottom of the lock and the concrete walls enclosing it, the air above and around ground zero would not have been as directly involved as is normally the case with a bomb exploded above the ground. Therefore, the molecular composition of fallout debris would have been significantly corrupted by the inordinate amount of vaporized water and subterranean materials that this explosion produced. The corrupted nature of this explosion was going to make scientific analysis to determine the bomb's DNA much more difficult.

It would be impossible to overstate the consternation Jack sensed upon learning that his two precious fourteen-year-old foster boys were missing on a fishing trip somewhere on Lake Huron. And, to make this nightmare even worse, some very noteworthy governmental experts were convinced that the huge surge of water, the one Jack feared had swept the boys away, was caused when some yet to be named "terrorists" detonated a nuclear device taking out the locks and dams that held back the waters of Lake Superior. To say the least, Jack's frustration was immense and well founded.

Had a nuclear device exploded in the air above the target, as is typically the case in war, the task of fallout analysis would have been much easier and substantially more predictable and reliable because it would have contained fewer isotopes. However, had the attackers opted for an above-the-surface detonation, while damage to the lock would still have been substantial, the explosion might have left intact much of the supporting bedrock beneath the lock, plus, it might not have totally destroyed the lock's sidewalls. And that was obviously not what the attackers wanted.

Another element that could have factored into the perpetrators' selection of a below-the-surface-explosion scenario might have been that they actually sought the added benefit of creating a situation more conducive to guarding their anonymity.

There was one more aspect of this bombing that was to prove dramatically atypical. While initially it went undetected, subsequent investigation eventually showed that the attack actually involved the use of two explosive devices. One of them was attached on the bottom of the huge iron ore carrier, and was then deposited, along with the ship itself, on the bottom of the Poe Lock before detonation. The purpose of that first bomb was to not only totally destroy the upper and lower gates of the lock, but also to exact as much damage to the lock's rock foundation as possible.

The second device was detonated in a secret compartment constructed near the pilothouse on this same one-thousand-foot ore carrier. Engineers later determined that the system used to trigger the bombs was designed so that the bomb placed above the surface of the water would detonate approximately one-ten-thousandth of a second before the one on the bottom of the channel. That way the one on top could achieve its maximum destructive force above ground before the one below could destroy it.

It became clear that the bomb placed near the pilothouse was much smaller than the one attached to the bottom of the ship. When the upper device exploded, the force was all upward, while the very large lower device was protected by thousands of tons of hematite iron ore that filled the belly of the ship.

The fact that two bombs were employed in the attack eluded the inspectors of the forensic teams for over a year. Even though no one could sufficiently explain the enormous damage that was done both above and below the surface of the water, neither were any of the forensic scientists eager to posit the possibility that two bombs were utilized. One reason for their hesitation to introduce such a theory was the inherent difficulty involved in detonating two devices in such close proximity—geographical as well as chronological. Such a thing was not known to have ever been attempted before.

Both Jack and his friend Henry had determined that they would not call off their search until they were successful in finding the two boys and Buddy—no matter what it took, or how long. The fact that they might be placing themselves in danger of radioactive poisoning did not deter them in the slightest.

Eventually, however, FBI forensics was able to turn one of the culprits. He not only filled them in on many of the details that had initially eluded them, the turncoat actually testified against the other perpetrators. He explained just how it was that they were able to so successfully put two bombs into play—one above the surface, and one below—in order to achieve maximum destructive force. ... And, the secret witness admitted, their use of two devices was to complicate the efforts of the Government's investigation.

Plus, whenever a nuclear device explodes on or beneath the surface of the earth, the nature of the fallout is dramatically altered by the physical composition of the surrounding terrain. Quite the opposite is the case when an explosion occurs above the earth.

It was later learned that the culprits had tried but were unable to procure a nuclear weapon. So, they developed their plan based on using conventional explosive materials. While they were not able to get their hands on a bona fide nuclear device, they were able to procure from the Russian black market a few bars of spent nuclear fuel. What they decided to do was to use a smaller device, exploded above the surface, to spew a fairly generic form of radiation into the surrounding air and water in order to create a diversion, thereby leading initial forensic scientists to the erroneous conclusion that the blast was the result of an old Soviet Russian nuclear bomb.

But, at the same time, they wanted to exact maximum damage to the two main locks and to the locks' rock substructure. That meant that they had to devise a conventional explosive device hundreds of times more powerful than any non-nuclear device ever before detonated. This is how they did it.

On the pretense of repairing the hull of a one-thousand-foot iron ore carrier, they attached to the bottom of the ship eighteen rows of steel tubes—port to starboard. Each of those tubes was five feet in diameter and thirty feet long. They attached thirty rows of the tubes, stem to stern. Each was then packed tightly with eighteen tons of H6 explosive. H6 was chosen over TNT for two reasons: first of all, H6 is substantially more stable than TNT, therefore easier to work with and deploy. The second reason it was selected is that it is nearly fifty percent more powerful than pure TNT.

When the time came for the bomb to be detonated, they sailed the giant bomb-laden ship into the lock, west to east, just as they would under any normal circumstances. But, as the pumps began lowering the water in the lock, the "ship-bomb" began pumping water into itself until it rested on the bottom of the lock. The crewmen on board then exited the ore carrier and rapidly departed from the area. Once they were safely out of range, they triggered the monstrous explosion.

Further compounding Jack's frustration was the recent loss of his beautiful, very dear friend, Millie Star. Not only did Jack blame himself for her death—she was hunted down and fatally shot by a contract killer hired by one of Jack's Deep State enemies—but, now he took full responsibility for the frightful disappearance of his two boys.

What follows is the backstory behind the situation Jack now faces.

Chapter 4

September 7 (Four Days Earlier)

In preparation for his "business trip" to New York, Jack had driven down to Grand Rapids, MI, to look up "Legend"—otherwise known as a fishing guide extraordinaire, Boy Scout leader, and all around interesting fellow. Legend, a long-haired sixty-one-year-old former hippie, had earlier endeared himself to Jack as well as to Jack's two foster boys due to his genuine *bona fides* with regard to his honesty, and an astonishing knowledge of life in general. He had become a friend to Jack's boys during the time Jack was solving the mystery of the Wealthy Street Murder case.

Legend possessed more than a couple of personal attributes that Jack found exemplary. For one, Jack had been particularly impressed with Legend's energy and willingness to work hand-in-glove with him in his successful effort to crack the infamous Grand Rapids case involving the murder of a number of nurses. A second aspect Jack appreciated about Legend's character was his almost uncanny success in winning the admiration of Red, Robby, and even Buddy. This eccentric angler was reputed to have pulled an absolutely remarkable assortment of fish out of the Grand River—the river that runs directly through the middle of Michigan's second largest city. Not only had Jack learned about Legend's prowess directly from his new friend's own braggadocious mouth, but he had also heard similar stories from numerous members of the Grand Rapids community.

Jack found that all he needed to do was to mention Legend's name in passing, and various members of the circle would be off to the races in their effort to share the latest story about their mutual acquaintance. Among numerous other things, Jack learned that his newfound friend would regularly catch fish when and where no one else could. Jack soon came to understand and appreciate the reality behind the *legendary* stories attributed to the man known as "Legend."

For weeks after their "Wealthy Street Murders" adventure had been thoroughly resolved, all Red and Robby could talk about was their new friend—Legend. At first Jack made it a point to learn as much as he could about the man behind the stories. Initially, Jack took all this attention in his stride. But then, after a month of breakfast-table *Legend* chatter, he determined that he needed to get to the bottom of it. Because he had remained in contact with the very attractive female detective in the Grand Rapids Police Department—Det. Lindsay Hildebrandt—Jack determined that he would give her a call first to see what her take was on this somewhat eccentric unmarried fisherman.

"What do you think about Ted Klanoski?" Jack asked her virtually as soon as she picked up. "Legend, they call him. Do you consider Mr. Klanoski a trustworthy sort of man for my boys to be hanging out with? What do you think?"

"Well," she replied through a surprised smile. "It's really nice to be talking to you too. ... Long time, Jack, Don't you think?"

Det. Lindsay Hildebrandt had, for nearly a decade, been widowed from her murdered husband, who, until his death, had also been a detective in Grand Rapids. Jack recalled that Lindsay had been very instrumental in solving the case of the Wealthy Street Murders, and he knew he could trust her. And now that he was preparing to spend some time out East in an effort to track down the killer of Angel's mother—his good friend Millie Star—Jack wanted to find a totally safe place for his boys to hide out during the mission. While former President William Fulbright had eagerly volunteered to back him up and protect his family, Jack knew that bad things could happen to his boys if it became known that he was participating in the effort.

"Think you can get away for a bit?" Jack asked. "Maybe we could meet for a cup of coffee?"

"Love to," she said. "How about that coffee shop you liked when you were in town before. You know, the *Passion Place*? Can we meet there?"

"I knew you'd suggest that," Jack said. "That's where I'm at right now. I'm sitting in the upper level."

"Great, I'll look for you up there."

Fifteen minutes later Lindsay gave Jack a big smile as she walked up the steps carrying a cup of black coffee.

"Were you actually asking me if I trusted Legend with boys?" Lindsay asked as she sat down.

Jack observed an element of attitude protruding through the tone of her voice.

"I suppose that's how it *appears*," he said. "And I certainly do apologize for that. But you must realize that I haven't seen or spoken to either you or Mr. Klanoski in almost a year, I would guess. Time has a way of changing things. ... Let me explain where I'm coming from. I'm really not in a position to put it all out there.

I'm sure you are aware that not all my cases are limited to what might be considered a pedestrian matter—domestic murders, major thefts, etc. My current job happens to involve principals and matters that I simply cannot discuss—not even with someone I trust, like you. That's just the nature of it.

"Suffice it to say, without a doubt, if the characters I'm tracking down had any notion that I might be closing in, they would be inclined to strike back. And my boys just might end up being targeted. I am looking for a safe place for them to stay until I can wind this shit up. But, I want them to have fun as well. … I'm sure you understand where I'm coming from."

"Yeah, Jack. I totally get it. Sorry about my tone. … How can I help?"

What Jack was not totally aware of is that during the short time that Lindsay had worked with him she had begun to think of him as something more than just a co-worker. It had been with his help that she had begun to understand who it was who had killed her husband. Plus, Jack had shown her the respect she had never received from her superiors in the Grand Rapids Police Department. And so, once the case they had been working on was solved, she was not ready to emotionally release Jack when he moved on.

Even though Jack never discussed it, were someone to have asked him how he felt about Lindsay, he would either have refused to respond, or he would have admitted that he had "feelings" for the woman.

It was clear from her response to Jack's inquiry that to one degree or another, she had at one time shared a similar interest in him.

But that time had passed.

Jack began to see that he had touched a nerve, and so he sat silently for a moment.

Lindsay took a deep breath and picked up the conversation.

"I can assure you that Legend is one hundred percent safe to hang out with your boys," she said, now totally attitude-free. "In fact, he and I have been living together for a while now."

"No kidding!" Jack replied in a little shock. "I never saw *that* coming. Not that I didn't think he had it in him. It's just that he always struck me as a very independent sort of fellow. I never pictured him letting himself become domesticated. Not even a little. … What the hell kind of detective do you suppose that makes me?"

Lindsay laughed out loud.

"Hey, my friend," she said. "We both know what kind of detective you are. Maybe you just misjudged me a little. I really respect his desire to be … self-determining. I think that's what I grew to love about him. … You never knew my husband. But, he was a lot like Legend, at least in that respect. I guess you could say that we have that attribute in common—Legend and I. If he followed around behind me trying to figure out what he should say or do next, somehow based on how he was reading me at the time, it'd drive me nuts.

"And he is the same way about me. He does not expect me to agree with him about everything. In fact, a lot of time I don't. … *In fact*, half the time I don't even have the slightest idea what he is talking about. And that's all fine. For both of us.

"But, if I need *anything*, all I have to do is make him aware of it, and he's right there for me. I'm the same way with him. … And, let me assure you of one other thing. Legend is totally trustworthy in every aspect of his life. The man's got true character. Granted, sometimes he comes off a little strange. He can be a bit eccentric. But that's just the way he is. He has some ideas that probably not another human being on planet Earth shares with him. That doesn't bother him a bit. He looks at all the evidence before him, and makes a call. … I find his methodology refreshing. In fact, as a detective, that's what I strive for. 'Sublime objectivity.' That's what I call it."

Jack was greatly relieved to see Lindsay acting like her old self.

"So," Jack said. "Do you think that he might be open to taking the boys fishing for a few days? Or do you have any idea who might be open to such an adventure? I will certainly cover all expenses. It's just critical to me that I get the boys safely away from me for a few days. Maybe a week."

"Really?" Lindsay asked. "When? When would you like us to do this?"

Jack could not really believe what he had just heard. *I think she just volunteered to help out with the boys,* he thought, but did not articulate.

"Oh, hell, ASAP, I suppose you could say. This job is a big one. And dangerous. Timing is a critical component. If it runs any longer than a few days, I can arrange to have Kate—you remember Kate, my daughter? If it turns into anything longer, she can step in and take my place. Do you suppose something like *that* could be worked out?"

"Maybe," she said. "But that depends on whether or not you'd let them go fishing with us. We're about to take three or four local boys fishing on the east side of the state. In Lake Huron. By Oscoda. We're planning to be up there for five or six days. Or, until they get sick of it. Or *we* do. I'm thinking that Legend wouldn't mind if your boys went with us. Our family had owned a cottage up there since before my husband died. I sold it a couple years ago to a local family—a friend, and the grandfather of one of the boys that Legend takes fishing.

"The new owners agreed to let us use it whenever we wished—as long as they're not using it. We don't get up there every year. But Legend and I went a few months back, and we had a great time. He thought it'd be cool to take a few of the boys from the local scouting troop. It's a huge cottage. It could easily handle your two—no problem."

"The cottage might," Jack said. "But could *you*? Wouldn't all those boys drive you nuts? Not sure *I* could do it. In fact, I'm quite sure I would pass on it. I'd love to take my boys up there fishing. But I'd draw the line with teenage strangers."

"I wouldn't dream of tackling it on my own. But I think Legend just might. If he doesn't like the idea he'll have no problem telling me so. He never does anything he doesn't want to. He knows your boys. If he doesn't think it'll work he'll let me know. … Let me give him a call and find out."

Jack did not verbally respond, but he did smile and nod.

Lindsay began keying her phone.

"Ted. …"

Chapter 5

T ed. Bet you'll never guess who I'm having a cup of coffee with," Lindsay said. "Yeah, you know him … he's from the Upper Peninsula. I'll give you a hint. You always referred to him as *Sherlock Holmes. That* tell you anything?"

Lindsay switched her phone to speaker.

"You gotta be shittin' me!" Legend said. "You can't mean … what the hell's his name? I always called him *Sherlock.* Jack somethin'. Reacher. Is it Jack Reacher? Oh, hell no. Reacher is that Tom Cruise guy. … What the hell is his last name? Is that who you're talking about? Jack … somethin'?"

"Jack Handler, yeah. That's him."

"Jack Handler," Legend repeated. "Of course. … Well, I'll be damned. Put me on with him. Can you put me on with him? That SOB saved my life. Those assholes had buried me alive. Remember that? And those two boys of his. Uh … what was their names— Red, and Robby. Red's the one who didn't talk. And their dog— Buddy. That was their dog's name. Buddy. … Can you put Old Sherlock on?"

"He's on already. He's right here."

"Hey, Legend," Jack said. "Jack here. How ya doin'?"

"Damn, Jack. When I woke up this morning I never expected

to be talkin' to you today. What brings you down to our neck of the woods?"

"Actually, I drove down here to ask a favor of you. I'll pay you for it, of course. But I think you are one of the few people I'd trust to pull it off. I'm wondering if you'd be interested in taking my boys fishing for a few days. I'll cover whatever you say."

"You've been talking to Lindsay, haven't you," Legend said, laughing out loud. "She told you that we were taking a few of our neighborhood boys fishing next week. Right? She told you about that?"

"Yeah, she did tell me about it. But I had my mind set on you before I ever discussed it with her. The boys never stop talking about you. And I need to go out of town for a few days. Work. Kate will pick them up early if you need her to. But, for right now, and the next day or so, she's tied up. What do you think?"

"What does Lindsay say about it? Is she good with it?"

"I think it could be great," Lindsay said. "Jack's kids are both Tom Sawyer incarnates. They're naturals. I can cook for two more kids, no problem. But you have to make the final call. It's *totally* up to you."

"Hell, yes. I miss those two. And, like I said, they saved my life. … All right. Yes. They can go with us, but only under one condition. You still listening to me, Sherlock?"

"I'm still here," Jack said. "I can hear you. What's your condition?"

"Buddy. You can send the boys with us, but only if you can include Buddy with them. Because, actually, it was Buddy that saved my life. I would just love to see that dog again. Can Buddy come?"

"Absolutely," Jack said.

"Lindsay," Legend said. "Are you guys at the same place we always go? *Passion Place*. Is that where you are right now?"

"Yup. That's where we are. Do you have time to stop over?"

"Hell yes!" Legend replied. "I can be there in twenty. Order me a hot chocolate and I'll be there before you know it. Whipped cream ... my usual. I'll be over in a shake. ... When can you bring them down? They're still in the Upper Peninsula? Right? I'd assume, at least."

"We'll discuss logistics when you get here," Jack said. "But, however this works for you, it'll work for me. I'll make it work. We'll discuss it when you get here. ... By the way, Lindsay and I are sitting toward the back, on the upper level. We'll be watching for you."

"See you in a few," Legend said. "I can't wait to hear how you're doin'. And I have a lot of ideas for you. I've heard all about the high water up there. In the big lake—Lake Superior. I've got some ideas, and I'm eager to hear what you think about them. You still live on Sugar Island? How's it look there? The high water levels—are they affecting your place?"

"Our resort is on a hill," Jack replied. "Not the boathouse, of course. The water's a little up on it. ... But, I think everyone in the UP is feeling something. We can discuss that when you get here. I really appreciate your jumping right in here. Look forward to seeing you."

"He really likes you, you know," Lindsay said when the guys disconnected. "Ted means everything he says. He doesn't butter people up. When he tells you how much he thinks of you and your boys, he's telling the truth. I couldn't count the number of times he has brought up your dog. He truly credits Buddy with saving his life."

"Well, that part of the story is pretty much correct," Jack said through a broad grin. "I can recall it like yesterday when Buddy jumped out of our boat and made a beeline to where they had buried Legend. Fortunately, they didn't do a very good job at it, and Buddy was able to free his head almost immediately. I have to admit it—I thought your friend was a goner. Even though they were too damn lazy to dig a decent hole, had Legend not been unconscious when they covered him up, panic would have undoubtedly set in and he would have succumbed to suffocation."

"Chalk that one up to a miracle," Lindsay added. "Maybe even *The Hand of God*. Whatever it was that saved him, we'll just have to conclude that it just wasn't his time to die."

"You're right," Jack agreed. "I guess it wasn't his time."

"Shall I pick up his drink?" Jack asked. "I think I heard something about *hot chocolate*."

"He does drink hot chocolate with whipped cream," she replied. "But, he'll pick it up on his way in. If we get him one now, he'll end up with two. I just know how he thinks. If we get it now, it won't be hot enough for him."

Jack smiled.

"I should give you a head's up before he gets here," Lindsay said. "He likes me to use his given name when I address him. So I will refer to him as *Ted*. But anyone else—he's fine with Ted, or Legend. Almost everyone in Grand Rapids calls him Legend. And that's okay with him. So, do as you wish. Just because I call him Ted doesn't mean you and the boys have to."

Just then the front door opened, and the man walking in was greeted by the barista, "Hey. Legend. How's it goin'?"

"Hey, man," Legend replied. "Pretty good. How about you?"

"Good, man. It's goin' good. … Hey, I'm supposed to be meetin' some friends of mine here—Lindsay, and an old friend. Do you know where they're sittin'? They said something about being in the back, on the second level. Is that right?"

"I don't know *exactly* where they're sitting, but I did catch a glimpse of Lindsay heading up those steps. I'm sure they must be up there. Do you want me to pour you your regular? A hot chocolate? Whip cream?"

"That'd be great. Perfect."

Legend handed the barista a five-dollar bill, thanked him, took his drink and headed up the steps.

"Hey, Jack," Legend said from twenty feet away. "What a surprise to hear from you out of the blue like that. How you doin'?"

Jack stood to greet him. Jack was wearing his black leather jacket, a shirt tucked into a pair of denims, and his favorite black leather cowboy boots.

Legend had his typical very worn jean jacket over his favorite tee with the Rolling Stones graphic on the front, black jeans and engineer boots. He had, since Lindsay, cleaned up a bit with a trimmed beard, baseball cap and a tasteful new "Lindsay" tattoo on his left arm.

Lindsay sat there in her "detective-blue suit" unofficial uniform. Her blonde hair was cut a bit shorter, and the bob was now highlighted by a soft curl around her face. She still wore little makeup, so just a touch of lip-gloss and mascara was all she needed to accent her features. She seemed very happy to be sipping coffee with her best friend and Jack.

"Well I'll be damned, my friend," Jack said, obviously quite shocked with Legend's appearance. "You look ten years younger than you did the last time I talked to you. Must be Lindsay here is a good influence."

"It's just the haircut," Legend said, feigning humility through a big affected smile. "Lindsay here has been setting me up to give paid talks all around Kent County. Schools, libraries, and places like that. The title of my talk is, "Legend's Secrets for Fishing the Great Lakes." I have notes that I sell, too. Lindsay says it's my book—*Legend's Book* she calls it. But it's not a book. But I do get ten dollars apiece for them. And, the school or library pays me a little. They give me a check for like fifty, or seventy-five dollars, every time. At first I turned it down. Maybe I was a little offended, or embarrassed. But Lindsay told me I should take it and say 'thanks.' These organizations have budgets for things like that. So, I got a haircut. And my beard trimmed. Now I accept their generosity. Pretty cool, huh?"

"Very cool," Jack agreed. "You've got a great story to tell. Worth every penny, I'm sure."

"I don't know about that," Legend said. "Most of the questions they ask have to do with my fishing secrets. I tell them just enough. But I don't give *all* my secrets away. … At first Lindsay told me that I should call my little talk 'Legend's Piscatorial Secrets.' I just laughed, because I'd never heard that word before. I told her that people were going to think I was telling them how to take a leak in the woods. I just—"

"They just *love* him," Lindsay jumped in. "It's so interesting to listen to him. I sit in whenever I can. And I'm still learning stuff. He's just great at it. … And in demand. They always want to get him back. Right, Ted?"

"We have fun," he said. "That's for certain. … Now, what's this about taking your boys fishing with us? You serious about that?"

"Yeah," Jack said. "But only if you're one hundred percent good with it. Did you have time to think it over?"

"No thinkin' over to do," Legend said. "I'm *totally* okay with it, if you and the boys are. I think it would be great. Lots of fun. … That is, if Lindsay signs on as well. She's going up with us. At least she *thinks* she can get away. … What do you think, babe? Think we could make it work?"

"I'm all in," Lindsay said. "As long as my boss lets me. It should be a real hoot. … I should warn you, though, that it's possible that I'll have to work … because it's just not for positive certain that I'll get the days off."

"Well," Legend said. "She's all in, I think. And I'm all in. That just leaves you and the boys. And, of course, Buddy. … Think Buddy would want to go fishin' with us?"

"I'm sure it'll be the highlight of their year," Jack said. "They know they're going on a fishing trip, but they didn't know that it'd be with you. … You're the first one they suggested. They will be absolutely delighted. I can promise you that."

"Terrific," Legend excitedly blurted out.

"Then, that's all set," he said, holding up his hot chocolate. "Let's drink a toast to it. Here's to a great fishing trip."

With big smiles Jack and Lindsay clicked their cups with Legend's.

"How do we get together on this?" Jack asked. "When and where? I'll drop them off as long as I have an address and a time."

"It'd probably save time and gas if you just dropped them off at the cottage. All they'll need are a few changes of clothes. … And some dog food. We have plenty of people food, and fishing equipment. We're all set there. But we don't have any dog food."

"When?" Jack asked.

"We're headed up early tomorrow. We'll be leaving *very* early—especially if you ask Lindsay. Probably be up there by nine. Make that nine-thirty, just to be safe. So, any time after that would work. No phone up there. Cells work some of the time. I'll give you the address, and the coordinates. It's pretty easy to find. … Damn! I am *so* looking forward to this! We are going to have an absolute blast! I just can't wait to get going!"

"Well," Jack said. "Neither can they. They have no idea I'm setting this up with you. But, from what they've said in the past, they're going to welcome this opportunity. … And when would you be winding it all up? If *I* can't do it, I can have Kate pick my boys up there, or in Grand Rapids. Your choice."

"Shall we say one week?" Legend suggested. "We'll be fishing for one full week. And then we'll be back here in Grand Rapids, at Lindsay's house, in nine days? That will give us one full week at the cottage. Does that work? If it doesn't work for Kate we can make other arrangements. Nothing carved in stone. We can talk if things change. But if that sounds okay, let's go for it."

"Deal's done," Jack said.

"Now that we got that all figured out," Legend said. "Tell me what's goin' on with the lake levels. I've got some theories about that. I'm eager to see what you're thinking."

Chapter 6

T heories?" Jack queried. "What do you mean by that? Are you talking about the Great Lakes water levels?"

"I've been doing a little research on the whole subject, and I have come up with some ideas. I'd like to see what you think about them. Interested? Can I tell you what *I* think?"

"Sure," Jack replied. "There's no doubt that there are a lot of landowners on Superior who are being threatened by the high lake levels."

"What is it up there on Superior?" Legend asked. "What would you say? I've seen pictures—befores and afters. Looks to me like the Big Lake is up nearly three feet—give or take. Would you say that's about right?"

"I've heard that too," Jack said. "But, officially, I think it's generally acknowledged that the levels of all the Great Lakes are up."

"Yeah, that's what I've heard," Legend said. "I like to fish Lake Michigan in Grand Haven and South Haven. And it looks to me like the water levels are very high there. Do you know why that would be? Can't even use the piers anymore."

"I've read about several theories, global warming being one of them. Do you have a *different* idea?"

"Maybe. I like to fish in Lake Superior, too. I have a friend up there. He has a boat that works fine in Lake Superior. We drop it in at the Whitefish Point State Dock. That's where a lot of the Native American fishermen drop their boats. Good fishing up there—whitefish, especially. But what got my attention are the breakwaters by the lighthouse at Whitefish Point. I've gone up there dozens of times. And, to me, it certainly appears like the waters around those breakwaters is up nearly three feet—give or take. Three feet! That is one hell of a lot of water. A *hell* of a lot. Don't you agree? Why do you suppose that is? Any ideas? I've got some, if you don't."

"So, you're not buying the story about global warming?" Jack asked, trying to draw Legend out.

"Can't rule it out altogether, I suppose. But consider some of these facts, and then tell me what you think."

"What facts?" Jack asked.

"For instance, in May of 2019, the Army Corps of Engineers reported that the level of Lake Erie rose six inches. *Six inches!* That's one hell of an increase to take place in stinkin' one month. But even more significant is that Lake Ontario rose over a foot and a half—in May alone! That's a foot and a half rise in a single month! How could that be?"

"What do you think?" Jack asked.

"I have some ideas," Legend said. "But there are some other facts that ought to be considered. First of all, did you know that the oceans are pretty stable? They're rising a little, but nothing like Lake Ontario. For instance, since 1880 the Atlantic Ocean has risen about eight inches. That's in a century and a half—eight measly inches."

"Melting of the glaciers," Jack offered. "What do you think?"

"Eight inches is nothing—not in the grand scheme of things.

That's eight inches in one hundred and forty years. A mere eight inches. Lake Ontario grew a foot and a half, that's eighteen inches, in one stinkin' month alone. Can you explain that?"

"Hadn't given it that much thought," Jack said. "Can you?"

"Well, if Lake Superior is up two or three feet since 2014. And if the rest of the Great Lakes are also up markedly. Lake Ontario being up a foot and a half in May alone. I don't think that it could all be due to rain."

"Then why?" Jack asked.

"You're a man of the world, Jack. What would you say? Where would you start looking for your answers?"

Jack looked deeply into Legend's eyes as he carefully considered his words. He then pushed his almost empty mug across the table, leaned back in the coffee house chair, and took a deep pondering breath.

"Generally," Jack said after a long moment, "When I'm looking for answers about such matters, my first thought is to always follow the money. That's what you're getting at, isn't it?"

"Maybe."

"Maybe?" Jack repeated. "But how do you propose that the 'follow the money' principle could be applied to this situation?"

"Consider this for a minute." Legend began to elaborate. "Almost all, if not all, of the iron ore used in American industry passes through the Great Lakes. It ships out of Duluth and such places, and is processed at various steel mills along the way throughout the Great Lakes System. If Lake Superior is allowed to grow even two feet, do you know what that would amount to as far as what a freighter or an ore carrier could move?

"Poe Lock between Lake Superior and the St. Mary's River can pass a freighter or ore carrier up to one thousand feet long, and one hundred feet wide. That additional two or three feet would allow one of these transports to carry an additional two hundred thousand cubic feet of iron ore—at virtually no additional cost. The same could be accomplished by dredging the channel out, but that is just incredibly expensive. While it would cost *nothing* to raise the level of the lakes."

"So, that's your theory, is it?" Jack asked. "What would they do? Seed the clouds to make it rain more?"

"That might be one way," Legend said in feigned concession. "But, it wouldn't work. However, there is an easier, faster way. And it *would* work."

"I think I know where you're going with this," Jack said, smiling. "I like the way you think. You're talking about damming up the channel to force the waters to grow up stream."

"It could be done just like that, you know," Legend said.

"Through the system of locks from Lake Erie to the Atlantic? Is that what you're thinking?"

"Exactly. There are a total of fifteen locks east of Lake Erie, which are nothing more than adjustable dams. All they would have to do is to use the locks to restrict water flow enough to accomplish their ends. After all, there really exists no other major outlet for the Great Lakes—just the St. Lawrence Seaway. That's virtually it."

"Well, you've got a point there," Jack agreed. "The Chicago River does eventually run into the Mississippi River, but the flow of that river is incredibly slow. It drops very little. I used to live a block off it. I know about it first-hand. The river as it exists today is basically a manufactured phenomenon. Originally it flowed *into*

Lake Michigan, but the engineers changed its direction to prevent
it from dumping pollutants into Chicago's water supply. But, that's
a whole different story.

"So, what you're suggesting here, Legend, my friend, is that
the shipping industry has *manufactured* the new higher lake levels
simply to pad their bottom lines. Is that about it? They deepened
the lakes to accomplish an increase to their bottom line. Is that
what you're saying?"

"Think about it. The cost of dredging is just *unbelievably* expensive. And extremely disruptive. But the cost of *raising* the levels
instead—virtually zero. At least for them. Not the case, or course,
for property owners. It has forced many homeowners along the
lakes to spend hundreds of thousands of dollars each to try to fight
back the water's aggression. Many have actually lost their houses.

"It would take a solid year to dredge out just the straits between
Michigan and Canada, and to deepen the locks through that area.
Shipping during that time would be dramatically affected."

"I always wondered about that," Jack said. "About the role
dredging might be playing in this whole matter."

"For me," Legend said, "the concern is for some of my fishing
sites upstate. The high waters are pushing back in the rivers and
changing the whole ecology."

"That is, in *Legend's* opinion, it's bad because it's disrupting
your fishing," Jack said through a chuckle.

"Well. Yeah. I suppose you could put it like that," Legend responded in a confessional tone. "And it would be true. I sure as
hell do like to fish. But so do a million other people. You know
that. ... But there's more to it than just my fishing. If they're doing what I'm *positive* they're doing, solely to make more money,

it's just too damn selfish for me to stomach. They're changing the whole ecology of the Great Lakes, simply to pad their pockets. It's just not right."

"If that's what's going on," Jack said in an effort to placate his friend, and to begin gently extracting himself from a discussion that he could not control, "then the whole story has to be told. The people do have a right to know. That I certainly agree with."

Jack then rose to his feet and began shuffling through his jacket pocket for his car keys.

"How else could it be happening?" Legend countered, not wanting to have his arguments dismissed. "The glaciers are not melting—and certainly none on land. The ocean is up a total of a mere *eight inches* since *1880*. That's almost a century and a half—and increase of only *eight inches*! That's nothing. ... In fact, some are saying that the ocean has dropped in recent years. Jack, I have even read that the world is in the second year of a mini-ice age. There are virtually no sunspots—that always drives temperatures down. Fewest sunspots in two hundred years. We're entering an ice age. ... I wanna know how the hell can that be driving *up* the levels of the Great Lakes? It's impossible!"

"How about the other Michigan Lakes?" Jack asked, still standing but sensing the need to re-engage. "The ones not tied directly to any of the five Great Lakes. Are they up the same way? And if it involves these other locks, wouldn't Canada have to be somehow involved?"

"I suppose Canada must at least be aware of what's goin' on," Legend replied. "If not in it up to its eyeballs. ... But, Jack, it's not limited to just the five big lakes. It involves the inland lakes too. They're part of the whole problem. It just so happens that there does not exist a lake in the state of Michigan that is not somehow tied into the whole Great Lakes ecosystem. *All* the inland lakes are fed and drained by rivers, and basically all of the rivers in the state empty eventually into one of the Great Lakes. That's just the way it works."

As was typically his way, Legend was engaging fully in the discussion, while Lindsay pulled out her phone and checked to make sure she was not neglecting some emergency back at her office. She enjoyed the repartee, but she viewed it more as Legend's forte and not her own.

"What's this business about building a new lock up in Sault Ste. Marie?" Jack asked, still wanting to change the subject and settle Legend down a little. "Didn't I read that the U.S. has just authorized the building of that new lock?"

"Yup," Legend said. "That's *exactly* right. The project has been thirty years in the making. I think it was back in the mid-1980s that President Reagan gave the go-ahead. But nothing has happened since then. Not until the present administration authorized funds to get it going. I just wish Bush would have given them some money to dredge the channel out a bit, and not screw everything up by raising the water levels. That would have solved the problem.

"Instead," Legend continued, "they took the easy way out and raised the level of the lakes probably thirty-six inches. I read that all they would have to do is to open up the gates and dams, and allow the levels to recede to where they used to be. Wouldn't take long at all. They could get the levels back to where they were ten years ago and it would raise the level of the Atlantic Ocean barely more than the thickness of a couple sheets of copy paper—half the thickness of a damn potato chip. That's nothin'! … That's just *got* to happen! It's only right that they fix what they broke!"

Initially, Jack had some difficulty buying into Legend's theory. Plus, he wanted to avoid an argument. So, he determined to keep his mouth shut and do a little research for himself later. As a result of that brief study, this is what Jack emailed to himself:

> The oceans form a single contiguous body of water that covers approximately 139,799,000 square miles. The five Great Lakes also form a single contiguous body of water, and it covers approximately 94,250 square miles. Legend is suggesting that the existing gates, locks and dams along the St. Lawrence Seaway should be opened a little to allow built-up waters to flow through to the Atlantic Ocean. By doing this they could within two months lower the Great Lakes 36 inches (which is approximately the amount Legend contends that the lakes have been forced to increase over the past several years). Not only would this restore the Great Lakes to their original levels, but by so doing, it would only increase the ocean level merely .024 of an inch—that actually is, as Legend says, only half the thickness of a potato chip! I would have to pursue this more deeply, but I think Legend might have an argument, at least his case appears to be one worth looking at more closely.

"Well," Jack said in a continued effort to change the topic of conversation, "It's clear that you will be keeping my boys engaged and entertained on this fishing adventure—perhaps even educated a little. … I have to tell you, I am eager to let them know that we finalized the trip. They were excited when I suggested that they go fishing. And they asked if they could pay you a visit. They're going to go nuts."

"Really?" Legend responded. "They remember me?"

"More than that," Jack said. "Ever since they met you they have frequently made you the topic of conversation over dinner. *Numerous* times. In fact, you come up at least once a week. I told them that I would see if you could be talked into taking them fishing sometime. I'm thinking that would be the perfect thing to do while I go on this business trip, and—"

"Whereabouts are *you* headed? And for how long?"

"All up in the air," Jack answered. "But, not to worry. Kate—my daughter ... you remember her?"

"Oh, sure, she was in on my rescue too. She was right there with Buddy and the boys. I remember her well."

"Kate is tied up during the first few days of my assignment," Jack replied. "She can either pick the boys up here in Grand Rapids, or, she can drive to your cottage and pick them up there. Not sure how well that's going to work if you have no phone service. What do you think?"

"It'll be fine. She can call into my message board and leave a note, and I can be on the lookout for her. I check that every night, no matter where I am. ... She still living and working in New York? She's a detective there. Right? A lieutenant now, I think."

"Right on all counts. She's in the middle of a big case right now, and she has to be in court every day for the rest of the week. But come Saturday, she can be wherever needed."

"And you?" Legend asked. "You don't really know when you'll get freed up. ... What sort of a project are you working on? Is it in Michigan?"

"I'm not trying to be vague," Jack said, "but I'm not at liberty to talk about it. It's no big deal, but my client wants me to remain silent on his case. Just can't talk about it. ... It might only take me a day or two to wind it up. Or, it could be a month. Just don't know."

"Fair enough," Legend said. "I don't need to know about your business. You just drop them off, and all will be cool. ... Like I said, I'll text you the coordinates for the cabin. It now belongs to the parents of one of the Boy Scouts. Used to be in Lindsay's family. ... I don't think the cabin even has a number on it. At least, I've never seen one. No mailbox. Hell, no telephone or electricity, either. We do have a big old generator, and we burn wood and some fuel oil for heat. Sometimes. Usually, we just use the fireplace for heat. I just love the freedom I feel when I'm up there. I wish you could stay and go out with us. You could teach me some of your fishing tricks. We'd have a blast."

"Thanks for the invite," Jack said. "But I'm sure I don't know anything about fishing that you don't. If there's any learning to be done it would be on my end. ... Maybe another day. I can't wait to tell the boys I got to see you. I know they'll have a great time fishing with you. ... What was the name of the owner? Just so I know."

"The scout's name is William McCarthy," Legend replied. "His father is Justin—Justin McCarthy. He's a friend of mine from way back. I've been fishing up there for years. ... Like I said, Lindsay's family used to own that cabin. ... Justin is a piece of work. Interesting guy. A *great* guy, actually. ... *Was* a great guy. Passed away two, three months ago. Cancer. That's the major reason I'm headin' up this trip. For William. He's been down in the dumps, and we thought this would be good for him. It's great that he'll have a chance to meet your boys. They'll all have a blast. A real blast."

"You probably already told me this," Jack said, "but how many boys in total will be up there? And, what is the age range? My boys are fourteen. Is that about the average age of your group?"

"They'll be perfect," Legend said. "The oldest of my boys is sixteen. That would be a lad named James—James Christopher. His dad, Garth, is Canadian. He's worked on a Great Lakes ore carrier for twenty years. James's brother, Billy, is the youngest. He just turned twelve. I didn't want to take him because he is really too young, in my opinion. But his dad insisted. He's trying to make a man out of him—at least that's what Lindsay thinks. I suppose it'll be okay, but the younger one is little even for his age. And sickly—"

"He's not *sickly*," Lindsay interrupted. "He's just a little smaller than the rest of the boys. But I wouldn't call him sickly."

"Yeah," Legend said. "I suppose. But I have to tell you that he worries me a little. I don't think he's ever been fishing off a boat—not in his whole short life. … We'll see."

"He will be fine," Lindsay said, trying to encourage her boyfriend. "James will help keep an eye on him. And now you've got Jack's boys. They will be helpful too."

Jack did not verbally respond, but it was obvious from his expression that he shared Legend's concerns.

That was virtually the end of that conversation. It was Sunday—1 P.M. Jack still had a lot of preparations to make in getting ready for his job in DC. Before he excused himself from Lindsay and Legend, he made sure he could communicate okay with Legend's cell, that he had logged into his phone the coordinates of the cabin where the boys would be staying, and that Legend had all the numbers for Kate and Henry in case of an emergency. He then said his goodbyes and headed back to Sugar Island. After that he called Henry and asked him to take the boys down to Legend's fishing cabin as early as possible on Monday.

Jack was barely ten minutes out of Grand Rapids when he received a call from his friend, Secret Service Special Agent Roger Minsk.

"Jack," Roger said. "I see you are in motion. In a vehicle headed north. Are you by yourself?"

While each book in the Jack Handler Saga will stand alone, if you wish to get to know Henry better, a very good book to read for that is *Dog Fight*. All fourteen books are available at better bookstores, and on Amazon.com. By the way, the book does not contain any actual dog fighting. The term is used in strictly an allegorical sense.

Chapter 7

I am. I was down in Grand Rapids making arrangements for the boys to go on an extended fishing trip with a friend from that city. What's on your mind?"

"We've got to move. And it's got to be now. Today."

"Really," Jack said. "I thought we were all set for Tuesday."

"Not anymore. I'm sending your ride into the Gerald R. Ford Airport to pick you up. It'll be there within the hour. I need you to circle back. Can you do that?"

Jack thought for a moment, and then responded.

"Count on me being back at the airport in forty minutes, or less. I've got to get hold of Henry again, and confirm the details. He's going to drop the boys off at the fishing cottage very early tomorrow. He can then catch a flight to DC to give us a hand."

"That's fine," Roger said. "You and I can work together tonight and tomorrow. And Henry can join us when he gets here. Except, it's not DC as we expected. Our people of interest—there are two of them. At *least* two—there may be more. They're arriving in New York as we speak. No indication at all that they are headed to DC. Not sure exactly what they are up to. But we've got some theories. We're going to surveil them closely. We can't let them out of our sight. Especially not until we can piece together the second leg of their journey, if there is one. And then figure out what exactly they're up to."

"Who have you got?" Jack asked. "Are there more than the two I know about—the ones that killed Millie? Am I right in that assumption?"

Millie was a good lady friend of Jack's. She had been gunned down in New York City nearly two months earlier. It was clear at the time that the hit on Millie was carried out because Jack and Roger had successfully thwarted an assassination attempt on POTUS in Singapore. It was during that episode that Roger suffered his two gunshot wounds. While his injuries were severe, he fought through them and was instrumental in assisting Jack in preventing the assassination.

It was assumed at the time that the hit on Millie was no more than payback targeted at Jack. However, were that the case—that Jack's quasi-inamorata was murdered to get even with him for foiling their attempt on POTUS—in the minds of the killers, the matter would have been ended with Millie's death. But of late, an abundance of intercepted chatter suggested that pure "get-even-ism" might not have been the principal factor in the hit on Millie.

The chatter between the two killers and the UNSUB (Unidentified Subject), the yet-to-be-identified third person, suggested that the UNSUB had an agenda of his own, and that it apparently even eclipsed that of the killers themselves. In fact, according to Roger's analysis, it appeared that the UNSUB was actually giving the orders. While Roger had not yet been able to entirely crack the cipher they were using, his training led him to this conclusion through his scrutiny of sentence structure and length and order of individual contributions.

"The UNSUB appears to be in charge of this operation," Roger had informed Jack. "That means that the driving force behind this new operation was not purely revenge."

"Makes sense to me," Jack agreed. "Especially given the fact that Buddy nearly tore the arm off one of the shooters. If revenge was the big deal for them, then I should think that they would have given that arm a little more time to heal up. I wondered about that. He's got to still be hurtin' big time. Major ligament damage, I would suspect. He can't be functioning at one hundred percent yet. ... So, whatever it is that they've got in mind here, or the real 'why' behind it, we might never know."

"Exactly," Roger agreed. "We're going to have to put ourselves out there as though we were assuming that we were only up against the original two, and that their only agenda was in payback for messing up their assassination attempt. ... I see it going down like this: we concentrate our surveillance on the original two subjects.

"We've got those two nailed down, and I think they know it—if they don't, they soon will. Intel strongly suggests that they're going to be here. But they appear to be meeting up with a third party immediately upon arriving. And, like I said, we have no info on that third person. But I'm pretty certain that whoever it is, he will be a major player."

"In other words, he will be a very *dangerous* person," Jack added. "And we don't have any idea as to who he is, or what he has in mind. Right? Or even the *why* behind the whole thing. Isn't that right? ... And, by the way, wasn't the original target supposed to be in DC? What happened to that plan?"

"I think the change of venue might have had something to do with current New York law."

"Really?" Jack asked. "What do you mean by that?"

"There are some serious law enforcement issues taking place in the big city right now. Morale in the department is not good at all. Big meeting at the UN. Might be a good time to pull something like this off there. … DC, on the other hand, is teeming with FBI and Secret Service. As is always the case."

"Okay, boss," Jack said, "I'm all turned around, and headed for Gerald R. Ford. Is my ride coming into one of the private strips, or the main terminal?"

"Main terminal. I've made arrangements. Just wait in the main waiting area. My pilot knows what you look like, and you might recognize him. His name is Harold Carp. I'm pretty sure you've met him. He's going to approach you and say, 'Can a guy get a decent hotdog in this place?' And you tell him to try the Fifth Third Ballpark. … Like I said, I think you'll remember him. He's run a number of errands for us over the years—some involved you. But still stick to the security protocol anyway.

"I'll pick you up myself in Newark. That's where I've got him coming in."

"Got it," Jack replied. "Can you tell me a little more about the object of this whole thing?"

"This is what we think is going down," Roger explained. "We believe the thinking behind the killing of your friend Millie was to get back at you for foiling the assassination of POTUS. Your boys were with her. No doubt they were on the hit list as well. Had it not been for their dog, Buddy, the end of that little saga would have been much different. It's just a damn shame that they were able to get to your friend. But, at least the boys came out of this okay. And Millie's daughter. She was with them as well. That's about it for now. I'm sure we'll be able to pull it all together as we learn more."

"Then you see the hit on Millie as pure revenge," Jack said. "Right? That's how I see it as well. ... But, what I'm not getting my head wrapped around is *this* latest stage. What could these guys be up to now? More of the same? Do you think that I'm still somehow the object of their attention?"

"That's what we're thinking," Roger said. "We're still learning. ... One thing that is a little puzzling is that these two assholes made it so easy to track them. They both hightailed it to Havana, almost immediately after Millie's shooting. Doctors there repaired the killer's arm. It required half a dozen surgeries. The crazy thing is that we did not initially know they were in Cuba. It's almost like they sent us a postcard giving away their location. They sent a communiqué, one that we could not miss, to one of the Deep State principals that we have been monitoring. Had to have been intentional. If not by them, then on the direction of the one giving the orders.

"They did the same thing when they began their trip back to the U.S. They made it easy for us to track them."

"So, what are you making of that?" Jack asked.

"We even knew what hotel they were headed to."

"How did you come by that info?" Jack asked.

"We've got ears in Intelligence. "

"Maybe they were trying to ferret out just who it is in Intelligence that works for you," Jack suggested.

"That thought occurred to me," Roger said. "But, again, it was almost as though they posted it on the bulletin board in the break room. They made no significant effort to secure that information."

"You're suggesting that they wanted us to know that they were traveling to New York," Jack concluded. "And exactly where they would be staying. That's what you're saying, isn't it?"

"It would seem that way."

"But this third party," Jack began wondering out loud. "Your UNSUB. Have you found it equally easy to track that person?"

"No," Roger responded emphatically. "That's one of the things that has really bothered me. We have no idea as to who that person is, or who he works for. Only that he appears to be in charge of this leg of the operation."

"I'll tell you how this feels to me," Jack suggested. "What if the whole point of this UNSUB is to kill me, and these two turds are flying in from Cuba to serve merely as bait on the UNSUB's trap? That would be one way to view this. God knows I totally screwed up their plans for POTUS. They would not want that to happen again. What do you think about that scenario?"

"We've been referring to them as the "Mutt and Jeff Killers'," Roger said. "Those old boys who killed your Millie. ... About your theory, that is one of the scenarios we've been considering as well. Mutt and Jeff being bait to draw us out ... mainly to draw you out. It's your face that is etched on their brains regarding their failure to take POTUS out. I'm not sure that they even associate me with that job. Pretty much I remained in the background. Don't know that, but I suspect that you're the one they seek to eliminate."

"Deep State did not know that you were in Singapore?" Jack asked.

"That's about right. They are aware that there are some major players who are heading up the resistance to them, but I have no reason to think that they know that Bob is chief among them. ... And, as far as we know, they still think that my only job is protecting Allison. ... Jack, my friend, we're pretty much convinced that yours is the only face on Deep State's most-wanted poster."

Jack did not respond immediately to Roger's comments. He was deep in thought.

"Then," Jack finally said, "Our task here is not so much to take these assholes out—your Mutt and Jeff—as it is to fart around until we draw out your UNSUB. Is that about right?"

"That would be an accurate assessment," Roger said. "Unpleasant as it might seem, that is just about right."

"Then Mutt and Jeff are the *bait* to draw me out," Jack summarized, "and my job is to expose the UNSUB. That makes for a whole different project than I anticipated. ... I was thinking that I could just slide in and take them out. And then be gone. I have to tell you, I don't much cotton to this sort of task. It's not my style."

"I get it," Roger said. "Totally. Do you want out?"

"I want to nail these assholes," Jack barked. "Hell. I am *absolutely* going to take them out. ... One way or another, that's exactly what I'm going to do. I am going to kill them both. And I'm going to make sure that I am standing right in front of them when I do it. They're gonna be looking me in the eye when I pull the trigger. ... I'm glad you told me about the UNSUB. I'll be watching out for him. But I can guarantee you that I will not allow him, or them, to dissuade or distract me from my objective."

"Then," Roger said, "I take it that you are all in on this assignment. Would I be right?"

"Yeah," Jack said. "I'm in. I owe you that. I'll play by your rules until we know who the UNSUB is, who hired him, and the motive driving it. But, once you're satisfied in that area, I'm going to personally deal with those two assholes—your Mutt and Jeff. How does that set with you?"

"Fair enough," Roger said. "Since we already know who they are, what comes of them is of no consequence to us. They are minor players. ... But, the UNSUB is a different story. We want him to survive and be on his way as quickly as possible. We want to take him down, and tag him with an injected tracking device, and then release him back in the stream."

"About the logistics," Jack said, "have you developed a plan to pull that off? You know, keeping him alive? That sort of shit is hard to accomplish. It'd be much easier to terminate your UNSUB than it will be to screw around trying to keep him alive. What do you have in mind?"

"I've got enough to get you started. I know where M&J are staying—hotel and room number. I've got a room all set for you directly across the street, and one floor up. And, I've assembled a lot of great hardware. But, as for exactly *how* you go about pulling it off, you're just going to have to do what you do best—improvise."

Jack sat silently for nearly a minute. That answer did not set well with him, but he did understand what Roger was looking for.

Finally, he responded: "Anyone in my room right now?"

"No," Roger said. "This whole job has to fly under the radar. Bob doesn't even know the details about it. ... Keep that in mind as you work it. If it should happen to go south, there'd be no one to bail you out. I won't be helping you, and there will be absolutely no paper trail."

"Bob's not been briefed?"

"Not even Bob, Jack my friend. It's just you and me, and your buddy Henry, if he makes it to New York."

"Henry will be heading your way as soon as he gets my boys squared away."

"What's Kate up to these days?" Roger asked.

"She's in the city. One of her cases is working its way through the court system. She has to be there to testify. Otherwise she'd be with the boys. She should be freed up by the end of the week, if all goes as planned. Once it goes to the jury, if we haven't completed the mission, she's going to fly back and pick up the boys."

"I have no idea as to how long this job might take," Roger said. "It could be a day, or it could drag on for a month. Or, all the principals could disappear. ... If the UNSUB figures out that we're onto him, I have no doubt that he'll simply pull out. Then it's all back to the drawing board. That's why I've kept this totally under wraps."

"If that's the case," Jack asked, "how in hell did *you* ever find out about it?"

"Jack," Roger explained, "sorry, but I'm not at liberty to share that with you. Sometimes I employ methods that must remain known only to me. This might be one of those situations. ... Trust me, my friend, should this go south, any part of it, we will all do well not to have too much information. I don't think you would last very long in a federal prison. You know what I mean?"

Roger was well aware of the problems that Jack had experienced in a federal prison camp a few short years earlier. It was there that a group of inmates had been contracted to kill him. And, they would have succeeded had Henry not been an inmate at the same institution. Henry came upon the hit team just as they were preparing to put the finishing touches on Jack's demise, and rescued him. That was, in fact, where Jack first met Henry. It was Roger that jumped into the situation and put the package together that sprung the two of them—Jack and Henry—before a second attempt could be attempted and carried out.

So, Jack fully understood where Roger was coming from, and did not pursue the matter.

"Can I assume that we will be able to hit the road running as soon as I arrive?" Jack asked.

Chapter 8

Pretty much," Roger said. "I'm still on medical leave, so to speak. I will be working with you very closely. I have rented a suite on the floor above M&J. It is also directly across the street from you. I have installed a whole shitload of surveillance and communication equipment in that suite above M&J, and in yours."

"What are you hoping to accomplish with all those electronics?"

"M&J will need to communicate with the UNSUB—at least in some fashion. We should be able to tell if there is any communication between them and the UNSUB. We might not be able to decipher it immediately, but we should be able to follow it back to its origin. … I've done much the same for you in your room. You will be able to record every movement they make, and monitor every word that they speak. Unfortunately, you have to assume that they are capable of doing the same with you."

"They will know that we are staying across from them?"

"Probably not right away. But as soon as they pick you up, they're going to home in on you. If the UNSUB is as sophisticated as I suspect he is, then he will have a whole organization working on his behalf."

"It would be very nice if we had some idea as to who is behind this. If we can learn the *who*, we very well might be able to deduce the why and how. As it stands right now, you are at a significant disadvantage. If you sequester yourself away too much, UNSUB will soon become suspicious. If you expose yourself, he will probably try to kill you. And it's quite likely that your termination is his main if not his *only* goal."

"How can I best utilize Henry?" Jack asked. "Any suggestions?"

"What do you think?"

"I'm thinking that we should have separate rooms. That way when I go down to eat, or hit the street, he could be discreetly watching my back."

"I've already reserved a room—directly across the hall from you. When does he get in?"

"That would be terrific," Jack said. "You think of everything. … Henry will get here as soon as he can after dropping the boys off. Probably late tomorrow. Or, even more likely, in the middle of the night."

"He's driving, I take it."

"I was going to fly him in, but it'd be better if he were to drive."

"It would," Roger agreed. "I can hide him better if he drives. … The room is rented under this name: Scott R. Blumberg, Ft. Lauderdale, Florida. Room number is 1519. Your number is 1520, by the way. An access control card is slid under his door, directly beneath the locking hardware. Same is true for your keycard. A pocket knife will retrieve them. You will find a second card for his room in the desk in your suite. I put it there so that you can access the room at will, and he can get the card in case he is unable to retrieve the one under the door. There is also a card for your door in his desk."

"So," Jack quipped, "Henry, the proud Native American, is going Semitic. What name is my room under?"

"Jack Handler, of course. We want our boys, and the UNSUB, to find *you* easily."

"Of course," Jack responded.

"I have a question for you," Roger said. "Millie's daughter—I think her name is Angel. Whatever became of her? Is she living with you and the boys?"

"As it turned out," Jack explained. "Millie had a twin sister—an identical twin. A woman named Mandy. Millie had only recently found out about her and had her tracked down. Millie had never met her mother. A year or so ago she decided she would like to trace her family back to find out as much as she could about her mother and father. She found out that there was no record of her father whatsoever, but there were papers filed naming her mother. That's how she discovered that she had the twin sister. Her mother is deceased—drug overdose. She had died shortly after Millie was born. But sister Mandy was a registered nurse. She was working at a hospital in Detroit. She was very surprised to learn that she had a twin sister.

"The two of them got together, only a few months before Millie was murdered, and they became good friends. Mandy was divorced some years ago, and she had no children.

"Millie named her sister as Angel's godmother, and bequeathed her entire estate to her and Angel. Mandy is now Angel's legal guardian. She left Detroit and moved into Millie's house in Sault Ste. Marie."

"Fascinating story," Roger said. "But, they—Mandy and Angel—are *not* coming with you to New York. Right?"

"Mandy is now working at the hospital in the Soo, and Angel

is continuing to attend school there."

"Do you talk often to them—Mandy and Angel?"

"Mandy pretty much blames me for her sister's death. She has made no effort to contact us since … the incident. The boys see Angel in school, but everything is different now. Not at all like it used to be. … And, along that same line, there's one more thing. The girl from out East—Jessie Childress—her parents were both killed as well, and she blames Millie for their murders. And, somehow, she's managed to bring Henry, Kate and me into her web of hate.

"The girl had become good friends with Angel. And so, Millie had agreed to let Jessie move into her house with them. Probably out of an unfounded sense of guilt. … Mandy then came in, and she made every effort to follow up on Millie's wishes. She welcomed the girl into the house with Angel.

"But, from what I've heard, it's not been a smooth transition. With Millie dead and all, neither of the girls are much interested in having anything to do with us. That's just the way it is."

"I get it," Roger said. "Stuff like that takes time. Can't rush through or around it. Time alone can heal it."

"Maybe," Jack said. "But both of these girls have lost their mothers to violence. And they have to have someone to blame. Anyway, that's about the size of it at this point. It is what it is. Really can't change the way people feel. … But, I can do something about Millie's killers."

"And we will," Roger agreed.

Sensing Jack's desire to drop the conversation, Roger quickly added, "Let's leave it at that. I think it best that I not be seen with you at all. So, you should head directly to the hotel upon arrival.

We'll touch base later. I'm confident the surveillance and communication equipment I've set up for you is one hundred percent secure. And, as always, your cell is secure. ... For the most part, I'm leaving you on your own. Do what you have to do to terminate your two targets. But not before I'm satisfied with everything we need to know about the UNSUB. He's my only concern for this mission. Is that all clear?"

"Got it," Jack said. "It works for me."

As planned, Roger's pilot was waiting for him at Gerald R. Ford Airport. They established their identities through passwords, exchanged pleasantries, and then embarked on the trip to Newark on the Cessna 172 that Roger had rented for the operation.

Chapter 9

J ack thought it best not to contact Henry directly about the changes in plans with regard to driving into New York. Roger had the more secure communication setup, and so Jack asked Roger to work out all the details with *Scott R. Blumberg* (AKA Chuchip Kalyesveh AKA Henry) regarding his part of the mission.

Roger instructed Henry to drive directly into Newark Airport, and there leave his vehicle in long-term parking. He then instructed Henry to contract an Uber to drop him off at Jack's hotel. He should take the elevator to the fifteenth floor, retrieve the key card from under the door of room 1519, and then begin using the name Scott Blumberg.

Roger also explained about the secure cell phone he would find in his room, and that he should always use it when communicating with Jack's secure phone.

It was exactly 5:05 P.M. when Jack arrived at the Midtown Gold Tower Hotel. He did not observe anything unusual when he went up to his room. Fortunately for him, he always kept an emergency travel bag in his Tahoe, so Jack was equipped with changes of clothes and personal items to accommodate his needs for up to five days.

Retrieving the keycard from under his door presented no problem for him. Immediately his eyes went to all the electronic gear Roger had fitted his room with, but he did not examine it. Instead he went immediately to the desk, and opened the top drawer.

There he found a spare card for his door. It was marked with a black permanent marker with a large "X." There was a second card. It was differentiated from the other in that in place of the "X," it was marked with a large "+1."

"That must be Henry's key," he said to himself.

In the rear of the same drawer were two brown paper bags. On top of each bag was a pair of surgical gloves. Jack put on the gloves, and then he opened the first bag. In it he found a stainless steel Ruger G100 .22 ten-shot revolver with a three-inch barrel. It was already fitted with a suppressor. Jack was curious as to the type of ammunition Roger might have provided for it, and he was pleased to find two boxes of .22 caliber longs.

"Perfect," he muttered out loud.

He then opened the second paper bag. It contained a loaded ten-shot Gen 3 Glock 29 Compact 10mm. semi-automatic pistol. In that same bag were four 10-shot spare magazines, a small belt holster, and a full box of ammunition.

"Damn," Jack chuckled, "I sure as hell hope I don't need all this firepower. I wonder what Roger was thinking."

Jack knew that any contractor with even a modicum of proficiency would use only two .22 long rounds for each of his hits. That ought to be it. "What else does Roger have in mind for me?" Jack muttered.

He did like the Glock 29—especially since it had mounted on the grip a very handy laser sight. It was designed to provide accuracy even at a substantial distance. All he had to do is pull the firearm and point it, and the laser would deliver the round with pinpoint precision for up to one hundred feet. It was just like the one he had back in Michigan. "Roger must have remembered what I told him," he told himself. "Very cool."

The ten-shot .22 caliber revolver, with its long rounds and suppressor, was, for a number of reasons, perfect for the standard run-of-the-mill contract hit. Because a revolver does not spew out the spent rounds, as does a semi-auto, it limits the evidence left at the scene. The suppressor not only muffles the muzzle blast, but it also makes it difficult for a person to determine the direction from which it came. And, while the .22 long round packs plenty of power to enter and destroy a man's brain, it typically does not pack the punch to exit the target's skull—thus limiting the amount of blood and brain matter deposited at the scene of the shooting.

"Absolutely perfect choices," Jack said to himself.

Jack attached the holster to his belt, and then slid the Glock 29 into it. The semi-automatic was intended strictly for self-defense. Jack was not worried about depositing his fingerprints on the Glock, so he removed the gloves and tossed them back in the desk with the Ruger ten-shot. He put one of the spare10-shot clips into his jacket pocket. He then began scrutinizing some of the electronic equipment Roger had left for him.

First up attracting Jack's attention was a color monitor and a sixteen-camera switcher. He turned it on.

Only a few seconds had passed before the monitor came alive. Six cameras emerged on the screen as they sequentially lit up the monitor. The first four appeared to be pointed at the building across the street. Jack discovered that he could stop any of those four by moving the joystick. Once the switcher had stopped on that camera, he could pan, tilt and zoom in and out. And when he was finished, he could hit a "resume scan" button on the switcher, and it would again begin sequencing the view provided by all of the cameras.

Cameras five and six were viewing the hall outside his door.

"Funny," he mumbled out loud. "I don't recall seeing a camera above the door—much less *two* cameras. Must be pretty well disguised."

Once he became comfortable with the configuration of the surveillance cameras, Jack clicked to stop camera #1, and then zoomed in.

The camera was focused on the window across the street. "Nothing there to watch," he said to himself. "Appears entirely dark to me."

He walked over to the window and pulled the drapes open slightly.

"Yup," he muttered, "it's dark over there. Must be nobody's home—or, they're in there with the lights off."

Jack could not determine which was true.

"Seems like Roger mentioned something like there being some infrared monitoring devices," Jack said. "I wonder what I have to do to get them working."

He then thought about it. Many cameras will switch from visible light to infrared automatically. He wondered if the cameras Roger gave him would do that.

So, he picked the first camera and zoomed in on the window across the street. He left it there for about twenty seconds. And then, because it was a very overcast evening, it switched to night vision. What had been happening was that when it was just looking at the side of the building, it was able to pick up enough available light—such as streetlights and headlights—to reflect off the side of the building. However, once he zeroed in on the window itself, it was so dark that the night vision kicked on. He then was able to view even dim shadows on the drapes. The shadows sporadically moved around, thus indicating that there were people inside the room.

Jack looked around and found a manila envelope with his name on it. He opened it. Inside he found stapled together twenty-three sheets of white paper. At the top of the first sheet were the words: Operating Instructions.

Jack looked around the room and spotted a four-cup coffee maker, with several packets of coffee, creamer and sugar. He turned on the tap and proceeded to make a pot of coffee as he began to read the documents.

The instructions were divided into a number of short, labeled paragraphs, each covering a given piece of Roger's surveillance equipment. Jack fingered through the first two pages until he found a section on the third page entitled: Eavesdropping. It read:

> The type of eavesdropping equipment we have set up for you is highly specialized. I'm sure you have used or at least encountered it already in your career. But I will summarize its use nevertheless.
>
> It employs Laser Microphones. This is how it works. The transmitter and receiver have been installed on the outside of your building. More specifically, on the window ledge of the suite directly below yours, which makes it exactly opposite the room occupied by our targets—Mutt and Jeff. Any conversation taking place inside that room

will cause the glass in their window to vibrate somewhat like an eardrum. The transmitter, which is pointed at their window, will pick up that vibration and reflect it back to the laser receiver, and the electronics built into the mic will pick those vibrations up and basically translate them into audible sounds.

The recording device will digitally record and store those sounds until erased. By the time you walked into your room, my technicians will have had the system operating for approximately thirty hours. When there are no voices in the room, the system will cease recording. That way it will not waste your time in replay. Enjoy!

Jack turned the equipment on *Live Play*. He was surprised at what he heard:

A: … a take a piss. You keep an eye out till I get done.

---three minutes of silence---

B: Feel better?

A: Do you think Handler's in there yet?

B: Hell if I know.

A: How're we supposed to know what he's up to, anyway?

B: Damn it! I don't know! … This is the shittiest job we've ever been on. … We're not getting paid enough for this kind of shit. That's all I can say about it.

A: What're we supposed to do? Just hang around this damn room until he takes us out? That's what's likely to happen, you know. He ain't some kinda stupid shmuck, you know. He's killed a lot of people. … At least that's what I've heard. …

B. Can't believe everything people say. That's how stories get started. So what if he's shot a couple losers. That don't make him some kinda Richard Kuklinski.

A. Who the hell is Richard Kuklinski?

B. You never heard of *The Iceman*? The notorious hitman for the Gambino family? I can't believe that you never heard of him.

A. No. I never heard of him. Is that who you're trying to be? … Some kinda famous contract killer? How'd he get that name, Iceman? Was he like a cool dude?

B. Iceman. He used to freeze his bodies to confuse the forensics. Made it impossible to determine time of death. He was a brilliant tactician. They say he killed as many as 250 men. Over a thirty-year career.

A. Damn. He must have been rich. What'd he get paid for each killing? Ten grand? More? I'll bet it was at least ten grand. That would work out to two hundred and fifty thousand dollars. Over a career, I guess that really isn't that much.

B. That's 2.5 *million* dollars, you idiot.

A. Oh. 2.5 million. That's still not very much, if you think about it. Over a whole lifetime. Not much at all, actually.

B. That's a whole lot more than we're making. Period. … What'd we charge for that bitch we offed? What'd they pay us, anyway? We split it. What was it? Ten grand. Right? And look at me. I still can't use my right arm. All because of that stupid dog. I still have to wipe my ass with my left hand. That whole job so sucked. … And now, here we are. Laid out like a piece of cheese on a mousetrap. All this to get this Handler guy to show his face, so the boss can blow it off. … What are the chances that he'll get a couple rounds off before the boss man kills him?

Jack sipped his hot coffee and continued listening.

A. Who did he hire? Did he ever tell you who he got to kill

Handler?

B. Didn't tell me. All I know is that we're supposed to draw Handler out in the open. How the hell we're supposed to do that—nobody's explained *that* to us yet. It's all just a big crock of shit.

A. All you do is com ...

---voices drop off as a fire truck went by down on the street, drowning out the voices in the room---

B. Ain't he supposed to be staying at the hotel across the street? Ain't that what they told us? Why the hell can't we just go over there and take him out in the restaurant? He's human—he has to eat just like the rest of us. Right? ... Why can't we just do it like that? That would be so simple.

A. Do you know what he looks like? *Really* know? Have you ever seen him? Like, would you be able to pick him out of the crowd? Besides, you ain't very good with a gun anyway. I don't think you could even shoot yourself in the foot with your left hand. ... Whoever it is that the boss has hired, I'm sure that he at least knows what Handler looks like. All we have to do is to show up and *make* him show up ... so the professional killer—the Iceman—can snuff him out. ... No big deal, really.

B. What are they paying us for this? Another ten grand? Is that it? And we split it? Is that what you agreed on?

A. Yeah. Something like that.

B. And when is all this supposed to happen?

A. When they tell us. We don't know if he's even in the city yet. When they know for sure that he's over there, they will let us know, and they'll tell us how they want us to lure him out in the open. Then, BANG! And it'll all be over, and we'll have some change in our pockets.

B. I'm getting sick of sitting around here. Can't we go out and get a hotdog and a beer someplace? Let's get the hell outta here for a while. Okay? No one will know. They're not watching us—not yet?

A. Sure. Let's do it. ... Are you ready?

B. I was born ready. You buyin'. Right?

---this was followed by laughing, and, eventually, the closing of doors. And then silence---

Jack immediately reached out to Roger.

"Have you been listening to those two clowns?" Jack asked.

"I have. Looks like that laser microphone's working pretty well."

"Yes it is," Jack agreed. "And they haven't yet given up who their boss is—the nameless person they keep referring to?"

"Not yet. And we might never—they might not know. It's possible that all we ever find out is who they send to do you. But, that should still tell us something."

"These fellows do not yet know that I'm in the city, do they? How are they going to find out? Am I going to have to go over there and introduce myself?"

"My guess is that the UNSUB is waiting for you to make the first move. I would be surprised, *very* surprised, if he was not watching those two guys. As soon as Henry arrives, I'd like you to begin to venture out. Get yourself in the same restaurant or bar with Mutt and Jeff, and see if we can't draw the UNSUB out."

"Where do these guys like to eat?" Jack asked. "Or where do they go to drink?"

"They've only been in town for one full day," Roger responded. "They haven't really established any significant patterns we're aware of. I've got someone monitoring the lobby of their hotel. We'll see where they go this time, and maybe we can start to figure them out—begin to predict them. ... I have no doubt that the UNSUB will remain out of sight until the time comes for him to act. But, I'm pretty certain that he's going to be monitoring our guys tonight, I would think. To see if you show up. It's just a damn shame that there are no indications as to who we are dealing with."

"And how about our boys—Mutt and Jeff, as you call them," Jack said. "I think you're telling me that they have no idea that I'm watching them."

"It seems that's the case right now," Roger said. "They appear virtually clueless. They understand and have accepted their role in this. They know that they are fresh meat and that you're the bear."

"Have we ever met? These two fellows and me?"

"To my knowledge, you've never met," Roger said. "They've undoubtedly been given pictures of you, just as we've provided you with headshots of them. But, as far as we know, you fellows have never been formally introduced."

"And Henry," Jack said. "Am I to assume that even the UNSUB is unaware of Henry?"

"About that," Roger said, "we just don't know anything about that for certain. We have nothing to suggest that Mutt and Jeff have ever actually met Henry. So, if he even wears a cap, and sunglasses, they would probably not pick him out. And Henry's smart. He can avoid standing out. But, as for the UNSUB, we just don't know. Likely, if not certain, the UNSUB has been provided an adequate dossier on both of you. That would include pictures. Plus, it is entirely possible that the UNSUB knows you ... perhaps even both of you."

Jack peered out from the small slice of view created by the almost closed drapery. The gentle late summer rain made everything glisten in the City That Never Sleeps. The running lights of taxis showed like shooting stars down the dampened street, interrupted only by the occasional careless pedestrian, overly eager to get home or wherever.

"You see," Roger continued, "what we're almost certainly dealing with are some very smart people. I'm talking about the people behind the whole thing. This means that our UNSUB is most certainly highly professional—unlike Mutt and Jeff. ... I share this with you as a warning. You had damn well better be *very* careful. Both you and Henry. Or you guys are going to get hurt. ... Dead, actually."

Jack savored another long sip of coffee before replying.

Chapter 10

I hear what you're saying," Jack said. "But, there are a couple things we have never fully discussed. One of them is the *why* behind this. If the whole point is to kill me and Henry, why are they even involving these two guys at all? Why not just do us? And the second thing I'm not terribly clear about is just exactly what sort of an outcome are you after? You've been pretty clear about Mutt and Jeff. You want them to stay alive until you have all the info that you're after—that is, regarding the UNSUB, and who it was that hired him. I think we both believe that there is a mastermind behind this whole mess, and it's not going to be our Mutt and Jeff. ... Once all that has been determined, your interest in preserving those two assholes is satisfied. But not until that point.

"My question is this: how exactly do we do this? So that everything is satisfactory in your eyes?"

"To answer your first concern," Roger replied. "We are not sure as to why the UNSUB is doing it this way. That is, why he is using Mutt and Jeff to draw you out. Just don't know the answer to that. Not for sure. ... It has been suggested that he is trying to make it look like your death and Millie's are all somehow tied to Mutt and Jeff. Fulbright thinks that they want to make it look like Mutt and Jeff took you out, and you killed them. As long as all of you die in the same room, evidence can be doctored to tell most any story. Bob is thinking that UNSUB is protected by Deep State operatives within the FBI and even the Secret Service. He thinks that they will try to make this operation fit the narrative, no matter how it goes down. ... And his reasoning seems the most logical. Bob is pretty good with sorting shit like that out.

"About your second question," Roger continued. "Regarding the end game for Mutt and Jeff. That is, when am I finished with them. ... About that, I will let you know as soon as I possibly can. All we are really interested in is nailing down just who it is that is paying the UNSUB. After we know that, we have no further interest in those two men. But I assure you that I will let you know about that as soon as I know."

"But," Jack asked, "until that point, I dare not terminate *any* of them. Is that right?"

"That is how I would like to see it go down," Roger said. ... "If, however, it ever comes to a life or death matter, for either you or Henry, I think you have to protect yourselves. I couldn't bear to lose either one of you."

"I couldn't agree with you more about that," Jack said, not entirely pleased with the box Roger had put him in. "I'll give it some serious thought and see what I can come up with. Before we make a move."

"And I'll do the same," Roger replied, obviously feeling more than a little guilty for the pressures he was applying. "Jack, I do apologize for this situation. And I do regret that I do not have an easy solution. ... But, of all the people I have ever worked with, I have always found you to be the most innovative of the lot. There are all sorts of words I could use to describe our working relationship. Efficient. Expeditious. Studied. Those are some of them. I could come up with a plan of action. But, I truly believe that you will develop a better one than I could."

"Well, I sure as hell didn't do so well protecting Millie, did I?" Jack protested. "Here I was trying to protect her ... and my boys ... and I get her killed."

"You're too hard on yourself, Jack," Roger said, trying to console his friend. "We still don't know who was ultimately behind Millie's murder. You did everything right for her. And your boys. *Everything*. And I mean that. As we ferret out the rest of this shit, we just might learn who put those assholes—Mutt and Jeff—up to it. It's a cinch that they didn't come up with that all by themselves. Someone *significant* hired them to gun her down."

Jack's eyes flashed. "Are you suggesting that ...? What the hell is it that you are getting at? Exactly?"

"Just that there's a lot of shit here that we just don't yet know," Roger said.

"Are you suggesting," Jack asked, "that the UNSUB is following orders from the same people that hired Mutt and Jeff? Is that what you're saying?"

"I'm not suggesting anything," Roger said. "The truth is that we just don't know who's behind any of this. ... Sure, sometimes we blame it all on Deep State. That's what we do a lot. We do that too much, I fear. Who the hell is Deep State? Is it ideological? Political? Economic? Is there a single driving force? Or many? Maybe it's all about serving oneself. ... That is, maybe it's a personal vendetta of some sort. Is China responsible? ... There's a lot of cash being poured in—where's *it* coming from? Offshore? If so, then to what degree are the globalists involved? If at all. ... Bottom line, Jack, this is what I'm trying to say. We've got a big problem here in the Good Ole U.S. of A. What I'm asking you to do is possibly bigger and tougher than saving POTUS's life in Singapore.

It would be much easier to just go, find out who the UNSUB is, kill him, and then shoot those idiot bastards that took out your friend. That would amount to the termination of a very successful job—you could take a shower, have a beer, and hightail it out of town ASAP. ... But, there is so much more involved here. I *really* need you to find out who is ultimately behind this whole mess. Unlike most of your operations, killing the perps is secondary at best, and perhaps not even desirable at all. ... The truth is, above all, I'm after info."

"I get what you're after, Roger. But I have an agenda as well," Jack said.

"Find out who they all are," Roger said. "Take it one step at a time. ... It would be ideal if in one week from now we know who's behind this. Period. ... It would be even better if we're both—hell, all *three* of us—are still alive."

Jack didn't respond directly to Roger's comment. In his gut, this was how he suspected all along that this was what Roger was really after. Now he knew.

"Just let me know where and what," Jack finally said. "I'll lay low until then."

"Sounds good, my friend," Roger replied.

Jack set the phone down and stared unfocused at the wall. "This is going to be like walking barefooted through a pit of angry rattlesnakes," he said to himself. "How is this ever going to work? ... Damn it all! I'd feel so much better if I came up with my own set of contingencies. Can always change or abandon if Roger offers something better."

Jack spent the next several hours designing his next move. Finally, long after dark, Jack looked down at his watch and mumbled to himself, "No point in waiting until Henry gets here. Waste too much time. I need to get started first thing in the morning."

But, before turning in, he first went downstairs to the late-night steakhouse and enjoyed what half of him considered to be a "final meal."

Upon his return he set his alarm for 5 A.M.

The first thing that Jack did after he rolled out of bed was to go through the desk to check out for a second time the goodies Roger had left for him. He found, along with the other keycards, two cards that bore the trademark name of the hotel across the street. Each had a handwritten post-it note attached. One stated that it was "For the door of Mutt and Jeff's room—#1479." And the other: "For the room above Mutt and Jeff's—#1579." He pulled the note off of the keycard for room #1579. And, tossing the note in the trash, he stuck the keycard in his pocket.

Typically, the first thing Jack would do on a morning like this would be to practice his daily exercise regimen, and then jump into the shower. But not on this day. Today he did work out, but once that exercise was completed, he simply stuck his head under the lavatory faucet, dried his hair off a bit, slipped on a shirt, and then slid his shoes on over his sockless feet.

Of course, he would never leave home without a weapon—the Glock 29 was belt-holstered under his untucked shirt at his lower back.

He took the elevator down to the ground floor and left the hotel.

The first thing he did upon entering Mutt and Jeff's hotel was to locate the concierge desk. As Jack walked up, the polite host stood up to greet him and said, "Good morning, sir. My name is

Carey. How may I serve you?"

Showing the host his keycard, Jack said, "I am totally out of shampoo and conditioner in my room. Do you suppose you could help me out a little?"

"Of course," the host said with a broad smile. "Would you like some soap and toothpaste as well?"

"Soap would be great," Jack replied. "I'm good with toothpaste."

"Here you go, sir," the host said, handing Jack a small paper bag prominently displaying the hotel's logo. "This contains a complimentary selection of items you might need during your stay with us. ... And how long are you planning to be here?"

"Two. Actually three more days, at least."

"Here you go," the host said, reaching out with a second bag. "Take these with our compliments. If you need anything else, don't hesitate to pay me a visit."

"Thank you so much for your help," Jack said as he received the items. "Oh, could you tell me what time the restaurant opens for breakfast?"

The host looked at his watch and said, "It's five minutes to six right now. Breakfast is served starting at six."

"Wonderful," Jack said. "I'll finish getting dressed and head right down. Thank you for all your help."

"My pleasure. Hope you enjoy your stay with us."

Jack smiled and headed for the elevator. He pushed the button for the fourteenth floor. When he got out, he looked around to get his bearings. There were two bronze wall signs. Each had two numbers and an arrow on it. He followed the one that said "1450-1500".

When he arrived at room 1479 he began to clumsily fumble around with the door hardware, making as much noise as a person could make without being reported to security.

He slid the card for 1579 into the reader, and then shook the door handle. And then he would curse out loud. He then repeated that procedure several more times, making a little more noise with each effort, and cursing loudly enough to be heard inside the room.

"What the hell is going on out there?" Mutt growled just loud enough for Jeff to hear. "Who the hell could *that* be?"

After the disruption continued to be repeated, Mutt finally pulled Jeff back and told him to pull his gun out and wait in the bathroom.

"I'll see what's goin' on. If it sounds like I need you, wait until I get him inside and close the door, and then shoot the sonofabitch. … Make sure you have the silencer on it. … And then shoot him. We'll worry about the body later."

Chapter 11

Who the hell is it?" Jeff asked.

"I don't know. Some drunk, I suppose. Now, get your ass in the bathroom. Get ready. If I call you, step out and shoot the bastard. Use the silencer. You got it? Right?"

"Yeah," Jeff replied. "I got it right here."

"Screw it on. Quickly. And get ready. Wait till I call you."

Jeff did not respond verbally, but he did start attaching the suppressor onto the barrel of a Taurus 9mm. semi-automatic pistol.

Mutt then walked over to the door and waited.

Finally, after about thirty seconds, the racket outside again commenced.

Nearly immediately after it started up Mutt growled, "What's goin' on out there?"

Jack reached behind his back to be sure his Glock could be drawn if need be.

"It's me. Jack Handler. This is *my* room. ... Just who the hell are you? And what are you doing in *my* room?"

Mutt was stunned. "What are you talking about? This is my room."

He turned toward the bathroom. Jeff was sticking his head out of the door with a big frown.

"*Your room!*" Jack barked. "The hell it is. This is *my* room. I just went down to pick up some shampoo, and you show up in my room."

"We've got keys and everything," Mutt said. "We've been here two days. This room is registered to me—Wilber Wright. This *can't* be your room. … What's your room number?"

"Must be the UNSUB thought they were too stupid to remember a fake name," Jack said to himself. "So he registered the room under *Wilber Wright*. That is really lame."

Jack thought Mutt might be looking through the peephole, so he took a step backward and examined the number on the door. "Fourteen seventy-nine, I guess," Jack said. "*This* room. This is *my* room. Just open the damn door and I can show you my keycard."

Mutt latched the secondary safety device and cracked the door open about two inches. "Show me your door key," he said.

Jack held it to the opening and showed Mutt. "See it? It's got this hotel right on it. I was just in this room. I spent the night in it."

"Nobody stamps the room numbers of the cards anymore. They use them over and over … program them for different rooms. You can't be staying in 1479. This is our room."

"What did you say?" Jack asked. "Did you say this was room *1479*? Fourteen seventy-nine? … I think I'm *1279*. Oh my God. How did I do that? What a stupid mistake. I am so sorry. So sorry. How stupid can I be? I must be suffering jet lag or something. … Damn it all. I am so sorry. Did I wake you up? Were you still sleeping?"

"You didn't wake us up," Mutt said. "Don't worry about it. We were just getting ready to go down for breakfast. It's alright."

"Then," Jack said. "You haven't had breakfast yet. Then join me—I'm buying. Anything you want. It's on me. I insist. Let me make this up to you? Okay? Not leaving until you agree to eat with me."

Mutt thought about it for a few seconds. And then he said, "Let us talk it over. Maybe we'll join you in ten. Appreciate the offer. We'll think about it."

"Great," Jack said. "I'll see you down there. I'll get a table, but I won't order until you can join me. So sorry about this whole mix-up. See you down there."

Jack turned and began walking down the hall toward the elevator. He listened intently to be sure that *Wilber Wright* wasn't stepping out to shoot him in the back. The closer he got to the elevator the better he felt. By the time he hit the *Ground Floor* button, he was smiling broadly.

How does that saying go, he was thinking to himself, *keep your friends close, and your enemies closer.*

Jack was pleased on several levels. First of all, he established beyond a doubt that Mutt and Jeff were now fully aware that he was in town.

Second, he left them thinking that he was registered at the same hotel as were they—just one floor beneath them. *Good thing I checked the elevator buttons on the way up, because some hotels actually do have a thirteenth floor. This one doesn't.*

Third, Jack successfully convinced Millie's killer that he did not recognize him. The truth is that Roger managed to dig up enough video footage for the forensic artists he worked with to come up with very accurate likenesses of both Mutt and Jeff. So Jack had immediately recognized Mutt. He did not have a real name to associate with Mutt, but there would be no surprises in that regard.

Fourth, Jack would now be able to set the table. He could have an enhanced role in determining when, where and how the battle would take place.

And finally, this breakfast should be relatively safe, even though Henry wasn't around to watch his back, as Mutt and Jeff did not have enough time to set up a trap.

When he reached the restaurant, he reserved a table for three. *Soon,* he was thinking, *I will get to know my adversaries better, and therefore be better able to deal with them. If they don't show up, then I will know that they are smarter than I thought, and that they were able to see through my little scheme.*

"Good morning, Mr. Handler," Mutt said with a smile. "I think you said your name was Handler. Is that right?"

Chapter 12

"Yes," Jack responded, "Jack Handler. That's my full name. And your name is Wilber Wright. Did I get that right?"

"Yes," Mutt said through an embarrassed smile, as he squeezed a quick *shut your mouth and don't say a word* glance at his partner. "My family name was Wright, and my mother was a big fan of the Wright brothers. So, my parents named me Wilber Wright, and my brother here, they named him Orville."

"I'll bet that was tough to live with growing up," Jack said with a perfectly straight face.

"You can't even imagine," Mutt said.

"What do people call you, Wilber, or Will?"

"Usually people call me Will. But, it doesn't really matter to me. As long as they don't call me late for dinner—or breakfast."

"Good one," Jack said. "What brings you to New York? Business or pleasure?"

"Both, I guess you could say. We're here on business, but we're going to have some fun on the side. Always like to mix business and pleasure whenever we can."

"I'm the same way," Jack said. He wanted to be careful and not pressure his guests at all. *Better not press this,* he reasoned.

"I think I need to take a look at this menu," Jack said, picking one up. "Remember, this breakfast is on me. So be sure to order anything you think looks good. As for me, I think their Deluxe Omelet looks pretty good. It says it's got ham, vegetables, and two cheeses. Sounds good to me. But you guys get whatever you want. … Hell, you can each get a couple of them. Or anything. It'll all be on my expense account. So eat up."

Mutt and Jeff looked at each other, and Mutt said, "I'll have that too. If that's alright."

"Yeah. Sure," Jack said. "With OJ and coffee. OJ and coffee sound okay? What do you think about that? Sound okay?"

"Orange juice and coffee sound great to me," Mutt said.

"How about you, Orville? OJ and coffee sound good to you as well?"

"Sure," Jeff/Orville said, nodding his head. "Sounds good."

"Then that's what it'll be."

Jack waved the waitress over and placed their order. When asked if he wanted to charge it to his room he declined, opting instead for his credit card. "I get points on my card when I handle it like this."

"By the way," Jack asked, "what sort of business are you two gentlemen in? And what draws you to New York?"

"We are here for the commemorative pen conference," Mutt said. "It's being held down in The Village—you know, Greenwich Village. We're both pen salesmen."

Jack had a difficult time keeping a straight face. *Must be they spent all of ten seconds coming up with that story. Those guys as salesmen? My ass. They'd starve doing that. And besides, no one books sales conventions in The Village. … Better change the topic,* he determined.

"What are you boys doing tonight?" Jack asked. "I've got a free pass to a gentlemen's club just a few blocks from here. So do you. All you have to do is show them your room key and they will let you in free. Want to meet me there?"

The two men looked at each other and nodded their approval.

"Great," Jack said. "Then that's settled. It's called 'Dolls and More Dolls.' You really can't miss it. It's located on Eighth Avenue near 44th Street. Somewhere in there. You can't miss it ... Your driver will know. They've got great drinks. I've been there before. In fact, I try to go there every time I'm in New York. They've got a sports bar, too. They broadcast all the major sporting events. ... And, of course, they've got the best young babes on the East Coast.

"Ten o'clock. I'll get in there a little early and get a table. You guys get there around ten. We'll have a great time."

Five minutes after the waitress brought out their breakfast, Jack suddenly looked down at his watch. "Damn," he groaned. "I almost forgot. I've got an appointment this morning. One that I *cannot* miss. You guys finish your breakfast, I'm gonna to have to run. Don't be offended. It's just one of those things. I gotta be going."

"Well, Jack," Mutt said. "Sorry you have to rush off like this. But we understand. It happens to all of us from time to time."

"Glad you understand," he said as he waved the waitress over so he could pay her.

"Tonight at ten," he said as he stood to leave. "All you'll need to get in is your hotel keycard. Ask for Jack Handler. They've got VIP rooms, but I don't think we'll need that, do you? Those are really some big bucks. We'll see. If we change our minds and decide to get a VIP room, we can still have them set one up for us. But I don't think that will be necessary. ... Anyway, we'll see you there at ten. The table will be under my name—Handler. Take care. Catch you later. If I decide on a VIP room, if you just ask for Handler, you'll find me.

"Oh," Jack said after he had taken only a step or two from the table. "Write a phone number down on a napkin for me. I'll give you a call to be sure it's all set for tonight. Your cell phone would be great."

"Here you go," Mutt said as he shuffled over a generic business card with his cell phone number handwritten on it. "Can we get your number, in case we have to reach you?"

"I'll call you. It'll be on your phone. I gotta run. See you tonight."

Jack's swift departure was fully intentional. His training taught him to keep moving. The story he implanted in his brain was that espoused by the most successful of the British fighter pilots during World War II—the ones behind the stick of the best fighting air machine of the era: the Spitfire. While it was as fast or faster than anything Germany was sending up at the time, the real trick to staying alive was to keep changing directions. "The German you worried about most was the one you couldn't see." The line Jack remembered best was lived out by one of the aces of the RAF—the Royal Air Force of the United Kingdom. "I stayed alive by changing direction every ten seconds, even if I thought there were no German Messerschmitt 109s anywhere in sight—every ten seconds."

Jack needed to make his exit quickly enough to sneak out of the hotel and return to his own room. *Those assholes are enjoying their free breakfast, they're not going to follow me,* he figured.

"Henry," Jack said. He had called his friend even before he reached his room. "Minor change of plans. Where are you right now? Can you talk?"

"Jack," Henry said. "I just packed the boys up and we are sitting on the ferry. You'd said you wanted me to get going as early as possible. I think the boys are still half asleep."

"No, Uncle Henry," Robby said, having overheard Henry. "We're all the way asleep. Can't believe you woke us up at six A.M."

"Did you hear that, Jack? Your boys are protesting their drill sergeant. … That would be me. … What's this about? A change of plans?"

"Instead of driving all the way into Newark, I'm going to have our pilot pick you up at the airport in Detroit. He'll fly you into Newark. There you'll take a cab, or an Uber, into the city. I need you to stop at the hotel and get settled in. And then step across the hall to my room and we can discuss what I need you to do. I need you to be at my door and good to go by eight-thirty. This assignment is proving to be a very tricky one. And it is likely to get even more dicey before we're done. I'll fill you in when you arrive."

"You talking Detroit Metropolitan?"

"Exactly. South end of the city. You'd take 275 to I-94E, and then just follow the signs. It's just a few minutes off 275."

"How will I find him—the pilot?"

"He has your phone number. He'll let you know where to wait."

"Sounds good," Henry said. "I'm still close to the house. Anything I should go back for? So I can prepare for *dicey*?"

"I'll have whatever else you might need. See you at eight-thirty. Don't be too concerned. We've had tougher cases."

Jack's own words aroused anxiety within his spirit. "Have I just lied to my friend?" he asked himself. "I do not recall ever having been faced with a more convoluted situation. I'm sticking his ass out there as well as my own. I hope I have not lied to my friend."

"See you later, boss."

A few minutes later Jack reached his room. He entered it, found the most comfortable chair, sat down and shifted his mind into overdrive. At 9:30 his phone rang.

"Roger," Jack said, answering his phone. "Glad you called. I'm going to need some specialized gear. I'm working a plan. ... Got something to write with?"

Jack and Roger talked for nearly an hour, carefully considering all the ramifications, strengths and weaknesses of Jack's plan.

Once Jack was satisfied that they had ironed out everything that needed to be, he asked, "Well, what do you think? Is it going to work? Do you think you can get me everything I'm going to need, and have it here by seven-thirty tonight?"

"Handler, if it was anyone but you, I'd say this hare-brained scheme doesn't have a shot in hell of working. But, you're a different animal. You proved that many times. You have a way of making everything turn out like you want. ... If anyone can make this happen the way I need it to, it'll be you."

"I think Henry and I can do it," Jack said. "And the sooner the better."

"This is how I'll get it to you," Roger said. "I'll deliver it in a van—a standard white delivery van. It will be tagged as an 'Emergency Vehicle.' That way it won't be towed. ... *Shouldn't* be towed—you are in New York. ... I will have the city clear a spot close to your club—Dolls and More Dolls. But it won't be directly in front of it. That would draw too much attention.

"Most of what you're requesting will be in that van. The rest of it—the gear that you will need to get started—I will drop off at your room in person."

"I look forward to getting this mission over with," Jack said, concluding the conversation.

Jack spent the rest of the day in his room, not even stepping out for food. He found a number of snacks and bottled water in the hotel minibar. He did turn on the laser mic and recorder in order to monitor conversations that took place in Mutt and Jeff's room. He appreciated the fact that while the equipment stored all sounds generated in the targeted room, it presented for *Standard Playback* only sounds during times when the laser mic detected bona fide human conversation. In order not to waste a lot of his time, he accessed only the *Standard Playback* option.

Some of what Jack eavesdropped on went like this:

"Are you sure that was really him?"

"Check the pictures for yourself. It sure as hell looks like Handler to me."

(There was a pause, so the recorder shut down. The clock indicated that twenty minutes passed. And then there was a one-sided conversation. Jack assumed it was the voice of one of the men talking over a phone to someone who was probably the boss.)

"I wanted you to know that we met with Jack Handler this morning."

(Pause.)

"Had breakfast with him. Both of us—Del and me."

(Pause.)

"No. Of course not. To him we were Wilber and Orville—just like you told us."

(Long pause.)

"We didn't contact him. He walked right up to our room and tried to get in the door. Said he thought it was his room. He said he made a mistake. That his room was 1279, not 1479."

(Pause.)

"Honest mistake, we think. After we convinced him that it was our room, not his, he apologized to us and invited us down to breakfast. We both believed him."

(Short Pause)

"Seemed like a nice enough guy. … He even invited us to go out to a strip club tonight. That's why I called you."

(Pause.)

"No. I'm not shittin' you. It sounded totally legit to me. He wants us to meet him at a place called Dolls and More Dolls at 10:00 tonight. We told him we would go. Do you think that was a mistake?"

(Pause.)

"No. He's not paying for anything. We can use our room key to get in. … I'm sure the drinks will cost extra. We'll take some cash."

(Pause.)

"Oh. It's him alright. Looks just like the pictures you gave us. And, when he paid for breakfast, he used a credit card that had "Jack Handler" right on it. … It's gotta be him."

(Pause.)

"Well, I suppose we wouldn't have to go tonight. We *could* just stand him up. He's in the city by himself, and I think he's a little lonely. … Hell, I don't know. *You're* the boss."

(Pause.)

"I don't understand how it could wreck everything."

(Pause.)

"Why can't we just meet him there at 10:00? Like he said. We'll go in and have a drink or two. All your guy would have to do is find us, and he will see Handler with us. He can do the job. And we'll all leave."

(Pause.)

"Yeah. It sounds pretty simple to me too. What could go wrong?"

(Pause.)

"If your guy changes his mind. Or gets cold feet. All he would have to do is walk out of the club. Handler and us could have a few drinks, and call it a night. That simple."

(Pause.)

"We're planning to stay there for a while … that is, if your man doesn't show up to do the job. … I'd say, we'll plan on keeping Handler there with us until at least midnight. That would give two hours. … Obviously, if your guy is satisfied, and is able to complete his mission. At that point we'll get out of there ASAP, or as soon as they'll let us. Be foolish to stick around then."

(Pause.)

"Okay then. Sounds good to us too. … Are you planning to be there? Or just your guy?"

(Long Pause.)

"Sorry, I know—"

(Pause.)

"You're totally right. I'm wrong. Whether you're there or not does not concern me. I apologize. I just—"

(Pause.)

"Yes. Yes. You're *absolutely* right. I am sorry. I was just thinking about how long we should stay there, if you should decide against doing it tonight."

(Pause.)

"Right. At midnight, we'll leave. Unless we hear different. Yes. That's good. That all works for us."

(Pause.)

"Okay. Thanks. Thank you very much."

There was then another pause.

"Holy shit, Del, I've never heard her talk like that before. She was one angry bitch. That's all I can say."

"She didn't like our plan?" Del asked. "Does she think she has a better one?"

"She didn't have any plan. That's why I thought she'd appreciate our offer. But *no-sir-ree Bob*. At least not to start with."

"But, she did come around in the end," Del said. "Right?"

"I guess she did. Pretty much. She gave us the go-ahead. So I guess everything's kinda okay. But she was *very* bitchy about it."

"What the hell does she expect?" Del complained. "We're giving her what she said she wanted. Shit! All she said she wanted was for us to flush Jack Handler out, and she would take care of the rest. She would see to it that he was taken out. ... We're gonna get paid. Right? I'm countin' on that money. She didn't say anything about that, did she?"

"She didn't say anything about money. And I was not about to bring it up. Damn bitch."

"I'm gonna have a beer," Del said, walking over to the mini-bar. "Want one?"

Jack could not wipe the smile from his face as he called Roger.

"Have you been listening to our Mutt and Jeff?" he asked.

"I did monitor it," Roger said. "Looks like it might go down tonight. ... But their boss didn't sound very happy about it."

"No, she didn't," Jack said. "You didn't pick up anything the female said, did you?"

"No, the equipment doesn't work like that. We didn't plant anything inside their room because we knew they were going to sweep it pretty well. And they did. They would have found any mics we might have hidden there. That laser mic requires people actually talk loud enough to vibrate the glass. It won't pick up the remote end of a cell phone conversation.

"But we did get some valuable information. For one thing, we learned that these guys are, at least were, taking orders from a woman. We didn't know that before. Of course, we don't know her name, other than 'The Bitch.' And I'm afraid that there are a lot of women sharing *that* name … at least in this line of work."

"And," Jack added, "one of the guys—probably our Jeff—actually goes by the name of *Del*. We didn't know that before either.

"How are you proposing to handle this tonight?" Jack asked.

"I'm just putting it together," Roger replied, "the equipment you requested. Not exactly sure yet. We want her, and the would-be killer that she hired. We want a positive ID on the two of them."

"Don't actually need to take them into custody then? Is that right?"

"Not unless he actually kills you," Roger chuckled. "At that point, I suppose we should make an arrest."

"Yeah," Jack moaned. "But we're not going to know if we've got the right guy until he puts a round in my head. Is that about right?"

"Just about."

"Okay, buddy," Jack said to Roger. "I've never known you to screw around like that. What sort of precautions are you taking? Care to share them with me? Because right now I'm not having a very good feeling about tonight."

Jack sat at the small black desk in his hotel room. His nervous energy led him to check and recheck the door locks, the video monitor, and the well-placed outside surveillance equipment.

As he leaned back in his swivel chair he thought, *I do believe that this stupid chair is the best piece of furniture in the whole damn room.*

"I will have two techs in the van," Roger said. "They will be monitoring everyone who walks into the club."

"Using facial recognition?"

"Right. If someone walks into the door who has any arrests or convictions for a violent crime on his record, it will alert us. And I will have four agents inside. Posing as regular patrons. They will have cameras on them as well. Theirs won't be doing facial recognition, but all video will be fed back to my field office, and they will be scrutinizing it there—real time."

"You talking about Secret Service Headquarters in DC?"

"No. I don't run anything through Headquarters anymore—never know who I can trust there. Deep State, you know. My field office is safe. And they can access all the databases DC can."

"Okay," Jack said. "Once we identify our would-be killer, what do we do? Should I take him out, or just ID him? How do you want this to play out?"

"Ideally, we would identify the contract killer, but let him live. That will tell us the most. And, over the long term, it could go a long way toward tracking down more of the movers and shakers. Kill him, and that is virtually the end of it."

That was the answer Jack dreaded but expected. Even a very basic manual on his line of work insisted that the assassin be taken

out as soon as identified ... not left around as a source of intelligence.

"What time are you getting here?" Jack asked. "Eight-thirty?"

"You said seven-thirty. So what is it to be? ... You trying to test
me?"

"Seven-thirty works for me," Jack chuckled. "That way we can
go over this face-to-face—just you and me. Maybe we can get all
the potential bugs worked out before Henry gets in. ... Are you
having the same pilot pick him up, as who flew me in?"

"Yup."

"Good, he should know the way."

"Nervous at all?" Roger asked.

"Hell no!" Jack blasted. "Jobs like this either work like expected, or you improvise. ... And if that doesn't work, then they plant
you in the garden. Never does any good to get worked up."

"How's your arm, by the way?" Jack asked, seeking to change
the subject.

Jack was alluding to Roger's left arm and shoulder that was
injured only a few weeks earlier in Singapore. Roger had taken
two 9mm. rounds in his left side before Jack was able to kill the
shooter.

"I can still feel it," Roger said. "Probably won't go dancing tonight. But my right arm still works pretty well. And that's the one
I use to point my Glock."

"We should sign off for now," Roger said after a brief period of
silence. "I've got a lot of running around to do if I'm going to pick
up and organize all this shit you ordered. Where shall we meet?
How about dinner in your hotel?"

"I'm going to sit tight in my room until Henry gets here," Jack said. "Never know who's watching. … Why don't you bring me a sandwich, along with that howitzer?"

"Singular," Roger fired back. "I thought you always asked for two. … What kind of sandwich would you like?"

"Surprise me. Grab one for Henry, too. Actually, he's a fan of New York's pastrami on rye. Two pastramis would do the job for Henry. … See you at seven-thirty. … And make mine a pastrami too."

With the curtains pulled tightly over his windows, and a hard-rubber doorstop driven tightly under the inside of the entry door, Jack rolled up a towel and wedged it into the gap at the bottom of that same door. He did that so as to make it difficult for anyone to slide a fiber-optic surveillance camera into the room to spy on him.

He then attached his own miniature wireless camera over the peephole so that he could video monitor any activity in the hall via his cellphone. Once he had these security measures in place, he set his Glock 29 on the table beside him, closed his eyes, and began running various scenarios through his mind.

Ten minutes later he popped his eyes open wide, and he rapidly started to search out other strip clubs in the area. He found one that particularly got his attention—*Ruby's Roost*. And he called them.

"What time do you open?" he asked.

"Doors open for drinks at six o'clock. Girls dance after eight."

"What time do you close?"

"We're open at six and close at four A.M."

"How about cover charges?"

"Weekdays, if you arrive before eight, it's waived. After eight, thirty bucks. And that is if we can even get you in. We get busy and that's it. You'll wait in the line outside."

"Can I pay for four reservations with my card?"

"Sure. Fifty bucks each."

"Really?" Jack asked. "Why so much?"

"Do you want 'em or not? Give me the credit card number right now, and the names. Otherwise you can take your chances."

Jack gave him his credit card number.

"That will be for four: one for me—Jack Handler. Two—Scott R. Blumberg. Three—Orville Wright. And, four—Wilber Wright."

"Are you shittin' me? Orville and Wilber Wright? Don't try to feed me that shit!"

"Just do it!" Jack barked. "You gonna be there yourself? Tonight?"

"Damn right, I'll be there."

"I will get there a little early. I'm Handler. There will be a Franklin in it for you if you can make sure there are no issues. What's your name?"

"I don't give out my name to nobody. And certainly not to some big-mouth asshole. I'll be at the door when you get here. Just ask for the big doorman. You won't miss me. I'm six four, go two eighty, and wear two large rings on my right fist. You show me the Franklin, and we'll be fine. Otherwise, I'm gonna give you a close-up look at my jewelry, and then you're gonna be scraping your ass up out of the gutter. I don't much like big talkers. And I think that's what you are."

"Sounds good to me," Jack replied. "I'll look for you—Mr. Big Doorman—when I get there."

"You do that," the doorman said gruffly as he hung up.

Jack was almost laughing when he rang Roger.

"Hey, buddy," he said. "Remember me?"

"Okay, Jack. What's up?"

"Change of plans. I need you to send your vans to a different address. A different strip club. Still in Manhattan, but on the Upper East Side—just across town."

"Should I ask you why?"

"Hell no," Jack replied. "We can discuss it down the road over a good craft beer back on Sugar Island. ... Here's where I'm going to need you. There's a strip club right off the Manhattan end of the Queensboro Bridge. It's called Ruby's Roost. Smaller than the one on the West Side."

"More *intimate*, I assume," Roger quipped.

"I don't know about that," Jack said. "But it'll work better, I think. ... I do want you to have your guys monitor anyone leaving the other club—Dolls and More Dolls. See if they can spot anyone leaving that club and heading for Ruby's. Will likely be around ten or ten-thirty. The ones we will want to keep our eye on are, of course, Mutt and Jeff. But, if there is a third or fourth that leave at the same time, heading east, then that might prove very interesting.

"You'll need one camera above the entry door at each of these fine establishments—there might be several entry doors at each. These must be monitored for facial recognition. If you detect the same person entering both clubs, then that just might be the one you're looking for. Make sense?"

"I get your thinking," Roger said. "Yes, it does make sense. Where, exactly, is this Ruby's Roost?"

"You can't miss it. It's just off the bridge west of First Street. ...

And, there is one more thing you can add to my grocery list. We should have two ambulances at the ready. And some uniformed officers right outside—not authentic, of course."

"Two!" Roger snapped emphatically. "Two? What the hell are you looking for?"

"Can you do it or not?" Jack asked. "I am going to need two. Maybe more. But I think two is a definite. One of them must be reserved for me. Will you arrange it?"

"Yes. Yes, of course. But you're tying up half my resources already. Now you want me to get you two ambulances. I can do that, but if there is a lot of blood spilled on this job, that can get really hard to explain."

"Two ambulances, then," Jack repeated. "And at least two, better with four, and a bunch of your guys disguised as uniformed officers. Are we good?"

"Sure."

"I'm not exactly sure about timing—that's with regard to the ambulances. Might not even need them. But, if we do, it will most likely be after ten—how much after that I can't predict. The club is open until four A.M."

"This is really starting to sound like a fun time," Roger said sarcastically.

"And, watch out for the bouncer," Jack warned. "He sounds pretty impressive to me. You'd better behave yourself, especially with your wounded wing."

After Jack disconnected the call to Roger, he sat back in his chair, closed his eyes again, and played all the various scenarios he anticipated they might encounter when the big show got underway.

As planned, Roger arrived at exactly 7:30. He brought with him two very large suitcases, both packed tightly with the equipment Jack had requested. He had used a large aluminum luggage carrier that he borrowed from the hotel's front desk.

"Well, my friend," Roger said when Jack answered his knock. "It's all here—what you asked for and more. Take good care of this stuff. Please. ... If I try to return it with bullet holes or blood stains, they make me pay for it. So have some pity on me. Okay? ... Oh, and here's your sandwiches. Two for you and two for Henry."

"I'll do my best," Jack replied.

"It is all there," Roger said as he walked toward the door. "Basically three of everything. That should cover what you and Henry might need, plus spares in the event they're needed. You've used all or most of this equipment before, so you should be good to go. I really should be running. I'm setting up a tech van at your West Side club, and two over on the East Side. If you and Henry have questions, just give me a call."

"Thanks, Rog. And good luck."

As soon as Roger had left, Jack began unpacking the gear. He laid half of it out on the bed, and the other half on the couch.

At ten minutes to eight Henry knocked on Jack's door.

"Greetings, Mr. Blumberg," Jack said. "Have you been in your room yet?"

"Yes," Henry replied. "I followed your original instructions. Everything was as you said it would be."

"Great. Roger was just here. He left some gear for us. If you're ready I'd like to go over the job. ... And, you should know, we have made some changes in the original plan. We should go over that as well. By the way, one—two—of the sandwiches on the table are yours—pastrami on rye. Hope you like them."

Henry glanced over and allowed his eyes to devour the four large slices of seeded rye bread, completely stuffed with pastrami, Swiss cheese, Russian dressing—aside from a generous bowl of coleslaw, all had earlier been grilled.

He finished one of the sandwiches within a few minutes.

"The plans have changed, you say," Henry said. "How have they changed?"

"For starters, we are going to a different strip club."

"We're going to a different strip club?" Henry repeated as a question, "Or, we're going to *both* but at different times? I think I would prefer it the second way."

"*They're* going to both, that is if they will. But you and I are only going to the second club."

"I'll bet you've got a good reason for changing it up. Right?"

"Yeah," Jack said. "I think I do."

"Feel like sharing it with me?"

"It's a long story, Henry," Jack said. "And it's not open for debate. I'll tell you what you need to know, but I don't want to slide my whole plan under a microscope, if you know what I mean. Too damn many moving parts. Too much to go wrong. Too many unknowns."

"I get it," Henry said. "Just tell me where to go and what to do, and I'll do my very best to hold up my end."

He then walked over to the table and lifted his second sandwich to his mouth and bean to eat it. Even though they had cooled somewhat by the time Henry got around to them, he could not have been more delighted.

"I know you will. And I am actually beginning to think we

might be able to pull this off."

"And come out walking on the other end?" Henry asked.

"Can't guarantee that," Jack said. "Fact is, I am bait on the trap. Roger is trying to figure out who engineered the hit on Millie, and now, this one targeted at me. He doesn't have a clue at this point. Initially he thought, as did I, that it was Deep State that had Millie killed. To get back at me for going to bat to save POTUS in Singapore. That's what we both assumed.

"But then, up popped *this* mess. Someone knows me well enough to conclude that I would be coming after Millie's killers. And they are now using my anger to isolate me so that they can put a hit on me and make it look like it was Deep State revenge. … I'll admit, some things about this don't add up. But, for some reason, this seems to be the way it's shaking out. So, we sort of have to play along if we're going to get to the bottom of it."

"But it isn't?" Henry asked. "I mean, Deep State was not behind Millie's murder? We both assumed it was, didn't we?"

"Yeah. That's what we thought."

"But it *wasn't* Deep State that hit Millie?"

"We just don't know. … One of the things that doesn't make sense is this elaborate plan they've gone to. It's almost like it's a personal thing. Hitting innocent Millie. And now going after me. Something else to this. And that's what I haven't figured out. … Roger is trying to flush out the killers, and who's behind it. That's what we're doing tonight. If all goes as planned, by the end of the night we will know who Millie's killers were working for, and, with any luck, one or both of us will fly back to Michigan—strapped in a seat and not a box."

"That bad?"

Henry carefully wrapped up the what remained of the second sandwich and put it in the mini fridge for later. He could have finished it off as he did the first one, but knew that he needed to keep his senses keenly aware during this mission.

"Potentially," Jack replied. "The powers behind Millie's killers have hired a real professional to take me out. Plus, I suspect that pro is going to kill the two men who killed Millie—it won't be that hard because the three of us will be sitting at the same table tonight.

"If the professional is totally successful, I will end up dead, and so will the two assholes who shot Millie. And, I believe that forensics will show that the same pistol was used on all four of us—Millie and her two killers, and me."

"How did the killer get hold of that pistol?" Henry asked. "Isn't it tucked away in some evidence locker? And, how is he planning to avoid capture?"

"The firearm picked up at the scene was not the one used on Millie," Jack said, as he poured himself a fresh cup of black coffee. He then took a seat at the small round table in the corner of the room.

"Can't explain it, but that's what Roger told me. My gut says that to complete this circle, it has to go down somewhat like I am describing. ... If the hitman is successful tonight, by tomorrow morning forensic testing will indicate that the two men sitting at the table with me were not the ones who shot Millie. So, they cannot be convincingly traced back to the party who paid for the whole thing. Which means that nobody will be able to effectively, or even somewhat convincingly, rat anybody out. ... Convoluted as hell, I know, but that appears to be how this is supposed to go down."

At this point, Henry looked a bit confused and tired. He had already driven from the UP to drop off the boys at a fishing lodge, he then drove into Detroit Metro in order to catch a waiting plane. And then, he didn't arrive at Jack's hotel door until 7:50pm.

On Roger's directive, the pilot gave him a Yankees cap to help him fit in with New York City residents. Henry was a large man, standing head and shoulders above most New Yorkers. So, the best plan to help him blend—short of seating him in a wheelchair— was to make him look like a Yankees fan.

"We can talk about this over a beer later," Henry said. "What I don't get is, how in hell are you going to survive this shit storm, while those other two guys, the assholes, get themselves killed. I don't see how you're going to pull this off."

"Frankly, Henry, I don't have a lot of confidence in the plan myself. That's why I don't want to discuss it any further. I can't have you trying to talk me out of it. You just might succeed. … Let's take our shot and see where we end up."

Both men remained silent for several very long, but not un-comfortable, moments. Finally, Henry spoke. "How about your boys, Jack? What will become of them?"

Jack did not respond.

Chapter 13

You have reservations for us, I believe," Jack said.

"Your names?" the cashier asked.

"Jack Handler and Scott Blumberg."

"Yes, I've got you down. … This is for four. You've got four names paid for. Are they here now, or are they joining you later?"

"The Wright brothers will be joining us around ten," Jack said. "You've got a big doorman, I believe. Can you point us in his direction?"

"He's right inside. Trust me, you can't miss him. He's gonna be checking you out to be sure you don't got any weapons on you. Just move along, please."

Jack and Henry walked through the door and immediately ran into the big doorman.

"You're the guy I need to see," Jack said as he handed the huge doorman a one-hundred-dollar bill. "My name is Jack Handler, and this is my friend Scott Blumberg."

"Step over here so I can wand you," the doorman said.

Jack complied.

When he passed his wand over Jack's crotch the sensor sounded.

"What the hell is this?" the doorman said. "You got a cast-iron cock, or what?"

"You could say that," Jack said, handing the big man another one hundred-dollar bill.

"You got a gun stuffed down your pants?" the doorman asked as he took the money.

"Get the hell out of my sight!" he said to Jack and Henry. "If either one of you give anyone trouble tonight, I'll break every bone in your bodies. Got it?"

"Sounds fair to me," Jack replied. "Keep your eye open for my other two friends—the Wright brothers."

The doorman looked away from Jack and Henry, and as he did he said more loudly than necessary, "You assholes just mind your own business and keep your homo hands off the ladies."

"That's it," Henry growled. He turned and started to go after the big doorman.

Jack grabbed him by the collar of his jacket and pulled him back.

"Not the time or place," Jack said. "We've got work to do. Save it."

The big doorman caught it out of the corner of his eye and pivoted around to face Henry.

"You'd better do what the old man tells you, jerkoff. Jack Handler's your daddy. He owns you. You'd better obey, you stupid shit."

Henry stared at the big doorman and pointed at him.

The big doorman flashed a prolonged middle finger at Henry.

"You'd better listen to the old man. Be a good little boy, and mind your master."

"I get it," Henry said still wearing the Yankees cap as he walked toward the bar with Jack. "But it's not my nature to let myself be talked to like that."

"No, it's not," Jack agreed. "But we've got a job to do here tonight. Putting the big guy down will only get us kicked out of here. It won't get us any closer to a win. We've got to concentrate on what matters."

Jack looked at his watch. "It's almost ten," he said. "Order me a club soda with lime. I have to make a call. … See if you can find us a table."

Jack stood and turned away from the bar and, using his personal cell, made his call.

"Wilber. Jack Handler here. Hey, buddy. There's been a little change of plans. Grab a cab and head over to Ruby's Roost. It's a really cool strip club just across town a few blocks. Ruby's Roost, on 60th Street by First Avenue."

"What the hell are you saying?" Wilber complained. "We've been looking for you for the past ten minutes. Then, you're not even here?"

"Yeah, I've found this better club. I've already paid your cover charge. For you and your brother—fifty bucks each. I've already paid it. Just ask for the big doorman and tell him that you're the Wright brothers, and that you're looking for Jack Handler. He'll bring you to my table. You're gonna love it here. The ladies are out of this world. Hurry on over. Remember to ask for the big doorman, and tell him you're with Jack Handler. It's all paid. See you shortly. The big show is just starting. It's great. You're gonna love it!"

Jack then disconnected his phone before Wilber could object. He then looked around until he found Henry, who was now sitting at a table virtually beneath the main stage. Jack discreetly acknowledged his friend, and then went over to see the big doorman.

"My two friends are on their way over here. The Wright brothers. When they come in they are going to be looking for me—Jack Handler. Don't mention that I am with my friend Scott. It would only make them jealous, and I don't want to do that. Just bring them to my table over there," Jack said as he pointed toward Henry. He then handed the big doorman another hundred-dollar bill.

"You got it, Jack," the big doorman said. "You know, I'm beginning to like you. Jack Handler—you alright."

"Yeah, big guy. I'm alright."

Jack pulled out a chair and sat down facing the stage. The room was smoky and dark. Even though NYC had a law against smoking in this type of establishment, the air was heavy with a thick fog of old nicotine.

"Okay," Henry said. "Your friends are on their way over here—right?"

"They're at least fifteen minutes away," Jack said. "If I'm right, Mutt and Jeff had to call their boss to relay the change of plans. So. It could take a little longer."

"Mutt and Jeff?" Henry chuckled.

"Yeah. We don't know what their real names are. Not yet. So Roger and I refer to them as Mutt and Jeff. You'll see why when they get here. … Don't know if I will even introduce you to them. But, if I do, I will call them *Wilber* and *Orville.*"

"As in the Wright brothers?" Henry asked.

"Exactly. I'm sure you'll agree that Mutt and Jeff fits them better."

"So," Henry said, "I'm not going to be sitting at your table. Right?"

"Right," Jack said. "And I want you to take this."

Jack then carefully pulled the Glock 29 10mm out from his pants and slid it over to Henry under the table.

"I figure something is going to go down tonight, and I do not want to be found carrying this," Jack said. "Do you have latex gloves with you?"

"Yeah, always."

"Good. Now I want you to turn on your ear bud and mic. That will put you in communication with me and with Roger. He will pass on what we say to his crews on a need-to-know basis. Don't forget—as long as the transmitter in your pocket is turned on, both of us will be able to hear what you say. And it will all be recorded. So be careful. Some screwy House Committee might someday be listening to our conversation from tonight. You never know what they're going to do next. They're crazy, sometimes."

"Got it."

"Now, I want you to take the Glock into the men's room and wipe it down thoroughly. When the night is over, find a way to dispose of it. How, I don't care. Just don't have it in your possession when the cops storm the place. You know all about New York City gun laws. Don't need that problem."

"Is it registered to someone?"

"No. It's totally clean and anonymous," Jack assured him. "Do your damnedest not to squeeze that trigger. Roger wants to be able to interview the hired gun. If you shoot him, this will all be a wasted exercise."

"Can't he just scoop up these two guys? And be over it?"

"These guys—Mutt and Jeff—they are not the hired gun he's after. The real professional should be coming in tonight. He's the one we want to identify."

"I'm beginning to get it," Henry said. "Jack—it seems to me like you're just screwed. Catching a professional killer without getting hurt is like cornering a skunk and come out smelling like a rose. ... How am I supposed to have your back? While you are telling me I can't stop the sonofabitch? How does that work?"

"It doesn't," Jack confessed. "Not by any equation I'm aware of."

"What exactly do you want me to do?" Henry asked.

"If you see anyone loitering around," Jack said. "Particularly if he's inordinately got his eyes on me. Let me know. I expect there to be two of them—the killer and his friend. Maybe to create a distraction. Or to watch his back like you're doing for me. They probably won't be standing together. But they will be communicating—the same way we are. ... The critical thing is this—whatever you do, don't kill them."

"Even if they attack you?"

At this point Henry was very glad that Jack had brought bulletproof vests for both of them.

"*Especially* if they attack me. Keep your eyes open. If you spot something, try to get in close. ... Those glasses I gave you are for surveillance. When you wipe down the Glock, put them on and turn on the camera. Like we discussed earlier. If you can get in close with your suspects, Roger might be able to do a facial recognition. Even if there are a few guys you think might be acting strangely, see if you can send Roger an image of all of them."

"I can't defend you?" Henry asked. "Then why did you bring the Glock in?"

"I wanted to see if I could," Jack said. "For one hundred bucks the big doorman was willing to disregard the rules at the door. If I could do it, so could the killer. So, I have to assume that he will be carrying a pistol with a suppressor."

Henry looked away and leaned back in his chair and just stared into oblivion.

"The boys, Jack. I ask you again. What will become of your boys?"

"I've got a job to do. Roger has provided me with a very large life insurance policy. Anything happens to me, Kate retires early and takes care of Red and Robby. We've discussed it already—she, Roger and I."

"And me?" Henry asked. "How can I help?"

"Kate will always know that she can count on you, my friend. Kate knows. ... Now, let's get this show on the road. ... I'll buy you a beer tonight. When this is all over with. I read about this craft beer place—just down the street."

"You're on," Henry replied.

He then arose from the table and looked for the men's room. On the way he pulled his handkerchief from his trouser pocket and wiped his eyes.

Chapter 14

Henry had not yet emerged from the restroom after wiping down the gun when Roger spoke through their ear buds: "Your guys appear to be on their way—Mutt and Jeff. But we haven't spotted anyone fitting the bill for the UNSUB. The two of them caught a cab. They should be over there in fifteen to twenty minutes."

"It's possible that they will not be arriving at the same time," Jack said. "In fact, that is how I would expect this to go down. They have never seen the UNSUB. Right? They would have called their boss, and the boss would have communicated the dispatch to the UNSUB. If that UNSUB is as professional as you believe him to be, he would have waited until it was confirmed that I was in the building."

"You're probably right," Roger said. "You've got Henry with you?"

A long moment passed in silence.

"10/4. He's listening, but he can't talk right now. He's in the restroom."

Just as Jack said that, Henry tapped three times on his mic.

"There you go," Jack said. "That's his signal."

"Where are you going to station yourself?" Jack asked.

"I'm around the corner from Ruby's Roost right now," Roger said. "I've got two vans here now, and one positioned at Dolls and More Dolls. I'll figure on leaving that unit in place for the duration. Found a good parking spot. And, we are still close enough we could call him in if need be."

"Hang on," Jack said as he pulled his personal cell from his jacket and held it to his ear.

"What's up?" Roger asked.

"Nothing," Jack said. "I just grabbed my phone. I had turned it off after I called our guys. But I'm starting to draw some attention talking, and no one is sitting at my table but me."

"I'm out," Henry said.

"Hello, Henry," Roger said. "Happy to have you onboard with us."

"Happy to be here, sir."

About ten minutes later, Roger spoke: "Looks like your two buddies are just arriving. Caught them on the camera we set up earlier."

"Still no word on possible candidates for the UNSUB?" Jack asked.

"None," Roger replied. "But they're starting to file in too fast for our equipment to keep up."

"No hits yet?" Jack asked. "Right?"

"Right."

Another few minutes passed.

"Here they are," Jack said. "Mutt and Jeff are headed toward my table. ... Signing off."

He then slid his cell back into his pocket.

"Wilber. Orville," Jack said, as he stood to greet them. "So glad you could join me. This is going to be a great show tonight. I've heard really good things about the ladies here. Glad you made it."

Ear-splitting rap blasted throughout the club. From some dark out-of-sight corner of oblivion, the DJ fondled his knobs striving to create the cheap atmosphere of a typical strip club. Sticky tables and crunchy floors were expected if not desired—always left for a cleaning crew that never showed up. Cold, greasy pizza was served at the long bar, along with halfway decent beer and cheap watered-down liquor.

"We didn't think we would," Mutt said. "You sort of hung up on me while I was talking. I tried to call you back, but your phone was off."

"Sorry about that," Jack apologized. "Reception isn't the best in here. And I don't think I'm even supposed to be using a cell phone in the club—might be taking pictures. You know what I mean. Anyway, I've turned it off. Don't want to antagonize that big doorman."

"Yeah," Jeff said. "He's big alright. But, you know what they say—*the bigger they are the harder they fall.*"

"Well," Jack said through a fake smile. "On that basis, that dude would crack the floor."

"What do you mean by that?" Jeff asked.

"I'm just agreeing with you," Jack explained. "He is one big man. ... And, one more thing—you can be sure that I ain't gonna be the one who tries to put him down."

Jack noticed almost immediately that both of the men were very fidgety—as though they were expecting something unpleasant to happen.

"Have either of you been to this club before?" Jack asked.

"I've never been to New York except for business," Mutt/Wilber said. "I've never been to any New York strip club. Are they all about like this?"

"I've been to a few, through the years," Jack said. "I think some are quite a lot bigger than this one. The one we were going to go to, Dolls and More Dolls, that was considerably larger, don't you think?"

Neither of the men answered. They seemed to be preoccupied about something toward the rear of the club.

"I gotta go take a piss," Mutt said. "I'll be right back. I had too much to drink today."

"Jack," Roger said, speaking into Jack's ear bud. "Credit card just popped up. It was just used over at the other strip club—Dolls and More Dolls. The image we have of him shows a very slender fellow—maybe five feet ten inches. Well dressed—almost feminine. Doesn't appear to weigh over one fifty-five. He was accompanied by a female. Nice looking redhead. ... Do you have a lot of women in there? If not, she should be easy to pick out."

"What do you think, Orville?" Jack said to Jeff, "Do you see many women in here? I mean, women who are not dancers—women who are not working. I see several. Maybe eight. Ten. What do you think?"

Jack's question was geared to evoke a response from his table guest. All, of course, for Roger's benefit.

"I see a few," Jeff replied. "Not many, though."

Jack noticed that the man answered his question, but did not look at him. Plus, he seemed disinterested in the women dancing on the stage right above them. His attention seemed directed behind Jack, away from the stage.

Henry detected that Jack was having trouble responding to Roger while sitting at the table with one of the men in question.

"Roger. This is Henry. What have you got for us? Anything?"

"Henry," Roger said. "We just had a tall slender man use a credit card over at the other strip club. And five minutes ago he used the same card at Ruby's Roost—where you guys are. He is with an attractive young lady."

"Can you describe the man?" Henry asked. "And do you have a name."

"Don't have it yet. That is, we don't yet have the facial scan. Name on the card was Miguel Montana. Probably a fake name—sure sounds like one. I have the image. He appears to stand about five feet ten inches. Wearing a double-breasted contemporary suit—European possibly—with a pocket handkerchief, and a stylish hat. The lady he is with is about five foot three. She is thin, with short, red hair. … See anyone like that?"

"Yes, I do," Henry said. "They just walked in. They're standing at the bar right now. Looks like they are waiting for a drink. … Pretty sure the girl he is with just checked out Jack and a guy at their table. The second guy with Jack is apparently in the john. But the couple is holding fast at the bar. Still waiting on their drinks, it looks to me."

"Why, again, are you wearing a cap?" Jeff asked Jack. "You're the only man in this whole damn club with a cap on."

"I know," Jack answered. "I realize it looks a little strange, but I'm just more comfortable when I'm wearing a cap. Believe me, it's not because I want to. But, chemo does that to a man." Jack then removed his cap revealing a bald head. … "In fact, I'm supposed to be wearing this stupid neck brace. I took a fall and sprained my neck really bad a couple weeks ago. I'm supposed to wear one of those ugly things around my neck, all the time, in fact."

Jack then pulled a neck brace out of his jacket pocket and held it up so Jeff could see it. And then he strapped it around his neck. "I suppose I should be wearing this contraption too, otherwise I might reinjure the neck muscle when—

"Holy shit!" Jeff blurted out. "What's that all about? Some kinda cancer?"

"Yeah," Jack said. "The doctors tell me it's in remission. That's the good news. But I still will have radiation treatments every two weeks."

"No shit. That's why your eyebrows look different too. Right? … Tell me, does your hair ever grow back? I mean, after you're cured, and they take you off radiation, does your hair grow back?"

"I'm surprised you could notice that my eyebrows are gone—that's why I wear the sunglasses. Guess they don't work. But the hair, it usually grows back eventually," Jack said. "Not always, though. We'll see. I should be off radiation in a month. Should be off it entirely at that point. If all goes well."

"Ahh! Then that's why the sunglasses."

"Right."

"How do you feel? Does it make you sick? I've heard that chemo can upset your stomach, like all the time. Do you feel normal, or sick? … Is that chemo shit the reason for the neck brace?"

"Not directly," Jack said. "I took a spill a couple of weeks ago. It was after a treatment, but we're not sure that's why I fell down. I suppose it could have been. Severely sprained my neck. Didn't break anything, though. That was good. Should be healed up in six weeks or so."

"Are you suing someone?" Jeff asked. "Often people wear neck braces if they're trying to sue someone for some accident thing. Or, do you really need it? You don't seem like the sort of guy who goes around suing people. But it's done a lot, I've heard."

"No," Jack chuckled. "I've never sued anybody. But I've always been on the other side of frivolous lawsuits. Been sued a time or two. ... Where's Wilber? Do you think he's okay? He's missing some fine ladies. Should I go see if he needs some help?"

"Here he comes," Jeff said. "He was just takin' a piss, I think."

"Hey, Wilber," Jack said as the man nervously slid his chair out and sat down. "We were getting a little worried about you."

Henry then said via the ear buds, "Second man just walked back to Jack's table. And when he did, the girlfriend of our subject followed his every move with her eyes. They're still waiting on their drinks. ... Something looks to be going down. Soon."

"What's with the neck brace?" Mutt said to Jack. "You going incognito, Jack? With the cap, shades, and now the neck brace ... wow, man. You afraid somebody's gonna recognize you, hanging out in a strip club? Got a reputation to protect, or somethin'?"

"I've had a spell of bad luck lately," Jack said. "First, the chemo, and then the neck injury."

"You weren't wearing a neck brace earlier," Mutt said. "I think the technical term is *cervical collar*—you weren't wearing that before, right? ... Did my buddy here knock you off your seat? Or did you sprain your neck flirting with the girls?"

Jack smiled, but before he could respond Roger excitedly spoke to him and Henry: "Just got a facial recognition hit on the tall skinny man. *He* is actually a *she*. Emma is the first name. We don't have a last name. ... But, Jack, you should remember her *very* well. She nearly killed you not that long ago."

"Sheeit!" Jack muttered.

Mutt and Jeff both took Jack's gruff response to indicate that he was offended at Mutt's comment.

"He didn't mean anything by it," Jeff said in an apologetic tone.

"No," Mutt said. "I was just jokin' with you. I just didn't—"

"No problem, boys," Jack said as he turned slightly to sneak a peek at Emma. But she wasn't at the bar. "This damn brace. It just gave me a little tingle on my skin. They can be uncomfortable at times."

"On the move!" Henry said. "Subject is on the move. Headed in Jack's direction. The second subject is headed toward the exit. Shall I intercept either of them?"

"Critical that we take Emma alive. Henry, if it becomes certain that she is the UNSUB that we're after, capture her. But we must take her alive. The same thing goes for you, Jack. She must commit before you take her down. But do *not* kill her. We've got too much invested in this case."

"I'm on my way," Henry said, pulling the Glock from under his belt as he bolted toward Jack. But he had taken only a few steps when a huge hand grabbed him by the back of his collar and stopped him in his tracks.

"Where you think you're goin' with that illegal piece of iron?" the big doorman barked. With his other big hand he grabbed the pistol and twisted it out of Henry's grip. He then put Henry on the floor by using the Glock as a club, striking him on the side of the head with a powerful blow.

"You asshole!" the big man said. "You're not supposed to bring shit like that into the club. It's against the law. And it makes me very angry."

Emma was pleased at the distraction because it drew everyone's attention away from her.

She moved swiftly in behind Jack. As she did she pulled a 9mm semi-automatic pistol out of her jacket, and from a distance of three feet she fired two quick shots into the left side of Jack's back. Both shots struck him squarely in line with his heart. Because the pistol was affixed with a suppressor, her shots were barely audible.

Her next two shots struck Mutt in the head, killing him instantly. She then fired a round into the left side of Jeff's chest. He struggled to stand, until her next round struck him between his eyes. He too died instantly.

She then unceremoniously tossed the pistol on the table between her last two victims. It bounced off the table and landed on the floor between Mutt and Jeff.

Jack fell forward on the table and didn't move.

Chapter 15

Henry caught Jack's distress out of the corner of his eye, but he could do nothing as long as he had the big man standing over him. Because all of the big man's attention was centered on Henry, he totally missed observing the shooting.

"Two suspects headed toward the door," Henry said for Roger's benefit. And then he turned his attention onto the doorman. As the big man stuck the pistol under his belt, Henry took advantage of him.

Leveraging his left foot around the big man's right calf, Henry mustered all the strength and speed that he could, kicking him on the outside of his left knee. The power of Henry's kick produced a compound fracture, dropping the big man like an old oak tree.

Henry sprang rapidly to his feet and delivered a powerful, perfectly executed sidekick to the head of the big man as he tried to sit up. Henry knew by the way the kick felt to him that the big man was at the very least unconscious.

"Jack's in trouble," Henry said to Roger as he spun toward Jack. "Our two suspects are at or through the door. We're gonna need doctors in here right away. It looks like she shot everybody at Jack's table. Including Jack."

As planned, Roger had two fully-staffed ambulances at the ready, along with a large contingent of fake New York City's best— eight of whom were virtually waiting in groups of two at the front door of the club. The apprehension of Emma and her girlfriend took place without incident. The uniforms cuffed them, read them their rights, swiftly escorted them to waiting vehicles, and rapidly whisked them away to an undisclosed location.

Henry, during his time working with Jack, had witnessed a number of killings, some of which were professional hits. Generally, the weapon of choice for an experienced hitman was a .22 caliber revolver. Usually two .22 longs were used for each target— one in the heart, and one in the head. Of course, that could vary. Sometimes there might be two rounds fired into a target's head, sometimes one in the skull and one in the brain stem. But, seldom would two rounds be fired into a man's chest because it would be just too iffy to count on shots to the chest to be instantly fatal.

In this case, Mutt and Jeff were hit as expected—at least one round was fired into their brains. But, that is not how Jack was hit. Both of the shots Emma fired were aimed directly at his heart— neither at his brain. Henry was not aware of that as he walked up to his friend.

"Jack!" Henry shouted. "Can you hear me? Where are you hit?"

Jack did not move.

Henry very carefully directed Jack's motionless body off the chair and onto the floor. He took his own jacket off, rolled it up and tucked it behind Jack's head.

The back and front of Jack's jacket were damp and red.

It was quite obvious to Henry that the two other men were both dead. He could see the hole torn through Jeff's forehead, and he could observe the fixed, bloodied glare of the man's open eyes.

Even though he did not physically check for a pulse in either of Jack's two table-mates, he had seen enough of death to know that those men were dead. He suspected the same for Jack. So, he was not surprised that when he reached for and felt Jack's left wrist for a pulse, he found none.

"Damn you, Jack!" Henry yelled. "You can't die on me! Not now!"

Within seconds two ambulance crews burst in and shoved Henry out of the way. "Get the hell outta our way!" they ordered.

Henry complied.

"What are you finding?" Roger asked.

"Three shot. Pretty sure they're all dead. Medical teams are on the scene."

Henry stood and watched as all three were loaded on wheeled gurneys. In each case their faces were covered. The uniformed "police" officers then pushed all onlookers back and established a perimeter. Henry, even though he was not close enough to hear what was being said, did notice that there appeared to be a lot of chatter taking place among the medical technicians.

One of the uniforms found and secured the semi-auto that was used in the slayings.

More quickly than Henry had ever before witnessed, all three of the victims were wheeled out of the club. He followed as closely as the uniforms would permit. As soon as they picked up on Henry making his way behind them, two of the officers approached him and put him in cuffs.

"You're goin' with us, my friend," they said to Henry. "Roger's orders." As soon as they were safely outside they removed the cuffs.

The bodies of Mutt and Jeff were both slid into the rear of one of the ambulances, and, with lights flashing and siren blaring, it pulled away from the curb.

Jack was gingerly loaded into the second ambulance. When Henry witnessed Roger pushing past the uniforms in order to get onboard with Jack and him, Henry said, "What the hell's goin' on here?"

"Sad day, don't you think?" Roger said to Henry.

Henry could not respond. His eyes were glazed over and his nose was beginning to run.

"You're damn right it is," Jack growled, throwing the blanket from off his face with his right arm. "I still can't move my left arm. Those damn 9mm slugs. They hurt like living hell. I swear, I have never felt anything like that before in my life. Any self-respecting contract killer ought to use a .22. I always had a higher opinion of Emma than that. ... Damn, that hurts."

"Jack, you sonofabitch!" Henry scolded, "I thought you were dead too. How the hell did you survive? Those rounds were fired in you at point blank. I saw it with my own eyes. You should be dead. What is that you're wearing, some kind of bulletproof jacket?"

"That's how Roger sold it to me," Jack said. "But the asshole sitting beside you did not tell me how much it was going to hurt if I ever had to use it. ... Now, damn you guys, won't you get this piece of shit off of me? It's hotter than hell under all that Kevlar. I already told you I can't move my left arm. Get this crap off my neck. Now! It's starting to itch!"

"Henry," Roger said, laughing. "Why don't you see if you can help him. I still can't do much with my left arm—not since the last time I worked with your friend. ... But be *very* careful. He might bite your hand."

Henry complied with Roger's request and helped Jack remove the cumbersome appliance. As he did he said, "That Emma was the babe who tried to kill you out West. A year or so ago. Right? Same lady?"

Jack answered Henry's question with a single word: "Yes." And he then shut up. He was a little embarrassed to have been so bitchy with his friends. However, neither Roger nor Henry could have possibly been more pleased. Henry was pleased that Jack had been spared. And Roger was delighted that he now had much of the information he had hoped for—not only did he have the hired killer in custody, he believed that, even without questioning the killer, he could determine who the killer worked for.

Roger strongly suspected that the person behind the murder attempt was his own charge—former First Lady Allison Fulbright. He believed this to be the case because it had been firmly established, at least in the intelligence arena, that it was she, Allison Fulbright, who had originally hired Emma to kill Jack a year and a half earlier. Both Jack and Henry were fully aware of that fact as well.

That revelation was not the only good news that Roger was to glean from their success. They later learned that ballistics indicated that the 9mm used in the shooting was the same as that of the firearm used to murder Millie. Plus, prints lifted from the weapon indicated that both Mutt and Jeff had handled the pistol in the past. That was of itself highly suggestive of the likelihood that they were the ones who had killed Millie. Once Jack had recovered from his ordeal, he quickly became satisfied that Millie's killers were dead, and he need not pursue the matter further—at least not that aspect of the matter.

Once Jack was relieved of the neck brace, he tamed the tone of the conversation.

"So," Henry said, "the neck brace was bulletproof. Then, I suppose, the cap was also part of the protective gear. Right?"

"Yeah," Roger said. "Jack anticipated he might have to take a round or two, and he wanted to direct the shots into his Kevlar jacket. He knew it would be from close range, and therefore, were he to expose his neck or head to the shooter, he would be killed. He figured that the killer would not want to fire into a hard surface, such as a neck brace. And bad things can happen to a bullet when challenged by a good Kevlar cap. So, odds were good that the round would be fired at his heart or face. So, as long as he did not point his nose at the hitman, the rounds would most likely be fired into the jacket, and he might make it through okay."

"What would have happened," Henry posed, "had Emma been using a .22 caliber long rifle round? And, say, she would have fired it from a four- or six-inch revolver? Would it have pierced the jacket?"

Roger smiled.

"Unknowable," Jack said. "It would *probably* have pierced the jacket. Might or might not have proved fatal. It would have flattened the round out and it would not have penetrated very well. … When I feel better, we can test that scenario. You can wear the jacket for that experiment."

"Henry," Roger said. "You've been to Vegas before—right?"

"Yeah. Sure. Hasn't everybody at least one time in his life?"

"Probably," Roger said. "And, have you ever played 21 when you were there?"

"Yes, I confess, I have played blackjack before—for money in Las Vegas. What are you getting at?"

"Here's my point," Roger said. "There's two principal ways

to play Vegas Blackjack—you can either count cards, or you can gamble. Those who are very bright, and know how to count cards, as long as they bet accordingly, they can often beat the table.

"But, those who *gamble*—they *always* lose. … Tonight, what Jack did, was gamble. And I helped him do it. We were both stupid … stupid, screaming assholes.

"Now, this is what I want you to do for me—for Jack and me. If you ever see us headed in this direction again—*ever!*—I want you to beat the living shit out of both of us. Jack tells me that you're very capable of doing it. So, don't take the time to think about it. Just knock us on our asses and walk away. Got it?"

Henry did not respond.

Neither did Jack.

Finally, after an inordinate period of silence, Henry said, "Whatever became of the big doorman? I'm afraid I was pretty rough on him. Did he make it? Do we know?"

"Compound fracture of the right leg, and a fractured skull," Roger said. "What happened to him? Did he take a spill?"

"Must have," Henry said.

"Just as well," Roger said. "My guys tell me that he was carrying an illegal weapon—unregistered in the City of New York, and radically illegal in an establishment serving alcohol. I'm afraid he might do some serious time."

After nearly ten minutes had passed, Jack finally broke the silence.

"Roger, I trust you got what you wanted out of this—information-wise. … But, were you surprised with what we learned?"

"That, my friend, would be a monumental understatement."

"How do you figure? We knew going in that those two jokers—Mutt and Jeff, we knew that they were the ones who killed Millie. Right?"

"Yeah. Sure. *That* we knew. And, once we run their DNA and prints through Quantico and Langley, we'll be able to pin a name on them—a real name. That part of it is all good."

"You can say that again," Jack agreed. "They're both dead and I didn't have to squeeze a trigger."

"Win-win," Roger said.

"Something else about that whole business," Roger continued. "Our shooter tonight apparently tossed the weapon down when she was finished. ... It will, I think, prove very interesting to do the forensics on it. She would not have left it behind without a good reason. When we searched her, we were shocked to find that she carried no weapons, other than the one she tossed down at the scene."

"I don't know about that," Henry chimed in. "That ass of hers looked pretty damned dangerous to me. I'm sorry, but—"

"Henry," Roger butted in. "What were you doing? Looking at that shooter's sexual equipment? She was *supposed* to be a man."

"Couldn't help it," Henry explained. "When you told us that his name was Emma, I had to check him out more closely. Once I stuck a different name on him, I started to think differently. And when she headed in Jack's direction ... I could tell by the way she moved, we were dealing with a woman. Sorry, but I suppose I'm old school. I still think that there is a difference between men and women.

"I'm just saying—that Emma person, or whatever her name really is—she had a dynamite ass on her. I'm just stating my opinion."

"Don't worry," Roger reassured him, "I'm not taking notes, so your sexist comments will not end up in some police crime file, or on any federal hard drives."

"Unless you write a book," Jack offered in humor. "You're not going to do that, are you?"

"Just forget I ever said that about her ass," Henry said. ... "But, Roger, why do you think she left the weapon she used tonight? You have a theory?"

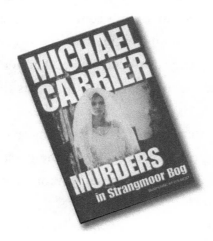

Murders in Strangmoor Bog is the seventh (and final) book
in the "Getting to Know Jack Series." This is the first series in the Jack Handler Saga.
The book is set in the Seney National Wildlife Refuge in Michigan's Upper Peninsula.
Millie and Angel Star are introduced in this book.

Chapter 16

I t's not that uncommon for a professional killer to immediately discard his weapon," Roger said. "But, combined
with the fact that 9mm semi-autos are not typically the
weapon of choice for a hit like this, the fact that she would choose
to leave it at the scene is suspect. I'll bet that her weapon tonight
has been used in other killings. And that was the point she was
trying to establish."

"So," Henry interjected, "You're thinking that the woman you
are in charge of protecting, that she is the person ultimately responsible for everything that went down tonight? Is that what I'm
hearing? Can't you just lock her up?"

Roger delivered a long stare pointed in Jack's direction. He was
hesitant to respond to Henry's question because of all the ramifications associated with that classified information.

Jack could see Roger's hesitance.

"Henry," Jack said. "You've been through a lot with me. We've
fought side by side several times. I know I can trust you with my
life. And I assume you know you can trust me as well."

"Of course I trust you," Henry said. "I'm pretty sure I get what's
going on, here. This woman, the one who hired Emma, she is undoubtedly a very powerful woman, with powerful connections.
I'm good with just dropping this. No need to tell me more than I
need to know. I totally get it."

"Hey, boys!" Jack roared, partly just to change the topic. "I promised Henry here I'd take him out for a craft beer after we'd finished there at Ruby's. I'm still game for it. How about you guys?"

"What about the hospital?" Henry questioned. "Don't we have to get you to a hospital?"

"Oh hell!" Jack said. "I certainly hope not. We all know that you don't take dead people to the hospital. It's bad for the white coats—hurts morale. Right, Roger? Where is this guy headed, anyway?"

"I was going to get you the hell out of town. That was the Queensboro that we just went across. We're in Queens right now."

"What do you know about craft beer bars in this area?" Jack asked.

"Not a whole hell of a lot," Roger said. "I work just off Central Park East—that's where Allison lives. But, my apartment is in Queens. I know some great beer joints in Queens.

"Let me see where we are," Roger said as he leaned forward to check their location. "Hey, driver. Where are we right now?"

"Jackson Avenue comin' up on Queens Plaza," the driver said.

"Okay," Roger said. "Let me think. ... How about swinging south and heading over to 51st Avenue—514 51st? To the beer bar. It's called the Alewife. Ever heard of it?"

"Oh yeah," the driver said. "Been there a few times."

"Open 'til one?" Roger asked.

"Yeah, I think so."

"Drop us off there," Roger said.

"You got it," the driver said. ... "I can't drink with you, but I can wait for you."

Roger thought about the offer and then rejected it.

"We appreciate the thought, but we'll use a taxi. … Where'd you get the ambulance, anyway? It looks pretty new. Where's it from?"

"We rented it from a Queens emergency vehicle rental service," the driver said.

"No shit!" Roger said. "You mean you can rent nice units like this? That's pretty cool. When does it have to be back?"

"Not until sun-up."

"Whose name is on the rental?"

"Yours. But I'm the one who's supposed to drive it. Because I'm the one with the license."

"Yeah. Just drop us off. See if they'll give me some money off— if you return it early."

The driver chuckled. "I don't think it works like that, but I'll give it a try. … By the way, that's right by the Midtown Tunnel, so there's a lot going on in that area."

"What do you do when you're not driving one of these ambulances for the Secret Service?"

"I drive a taxi."

"No shit!" Roger said, as he peeled off three one-hundred-dollar bills. "Then, on second thought. Since we're paying you anyway, here's a little cash to cover your time. Why don't you just get this billboard outta here, and see to it that we get picked up at one. Can we do it that way?"

"Anyway you want to do it, Roger," the driver said, pushing Roger's hand back with the cash still in it. "But I'm not taking your money. I've already been paid for the night. … Anyway, I heard what you guys went through in there, and I want you to know I'm behind you all the way. I'll be back at one."

"Cool," Roger said. "Very cool. By the way, what's your name?"

"My name is Roger too, just like you."

"Well, I'll be damned," Roger said. "I'm sure I'll remember that. Thanks for doing a good job for us tonight. I look forward to running into you again. You take care now."

"Hey, Roger," Jack called as he sat up. "Not you, Roger. I'm talking to the driver. Hey, driver. Would you have a spare jacket around that you could loan me? You can have it back tonight. I've got to get rid of this sweaty Kevlar. Roger, the other Roger, he's going to want it back. It's pretty much soaked in something that looks and feels like blood, but it's fake. Just toss it in a bag and bring it back tonight. You got something up there you can loan me?"

"See if this works," the driver said, handing a jacket back to Roger. "It's got my name on it, but don't worry about it."

"Perfect," Jack said. "I'm here incognito anyway. This will do just fine."

The three men walked into the Alewife and asked for a table. The bar was clean, dark and smelled like booze and desperation. The tall tables were 36" round black metal, with four ladder-back chairs tucked in around each empty table. The room was covered with movie posters, mostly of Humphrey Bogart and Lauren Bacall in black and white. There were TVs playing sports in each direction and the low hung lighting provided a magical ambiance to the bar. The floors were of well-worn hardwood—probably salvaged from an earlier application. The bartender recognized Roger and led him to his favorite spot.

"What do you recommend here?" Henry asked. "Got any favorites?"

"The Alewife has a very good name around here," Roger said. "They've got several that are available this time of year. But the last few times I visited I bought their Forged in Fire Oktoberfest brew. If they've got it, I think it's pretty good. Has a caramel flavor that I like. But pick one and try it. They're all pretty good. Very popular."

"That's a plan," Jack said. "Let's order a few different brews. Try them all until we find the ones we really like."

So, that's what they did. They had the bartender bring them two mugs each of what the house had available: *Lupulin Vibrations, RA WIT Witbier, Thousand Stars, Death to Ego* and *Summer Friday Session.*

Roger's favorite remained the Forged in Fire Oktoberfest, but they all switched it up giving each brew a shot. Truth be told, to a man they each just came off one of their toughest challenges in weeks if not years—or perhaps even longer. It is likely that they would have found almost any cold beer would have done the job just fine.

But, as closing time neared, they were all content to settle back with their last brew of the night. Conversation had slowed, partly because Jack and Roger had to be very careful what they said within earshot of other patrons.

Finally, Henry brought up a topic that they could all discuss freely. He sat back in his chair, took a deep breath, and with his deep brown Native American eyes, looked at both Jack and Roger intently...

"Hey," he said. "Either of you guys got any idea about what's causing the Great Lakes to swell up like they have in the last year or so?"

"Henry," Jack said through a large smile. "I can definitely see that you've been talking to my good friend Legend—AKA Ted Klanoski. Right? That's why it was important that Lindsay went along on the trip—to help temper Legend."

"You got that right," Henry said. "I did have a discussion with your friend, Legend. ... But he was by himself with the boys. Lindsay had to work."

"Oh, well," Jack said. "I suppose they'll all survive without a female onboard. She sort of warned me that might happen."

"About Legend's theories concerning the Great Lakes," Henry said, "do you think he's right?"

"When the hell did you have time to talk to him, anyway?" Jack asked.

"When I dropped the boys off," Henry said. "And he was very eager to find out what I thought about the whole thing."

"That guy doesn't miss a trick," Jack said. "Well, what did you tell him?"

"I said that I haven't researched it much," Henry replied. "Hell, I haven't researched it at all, to tell the truth. So, I really didn't know. ... He did have some compelling arguments, though. Don't you think?"

"What the hell are you guys talking about?" Roger asked. "Do you plan to let me in on this, or are you going to treat me like a mushroom?"

"Treat you like a *mushroom*?" Henry asked. "What does that mean?"

"You gonna stick me in shit and keep me in the dark," Roger said, definitely feeling his beers.

"Henry," Jack said, checking his watch. "Why don't you bring Roger up to speed on Legend's theory. And do it quickly, we only have forty minutes until our chauffeur arrives."

"I dropped off Jack's two boys yesterday to go fishing. With a friend of Jack's. And as soon as I arrived, this guy, Legend is what he goes by, he cornered me over coffee and wouldn't let me leave. Nice enough guy, but he just wouldn't stop talking.

"Anyway, he had a theory. To him, it was more than a theory. He was totally sold on it. What he was stating had to do with the water levels in the Great Lakes. They are, you know, very high. Historically high. As much as three feet higher than normal."

"Yeah," Roger said. "I've been reading about that. Scientists are saying it has something to do with climate change. Is that what he was thinking?"

"No. Not at all. He said that the Atlantic Ocean is up only eight inches over the past one hundred and fifty years. *That was over the past one hundred and fifty years.* Eight measly inches. And, he said, over the past two years it is actually down a little. But, during those last few years, the Great Lakes have risen two feet, or more in some cases."

"How about rain?" Roger asked. "Are you getting a lot more rain?"

"Same question I asked him. Legend says those figures are jumping all over the charts. Some are saying that rainfall is up, but he says it's not. The National Weather Service argues that it's just about normal. But, he has a different approach than just rainfall. That's what intrigued me. *He said we should always follow the money first.* I don't recall everything he said, but, from what I can remember, I think his argument did make sense."

"How do you follow the money when it comes to rainfall?" Roger asked. "And how does he explain it?"

Henry took the last of the now warm beer and continued with his explanation.

"He says that the St. Lawrence Seaway drains all of the Great Lakes. In that, he's positively right. I knew that for a fact. Water flows from Lake Superior into Lake Huron. And so does Lake Michigan—it also flows into Lake Huron. From there it flows into Lake Erie and then into Lake Ontario. And, finally, out to the Atlantic Ocean."

"Oh," Roger said. "I think I get what he's suggesting. He's saying that the locks along the St. Lawrence Seaway are keeping the water levels unnecessarily high. Is that it? But why? How does he arrive at his notion of following the money? What's water levels in the Great Lakes got to do with someone making more money?"

"It does seem farfetched," Henry admitted. "At least on the surface. But, when he talks about shipping in the Great Lakes, and all the way through the St. Lawrence Seaway, his theory begins to make sense—at least it got my attention.

"He says that by lifting the levels by two or three feet, they have allowed for millions of tons of freight to pass through the lakes, from Duluth to Detroit, Cleveland and through the Seaway all the way to Europe. Millions of tons means billions of additional dollars. He refers to them as billions of totally free dollars—all profit."

"And there's a market for all the extra freight?" Roger asked.

"I suppose so," Henry replied. "They're finding markets."

"Tell me," Roger said. "If these freighters are capable of carrying all that additional cargo, why do they need to raise the lake levels? Is it because the channels are not deep enough to support the additional weight?"

"So says Legend. He said that it has been suggested that the channels be dredged out to allow for larger loads, but they do not want to spend the money. Could cost hundreds of millions."

"I've heard people say that the problem is caused by global warming," Roger said. "Could not *that* be the case?"

"Who's to say," Jack said. "But what Henry said about the ocean level having risen only eight inches in the past one hundred and fifty years. What does that tell us?"

"Legend says that all they would have to do to fix the lake level," Henry said, "would be to open up some of the locks and dams that they have built to control these things. There's a dozen or more of them from Lake Superior all the way out to the Atlantic Ocean. If they were to allow the waters to even out to their natural levels, the problem would be solved. Lake Michigan, Lake Superior, Huron, Erie and Ontario, they would all return to their natural levels, and thousands of homes would be saved. He said the whole situation absolutely has to be the result of environmental manipulation— and the reason for it, unadulterated greed. That's Legend's story. But, it remains a demonstrable fact that without those dams and locks, lake levels would drop considerably."

"I did a little checking on that myself," Jack said. "Did you know that Lake Superior is artificially maintained at a level twenty-two feet above that of its neighbor—Lake Huron? It's a fact that, from the beginning, the locks at Sault Ste. Marie hold back a full twenty-two feet of water. And, the engineers responsible for maintaining those locks admit that the purpose of the locks is specifically to enhance maritime shipping profits. What Legend is saying is that these engineers have simply decided that there is more money to be made, so screw the public. At least, that's what Legend is saying. I have not done the research, so I don't yet know if he is right or wrong. But, it did make sense to me."

"Help me understand this better," Roger said. "Tell me again, why would additional rain *not* affect Great Lakes' levels? You guys have had some rainy years—more than usual, I've heard."

"The way Legend explained it is like this," Henry said. "Say you sought to soak the grease off a gear you wanted to use to rebuild your transmission. So you ran the bathroom sink—the lavatory—full of hot water. Right up to the overflow hole. But, when you put the gear in it, the water did not cover it."

"Pretty easy to see what sort of fellow your buddy Legend is," Roger chuckled. "But, go on with your story."

"So, you break out the duct tape and cover up the overflow hole. Then, you can run another two inches of water in the sink. The water covers the gear, you pour in the dish detergent, and you can clean the grease off the gear. Any substantial additional 'rain' merely raises the already high level in the sink, but that's it. … If, however, you run too much additional water into the sink—that would be like getting a lot of rain—you run the chance of over-flowing the sink.

"But, at any time you wish, you drop the water back to the original level. All you have to do is to remove the duct tape. And all is well. Of course, you won't be able to soak the very large gears or bearings, until you buy a larger sink. Or find another way to make it deeper."

"That does make sense—making it deeper," Jack said. "Shipping channels do require periodic dredging to maintain adequate depth. It's standard maintenance. … But, it does cost a lot of money. Do you suppose that is the problem?"

"Legend kept going back to his original story," Henry said.

"The Atlantic Ocean has risen only eight inches over the past one hundred and fifty years. That's not very damn much. Not when you consider that the Great Lakes are ranging up to three feet higher than only a few years ago. Some say it's over three feet. ... I asked him about dredging, and he said that the shipping channel is way overdue—everyone agrees that it needs a major overhaul. This business of artificially raising the levels of the lakes and channels is a temporary fix at best."

"I don't believe this," Roger finally interjected. "Here we are— three old men. Drinking craft beers and solving the world's problems. What shall we tackle next?"

"How about the unified theory," Jack said, laughing out loud. "No one's solved that dilemma yet."

"Yeah," Henry said as he adjusted his sitting posture. "If we can do that, we should be able to hit Vegas and run the tables."

"Great plan," Jack said. "I'd vote for that. ... Hell, after tonight, I'd vote for anything that sounds like it might pour a little fun into our lives. We have spent a good part of this last year solving life and death issues—always for other people. I'm good and ready to have a little fun. How about you guys?"

"Man," Roger said, "Enough of this bullshit. Vegas does sound pretty good to me right now. How about you, Henry? Jack and I might need some help—both of us have mending left arms. We would definitely need someone who can shuffle and cut a deck. What do you think?"

Roger's tone had changed dramatically. While all the conversation in that beer bar, up until that point, had been light and superficial, he was ready to put a serious plan on the stove. However, when he glanced over at his two friends for a reaction, he found their eyes glued to the television above the bar.

"Hold that thought," Jack said to Roger. "I've got to check this out. It looks like something happened in Upper Michigan—Sault Ste. Marie, it says."

Jack and Henry pushed their chairs back and headed for the bar to get a better look. Roger followed on their heels. All three stood in silence as a Special Announcement scrolled across the screen:

"Special Alert – A Major Explosion has Just Rocked the Midwest – We are now beginning to receive reports into our newsroom that a devastating blast has occurred on the Canadian border with Michigan. First reports indicate that the entire city of Sault Ste. Marie is ablaze, both on the Canadian and on the American sides. The blast, which occurred this evening at approximately Midnight EST, is believed to have taken place aboard a large iron ore carrier just as it was passing eastbound through the locks there. While we are awaiting eyewitness reporting on the explosion, speculation by residents of nearby Neebish Island suggest that the blast may have entirely taken out at least one of the huge locks located in Sault Ste. Marie. These locks adjust water levels there permitting the movement of large ships and freighters between port cities such as Duluth, Minnesota, to various ports east all the way to the Atlantic Ocean and beyond. Residents of Neebish Island report that within minutes after the explosion a huge surge of water rushed past the island, inundating much of the its shoreline. There has not been reports of injuries or fatalities, but it is still very early. Our national bureau has informed us that while the explosion does look like an act of terrorism, no one as yet has taken credit for it. We will provide more information as it becomes available."

"Holy shit!" Henry blurted out. "Look at that. Can you believe it? Did you see what I just saw? I can't believe it!"

Michael Carrier

Chapter 17

Well, I'll be damned," Jack said, slightly more calm than his friend. "That is just exactly what we were talking about! Not the explosion part, but the problem that the locks apparently have caused. And now look what has happened. ... Roger, Henry, pull in close to me. I've got something to say to you. It's important—very damn important. Come here."

Both Roger and Henry slid in very close to Jack to hear what he had to say.

"Do you think that anyone else has listened in on our conversation?" Jack asked. "I mean, even one of the waitresses. Or people at the table next to us."

"I really don't think so," Roger said. "But I know where you're going with this. If it turns out to have been a deliberate terrorist attack—even by a domestic terrorist, and if anyone can tie us to it as having prior knowledge—we could have a serious problem. ... As far as anyone overhearing us right here in the bar, I think we're in the clear. I don't think *that* happened. In fact, I'm pretty sure no one was paying attention to our conversation. At least, no one here in this building."

"But," Jack said. "You're seeming to be leaving the door open. What are you thinking?"

"Did any of us leave our mics hot?" Roger asked. "I turned

mine off when we got in the ambulance. Habit. How about you guys?"

"Same," Jack said. "I cut mine off when they pulled the sheet over my face on the gurney."

Henry reached into his pocket and pulled out his transmitter. He switched it off so that the other two could witness it. "I removed the ear bud, but not the mic," he said. "Is that a big problem?"

"I need to get to my office and take care of it," Roger said.

"Does that go through the whole network, or is it proprietary to your field office?" Jack asked.

"Normally it would hit the network," Roger said. "My field office is on the network. Regulations *require* it. But with this whole Deep State situation, I don't trust very many people, particularly those who have access to all that shit. My so-called 'field office' is now pretty much limited to those who have a key to my apartment."

"How many fit that description?" Jack asked.

"You're looking at him," Roger said. "That's why I said that I have to get back right away. If that shit ever got out, no one in their right mind would ever accept the fact that we did not have some sort of inside track on that whole nasty affair. That's not to say that there are very many members of Deep State who are actually in their right mind, but I need to take precautionary measures, ASAP. ... But, don't worry. Really. This sort of shit goes on all the time. I'll get over there and take care of it."

"My boys!" Jack said with a worried look on his face. "I've got to get back and check up on them. They should be fine down there on Lake Huron. They're over a hundred miles south of ground zero. But, that surge of water is not going to subside anytime soon. ... If that explosion actually did take out a lock, if it was big enough to take out both ends of the lock, that means that the top twenty-two feet of the largest inland lake in the world will be flowing into Lake Huron. It will eventually reach the boys. I need to get up there, *pronto.*"

"Me too," Henry said. "I'll go with you."

"Good," Jack said. "I do not want to go back to the hotel if I don't have to. ... Roger, do you think you could see to it that my room gets cleaned out? And Henry's?"

"Sure," Roger said. "I can take care of that. I'll get yours too, Henry."

"Thanks," Jack said.

"No big deal," Roger said. "Remember, counting both hotels, I've four rooms in total. And all my equipment. As soon as I take care of the recording, I'll get a crew over to the hotels. ... I'll get a car over here for you to take to LaGuardia. It'll be a lot quicker for you to fly out of LaGuardia. I can get our plane over there for you. Drop you off at Detroit Metro. You can take it from there. ... How about your personal stuff at the hotels? Anything irreplaceable?"

"Pack it all up and dispose of it as you see fit," Jack said.

All three men were deep in thought, so not much more was said. Roger the taxi driver was already in the parking lot waiting for Agent Roger. And so he left. Because the bar was closing, Jack and Henry walked out and waited on the sidewalk. Within ten minutes after the Rogers' ride pulled out, a car arrived to pick up Jack and Henry.

"Think you can find that cabin again, maybe in the dark?" Jack asked. "The cabin where the boys are staying?"

"Yeah," Henry said. "It's well off the beaten path, but I should have no problem finding it. I'm usually pretty good at that sort of stuff. ... But—"

"But what?" Jack interrupted. "I hate those damn buts. But *what*, Henry?"

"I had a lengthy conversation with your friend Legend. He told me that they were planning on spending one or two nights on a nearby island."

"An island in Lake Huron?" Jack asked. "Or on the river?"

"An island in Lake Huron. That's what Legend was talking about. It was tiny. I don't think it even had a name. No one lived on it. It was much too small. But Legend said his dad used to take him fishing up there and they would camp out on the island some of the time."

"Damn it!" Jack barked. "And we don't have any way to get hold of them, do we? Their cells don't work at the cottage, Legend told me."

"Might work on the island," Henry said. "If they're even on the island. ... Actually, I would think that they're probably at the cottage. This being the first night and all."

"I guess we'll soon find out," Jack said. He was not a very happy man right then.

Chapter 18

The ride out to LaGuardia was uneventful. Jack did try three times to call the boys' cell phones, but the calls did not go through.

It was still very early by the time they hit the Brooklyn Queens Expressway. If their pilot could get them in the air quickly enough, they would be able to pick up their car in Michigan and head right out to find the boys, taking turns driving and sleeping.

The unanswered calls could mean a number of things, Henry was thinking. *Could mean that they were at the cabin, and that they had no cell service. Or, it could mean that they were on that unknown island, whatever the hell it's called. Cell phones might not work there, either. Just no way of knowing.* Henry then began reading the news on his phone.

Jack caught what he was doing and asked, "What are you seeing? You're checking the news. Right?"

"Still not much. Says they're flying in the FBI. That's not news. If terror is even suspected, it has to go to the FBI. ... Doesn't look like there's anything really new. Just what we saw on that TV at the bar. ... Wait! *That's* new. Want to look at it, or shall I read it to you?"

"Just read it," Jack said. "What do you have?"

"A retired nuclear engineer who lives on Neebish Island has suggested that the explosion in Upper Michigan has all the earmarks of a terrorist bombing, and he further thinks it possible that a low-yield nuclear device was employed. He thinks that because he has taken measurements around his house, and of the water, and has found both the air and the water seem to indicate an unusually elevated level of radioactivity."

"*That* does *not* sound good," Jack said. "I don't like that at all. Neebish. That's where that other guy was from—the one who talked about a large water surge. Wonder if it was the same fellow."

Henry could tell that Jack was really affected by the news. So, when Jack looked away from his cell, Henry closed the app and put his phone away.

Just as they arrived at the airport Jack's phone rang. He looked at it and saw that it was Kate. He said, "I wondered how long it would take you to find out about this. … Yeah. Henry and I wound it up in New York and are on our way back to check on the boys. … We're still at LaGuardia. Roger got us a ride on a single engine prop. His personal pilot. … No, we're flying into Detroit Metro. We'll pick up the Tahoe there, and drive up to the fishing cottage. … What have you heard? … Hold on, I'll put this on speaker so Henry can hear. Would you repeat that?"

"I received a wakeup call about a half an hour ago. From my boss, Captain Spencer. He called me because he knew that you and the boys lived up there, and he wanted to find out if I knew anything about what happened. Of course, he woke me up with the news. I had gone to bed much earlier. … He seems to think that it was a terrorist attack. He has been in contact with the FBI. They automatically put New York on high alert when anything like this goes down. They told him that it was too early to know anything substantial about the blast, only that it appears to have been aboard a thousand-foot ore carrier, and that when it blew, it took out the big lock in Sault Ste. Marie. Blew it totally away. Totally destroyed it, and all the surrounding buildings. *Huge* blast."

"Does he suspect that it was nuclear?" Jack asked.

"The FBI is of the opinion that it could have been. The blast was huge by any measure. So, it could have been a small nuclear device, they are saying. One of the news agencies has interviewed a caller from the area, an engineer, and he is thinking that it might be nuclear. He is in possession of testing equipment that suggests that it could be. Too soon to say. It is very good to know that the boys are not on Sugar Island. No matter what sort of explosion it was, they have a better chance of coming out of this okay, being so far away from it."

"Yes and no," Jack said. "I need to tell you that Henry thinks the boys might be camping out on a small, uncharted island located in Lake Huron. That's the way Legend left it with him. We're going to be checking it out."

Jack talked for a few minutes longer. Kate told him that she was cancelling her schedule for the rest of the week and would be headed to Detroit as soon as she could book the flight.

As Jack disconnected the call, Henry asked him about the single-engine prop. "I thought we would be taking the private jet."

"I texted the pilot to see if he could get us on a propeller plane—single engine. I wanted to leave our options open with regard to searching for the boys. Can't do that in a jet, no matter how small. ... What have you got on them? Do you have any maps or anything showing where that island is?"

"I scribbled out some notes when I was talking with Legend," Henry said. "I didn't think it was that important at the time. But I wrote down some coordinates. A set for the cottage, and a set for the island—Legend had them recorded already, so he just gave me a copy of them."

"You texted me the coordinates for the cabin," Jack said. "I'm looking for those. That will help this pilot find the island. Just text them to me."

"Right. Here you go. The island is uninhabited, but it does have a name. It is called Gull Island. It is about half a mile south of a larger island—that one is called Charity Island. It is occupied—has buildings on it. But the coordinates for Gull Island are 44.017559N, and 83.441075W. Like I said, no one lives on Gull Island. It is only about 500 feet long, and 200 wide. ... Legend said that there were three or four other Gull Islands listed in the state, but this one is a small island just east of the cabin. He said the fishing there is incredible, if you hit it at the right time of the year. His father used to take him fishing on the island."

"After we take off," Jack said, "I'll check with the pilot and see if we can do a fly-over of the cabin, and maybe the island. He might not be able to do that, because of the explosion. But, they're still allowing flights in and out of Detroit Metro. So I guess we'll see. ... It might be too dark yet. If there's a lot of cloud cover, with the sun not up yet, it would be a senseless waste of time. He thought we could be landing about five-thirty in Detroit. So, it might work out okay to head straight for the island and at least do a flyover—if we can get clearance. ... I wonder if they have a strip on Charity Island."

"From the way Legend described it," Henry said. "I sincerely doubt it. It's like less than a square mile in size, he said. I doubt that it would have a strip."

"I checked with the pilot," Jack said. "And he told me that the plane we're taking is not equipped with pontoons, just parachutes, but not pontoons. The parachutes might be useful as a last resort. Unless we spot something dramatic, I would rather rent a boat and check it out like that—something large enough to get all the kids back to safety."

The flight back to check on the boys was uneventful. At Jack's request, Roger and his pilot were able to secure the rental of a Cessna 208 Caravan turboprop. Not only did that unit provide more room just in case they needed it, its range was over twelve hundred miles. That way they would be able to fly directly to where the boys were thought to be without refueling. Jack was convinced that time was critical, especially if there was even a remote chance that the explosion causing all the uproar might have been nuclear.

Before taking off, the pilot had cleared a flight plan that took them over Lake Erie, and then through a large stretch of Canadian airspace, before reaching the vicinity of Charity and Gull islands. Roger had expressed some concern about their being permitted to fly over Canada due to flight restrictions imposed as a result of the suspected terror attack. But permission was quickly granted.

Even though it was totally black outside, Jack's eyes were glued to the earth below. The same was true of Henry—neither man slept a wink. Neither spoke, either—at least not for the first two hours of the flight.

Finally, Jack broke the silence that was the white noise caused by the sound of the large propeller beating against the air. "Must be over Lake Erie. Haven't seen a ground light for forty-five minutes."

"That's what I was thinking," Henry said from the other side of the plane. "Sun should be breaking through soon."

Jack looked at his watch and said, "Right. Looks like we will have at least some light. I wonder how low he intends to take it."

Just then the pilot spoke over the intercom.

"Jack. Would you please join me up here?"

Jack glanced back at Henry, and then unfastened his seatbelt.

As he entered the cockpit the pilot motioned for him to slip on the headset that was lying on the other seat.

Jack did as the pilot requested, and then sat down and buckled up.

"You ever fly one of these?" the pilot asked Jack, after he had settled into the other seat.

"Not the 208," Jack said. "I think this bird is used primarily as a regional passenger plane. Right?"

"Exactly. But this one is a little different. It has been specially fitted for use by the various federal agencies. They keep one in DC, one at Kennedy, and at half a dozen other major airports throughout the rest of the country. This one just happened to have ended up at Kennedy. So I—actually, Roger—commandeered it and had it run over to LaGuardia. You said you needed an extended range, and this fit the bill."

"You said it was 'specially fitted.' What does that entail?"

"It has a lot of additional equipment that doesn't really relate to what we're using it for today, so I won't bore you with those details. However, it does come with a very high-gain military-grade video camera. I think we will power that puppy up and see if it helps us look for your boys."

"Really?" Jack said. "Does it enhance light?"

"It doesn't exactly see in the dark, but it does a great job at capturing and magnifying existing light. It'll amaze you, I think. ...

Of course, it doesn't see through the clouds, but it looks to me like that's not going to be a problem this morning. We should be able to drop well beneath the cloud cover and perform some relatively low-altitude reconnaissance."

"Does it, the camera system, is it equipped with an infrared sensor?" Jack asked. "Can it detect body heat? So that we might locate a human being from the air?"

"The camera does not do that, but we do have a thermal sensor—I refer to it as the Grid-EYE. It's pretty new. The older infrared sensors required that a person be in motion. But this one can detect a warm body even if that warm body is trying to hide."

"So, if one of our boys is on Gull Island, that sensor will see him?"

"Yes. … That is, if he is still warm. I'm sorry to put it that way. But, if a human body has cooled to the temperature of its surroundings, the onboard Grid-EYE is not going to see him."

"I get it," Jack said. "… How far are we from the island?"

"Fifteen minutes, I'd say. Give or take."

Jack inhaled more deeply than usual. He held that breath for over ten seconds, and then released that air with a noticeable quiver. Jack was very uneasy as to what they might find. He was still running on nervous energy and beer. "I could sure use a cup of coffee," he said to himself. He looked over at Henry, who was sitting with his head back, face up, as though he'd fallen asleep. But he hadn't. He just did not feel like talking right at that moment.

Fourteen minutes later the pilot began to cut back on his speed.

"This is a large plane," the pilot said to Jack. "Not exactly ideal for what we're doing. We do not want to gamble on a stall, so we will not back off on the throttle excessively. And we are not going to go in terribly low. But I think you'll be able to get what you need. … Get ready. … We're coming in from the south. … That's the islands up ahead. Charity Island, by the shape of it. Gull Island's just south and a little west of Charity. It is the tiny little— … Damn! Did you get a good look at *that*?"

"Yeah," Jack said. "It's *not* there!"

"Oh, it's there," the pilot said. "But, it's covered with water. Or mostly covered."

"Well," Jack said. "I know damn well that my boys are sure as hell not on it. … Fire up that telescopic camera. Let me take a look through that."

Harold the pilot already had the camera ready to go. "I'll put the coordinates in it—the ones for Gull Island. Otherwise it would be impossible to lock it in." A minute later the camera snapped in and auto-focused on the middle of the island.

"I'll circle around and come back over it," he said. "You should be able to get a good look at it when I do."

"Could you turn that thermal sensor on, too?" Jack asked. "I don't know how tall or big those trees really are, but I'd like to see if any of the kids might have climbed up one of them."

"Here," the pilot said to Jack. "When I come back in I will be directly over the island. Use this joystick and point it at the island. It will be directly beneath us when I fly back. See if anything comes up on the screen. If there's even a raccoon in one of those trees you'll see it. And you point that thing at it. There'll be no missing it."

Henry got out of his seat and walked up to the back of the cockpit. Jack looked back at him and shook his head. The Cessna passed directly over the island, and they saw nothing.

"Nothing?" the pilot asked. "I didn't see anything. Did you guys?"

"No," Jack said. "Can we do that again?"

"Sure. I'll swing around and come back over," the pilot said as he handed Henry another headset.

The pilot circled and flew over the island two more times, but still no one saw a thing—not on the camera, and not with heat detection.

After the third time over, Jack said to Henry, "Got your cell phone handy? Find the coordinates for the cabin and give them to Harold."

The pilot heard what Jack said, and he spoke up: "I've got them right here from earlier. If you're satisfied that we've covered the little island well enough, we'll take a look at the cabin. See what we can find."

"About how far is it from the island?" Jack asked.

"I'd say it looks to be about thirty miles," the pilot said. "As the crow flies."

"That far?" Jack asked, a little surprised. "They did that by boat every day?"

"Not every day," Henry replied. "Legend is quite the fisherman. I got the feeling that he intended to head there in the afternoon of the first day. Spend the night camping out—they had a couple tents—and then head out fishing early the next morning."

"That would be today," Jack said. "And now the whole island is under water. … But, we can't be *absolutely* sure that they were headed out the first day. Right? It could have been that they would decide to spend the first night in the cabin, and then go fishing around there for the first day—for the first *whole* day. And then venture out to Gull Island for the second whole day. Could that have been the way it worked out?"

"I think that's how you and Kate would have done it," Henry replied. "All the boys would be tired after riding for that long. And they would have wanted to get a good night's sleep on that first night. ... I sure hope that's how it went down."

The pilot then said, "We can take a couple circles around that area, but then we should head to Detroit Metro. We're still good on fuel, but with all this stuff going down—that business up north—they could end up closing airports, and it might take a while to be cleared for landing. We would not want to get ourselves in trouble by running late on this."

"If we find something at the cabin," Jack said. "Is there any place to set down around there?"

"I checked that out. There's a strip in Alpena. But, it's not that much further to take it back to Detroit, where they were expecting us. This machine is about a 1.5 mil. I don't want to get stuck working that off, if you know what I mean."

"Let's take a look at the cabin," Jack said. "We just might find the boys running around there."

He then smiled and continued, "Probably not running around at this time of the morning. ... Henry, do you think you can identify the cabin from the air?"

"I would think so," Henry said. "But I'm sure I can identify Legend's vehicle. Pretty distinctive. Can't miss that."

"What is it?" Jack asked. "What's he drive?"

"He has a converted school bus. Very fancy. Didn't you catch it when you talked to him in Grand Rapids?"

"No. I didn't see anything like that. Did he paint it, or is it still school-bus yellow? What should I look for?"

"It will be the only cranberry-red former school bus that you're gonna see today."

"Cranberry-red!" Jack said. "He must not keep it parked at his house. I spent a lot of time in Grand Rapids a while ago, and I don't recall ever seeing a cranberry-red school bus."

"He has spent years customizing that bus. I'd doubt that he would ever park it on the street."

Less than a minute passed before Jack barked, "There it is! That's it. It's got to be it—fancy red school bus. ... And it's almost window deep in water. Look at that shit. The water is actually all the way up to the top of the wheels. ... Which cabin is it? The closest one? There, under the trees?"

"No," Henry said. "It's not that one. There's no road leading up to Legend's cabin. No electricity or telephone. You have to hike everything through the woods a hundred yards or so to get to it. ... That's it back there. It's *totally* flooded all around it. ... Can we take another loop? I'd like to see if there is any smoke coming out of the chimney."

"Yup," the pilot agreed. "We'll take one more run over it and then head to Detroit Met. Is that cool by you, Jack?"

"Makes sense," Jack replied. "The sooner we get on the ground, the sooner we can get back here and find our boys."

Chapter 19

As it turned out, the blast was accomplished by affixing over one hundred MOAB bombs, each of which had the explosive force of a small nuclear device. They were attached to the bottom (outside) of a 1,000-foot ore carrier. Inside the freighter was 100,000 tons of iron ore. ... It had entered the Poe Lock in Sault Ste. Marie from the west, coming from Lake Superior. As soon as the western gate, which is in reality a "moveable dam", closed, the ship began rapidly taking on water via a series of recently installed bilge pumps running in reverse. At the same time, a group of eleven crew members tossed a ramp over the starboard side of the ship and onto the side of the lock, and they quickly got off the ship. They walked briskly to the west end of the locks, and there boarded a Zodiac Rigid Hull motorized extraction boat. Before authorities could react, the boat sped west at over 40 knots.

While this was taking place, the lock pumps began removing water inside the lock, and the freighter continued taking on water. Finally, the ore carrier rested on the bottom of the channel, driving the MOAB devices deep into the mud at the bottom.

Once the water had been dropped to the level of the Saint Mary's River, but still before the eastern gate had opened, the operators of the escape boat actuated a wireless transmitter. That device simultaneously triggered the detonators on all one hundred MOAB bombs. The force of the explosion was horrendous. Not since World War II has so much explosive force been released except in a mid-ocean test environment, which was always totally void of victims. The destructive force of that blast was akin to that which devastated Nagasaki and Hiroshima.

Because the explosive devices were so tightly compressed beneath the heavy weight of the iron ore, the force of the blast was directed down and out. Not only did it take out both ends of the Poe Lock, it absolutely decimated all the rock and masonry infrastructure comprising the whole of the Soo Locks. In fact, the downward force of the explosion created a crater directly beneath the Poe Lock that approached a depth of two hundred feet.

Initially, workers were not only entirely blocked from attempting temporary repairs on the locks, they were prohibited from even assessing the damages. It took nearly one full month before engineers were permitted to perform an on-site evaluation of the damages. That was because sensing equipment at various locations downstream from the locks, as well as at near ground zero, indicated that there were substantially elevated levels of radiation. It was feared that the excessive radiation detected resulted from the type of explosive device used to wreak the horrific damages incurred. "It must have been some sort of nuclear device," some suggested. "That means we must evacuate the entire area in order to prevent the long-term side effects of radiation, such as severe skin problems, chronic fatigue, cancer and other major health issues."

Only after it was conclusively determined that the explosives used, even though surprisingly powerful, were totally conventional, were engineers permitted to set foot on the ground in order to perform the exhaustive damage assessments necessary in order for repairs to begin. It was, therefore, three months after the explosion before the clearing of debris could even start.

Six months after the formal assessment was initiated, a preliminary report was submitted to the Army Corps of Engineers regarding findings and recommendations of the initial team of inspectors and engineers. A summary of their determinations is as follows:

Upon our thorough examination of the so-called "Ground Zero" of the "Soo Locks" explosion, we have arrived at the following conclusions:

1) Because the Soo Locks, and the bedrock upon which the Soo Locks were initially constructed, has been disturbed (and thereby irreparably damaged for this use) by the explosion, we therefore recommend: that all future lock construction be relocated a minimum of fifteen hundred feet west of their current location, but east of the International Bridge.

2) That the channel be cleared of debris and dredged to the proper depth through the west narrow channel at Neebish Island, and beyond as deemed necessary by the USACE (U.S. Army Corps of Engineers).

3) That the channel walls from the site of the new locks, downstream be repaired and strengthened where necessary to a point past the end of the west narrow channel at Neebish Island.

4) That the St. Mary's River Bypass System (and its electrical power generation infrastructure) be repaired, upgraded or replaced as deemed necessary by the USACE.

5) That necessary repairs (if any) be made to the International Bridge, leaving in place the existing bridge supports and

foundations (as they appear not to have been damaged by the explosion). And,

6) That the current low water level in Lake Superior since the explosion be maintained until construction is completed.

There were many questions that arose surrounding the event (which came to be known as the "Soo Locks Bombing"). Chief among those questions were two: first of all, *Who* was responsible for this destruction? And, second, *Why* would anyone in their right mind ever choose to perform such an egregious act? Regarding those questions, the passage of time not only provided the answers, it revealed that the *Who and the Why* were inexorably tied together in the most intricate fashion.

Initially, the consensus of thought held that it was an act of terrorism, and that most likely the source of the attack originated in the Middle East. That theory was helped along three days after the bombing when a message, handwritten in Farsi, arrived at the White House. The first part of the note took credit for the bombing, and the paragraph at the end translated into English as "Death to American infidels." It was at first thought genuine. Upon examination, however, Islamic scholars declared it to be a fake based on the idioms it used. Plus, the scholars believed that if the note were genuine the writer would not have waited three days to present it.

So, it was back to the proverbial "drawing board" as to the *Who and the Why* behind the bombing.

As is frequently the case in matters like this, both questions remained largely unanswered for several years. In the minds of most people from New York to California, the suspected culprit was the nameless/faceless/ubiquitous Middle Eastern terrorist. If you were to ask fifty citizens of the U.S. about it, forty of them would say something like, "The ship was blown up by Middle Eastern terrorists." While the remaining ten wouldn't have had a clue that it even happened.

But then, one of the most interesting things you can imagine occurred. It all started when a wealthy retired Detroit attorney purchased a million-dollar home just west of Whitefish Point in Michigan's Upper Peninsula. His name was Lawrence F. Burns, Esq.

It was a lovely home. Overlooking Lake Superior, it boasted a beautiful beach, which extended three hundred feet east to west, and ran nearly three hundred feet north to south—if measured between the large Lake Superior waves.

As a very successful business law attorney, Mr. Burns always exercised caution when spending his or his clients' money. Before he laid down his cash to buy his dream home, he checked with the Army Corps of Engineers to see if it might be in danger of erosion. He was pleased to learn that the U.S. Army Corps of Engineers (USACE) had declared the area surrounding his home on all sides as a "Low Risk Area" with regard to water erosion.

Once assured that the home had been declared safe to buy, he made his offer. And it proved to be a successful offer, allowing him to pay the money and take possession.

However, three years after making the purchase, the level of Lake Superior had risen nearly a full foot. It continued on that path for the next three years, rising nearly three additional feet. And because of its higher level, it chewed away at the bank in front of his house. At the end of that sixth year, the distance between his deck and the big lake had dramatically shrunk. While once two hundred and fifty feet separated his house from destruction, now it was less than forty feet. And the situation was continuing to worsen.

So, Attorney Burns hired a local contractor to protect his bank before Lake Superior turned his million-dollar home into a houseboat. At a cost of nearly a hundred thousand dollars, the contractor affixed heavy asphalt-treated felt underlayment to the entire bank, and then arranged for over a thousand tons of large quarried boulders to be placed on top of that black fabric.

Thinking he had solved the problem, Attorney Burns accepted the opportunity to represent a large Ukraine-based multi-national energy corporation. The downside of the job—it required that he relocate to Eastern Europe for eighteen months. But, there was a lucrative upside to the opportunity. If he were successful, when he returned to the U.S. after a year and a half, he would have earned money to buy two or three more homes much like the one he owned. He accepted the offer.

When he arrived back in the country, his first move was to head up north to check up on his beautiful vacation home. What he found when he arrived shocked him. The level of Lake Superior had risen nearly another foot, and when it did, it totally devoured his investment in erosion security. Now the lake had not only taken out all his boulders, it was threatening the very deck he loved to go out on to watch the sunset. Neighbors told him that he was about to lose his home. "One more harsh winter, or severe wind storm, Old Lake Gitche Gumee (which means ‹big water› in a Longfellow poem) will have consumed your home."

Attorney Burns was beyond frustrated. After taking a short

walk down to the bank to observe the destruction for himself, he turned around and immediately drove his Escalade ten miles south—to the little town of Paradise. He found his favorite little party store/fuel station, went in and purchased two bottles of dry red wine. His plan was to take the wine back to his house, and drink it all, or at least a good share of it. And then in the morning, he would head back to the house he still owned in a nice Detroit neighborhood. "No point sticking around here any longer," he told himself. "I've already done everything possible."

However, when he arrived back at his house, he found an envelope that had been pushed under his door. *I undoubtedly walked right over this when I was here before,* he reasoned. *I suppose I was just too distraught at the time to notice it.* So, he poured himself a nine-ounce glass of dry red, and then sat down to read the missive he had totally missed before. It said:

From the Law Firm of Crighton, Crighton and Holmes.

Dear Mr. Burns. I regret to inform you that you are about to lose your home to Lake Superior. I have no doubt that you are already aware of the problem, because I can see that you have already spent a small fortune on a water break. Unfortunately, that money has been wasted. Lake Superior is up over three feet already, and it is likely to get even higher. The rock is not going to save your home.

Hundreds of other residents who live along the Great Lakes, and Lake Superior in particular, are experiencing the same problem. Thousands of homes, some even more expensive than yours, have already succumbed to the rising waters of one of the Great Lakes. And, most of them have found that no amount of expensive break-water constructions can protect their investments over the long haul. Eventually, the big lake will inexorably take your home.

What this note is designed to do is to serve not so much as a warning of the plight about which you are already aware, but to inform you that you do have a solid and reliable recourse. What this class action case maintains is that you are not battling Mother Nature. What we contend the evidence shows is that the problem was brought about by the rapacious greed of some very wealthy businessmen, and of their even more greedy investors. We believe we can definitively show that they are the ones responsible for the destruction of hundreds of private and public beaches, of hundreds if not thousands of homes, of dozens of streets and roads along the shores of all the Great Lakes, and that their callous actions threaten to decimate thousands of more homes.

Following is the history surrounding this problem—how we hold that the trouble began, why it persists, and what now needs to be done:

1) Back in 1986 preliminary plans and authorization were made to build a "Super Lock" where the dormant Davis and Sabin Locks lay. Three of the arguments proposed prompting the project were:

> A—The Poe Lock (the only lock large enough to accommodate the newer one-thousand-foot ore carriers) occasionally has to be closed for repairs. Usually those repairs can be made when the locks are closed for the winter. But, were the lock to go down between March 25 and January 15, it would basically shut down the nation's ability to produce steel, thus creating a national security emergency. The United States Department of Homeland Secu-

rity estimated that a six-month closure to the Poe Lock during shipping season could cost the U.S. $1.1 trillion and the loss of over 10 million jobs. A new Super Lock would prevent that loss.

B—A second larger lock would streamline navigation, and thereby encourage the growth of the Great Lakes shipping industry.

C—It was estimated that the new lock would directly produce over 1,000 new jobs.

2) The Super Lock was approved for construction in 1986. Those in charge of planning believed that the new lock would be constructed in the imminent future. However, the project was not formally funded at that time, and it was even further stalled by subsequent administrations. Therefore, we contend, necessary maintenance efforts on the existing locks and the downstream channel (such as dredging) were not performed in a timely fashion. This meant that the channel east and south of the existing locks grew more and more shallow due to the buildup of normal-use debris carried downstream by the swift flow of water through the bottom gate. Unfortunately, due to this procrastination, necessary regular maintenance was inappropriately postponed in anticipation of the construction of the new lock. The reasoning: we contend that it was determined that since the construction of a new lock would require massive dredging, significant savings could be achieved by combining the projects—regular maintenance and the construction of the new lock. Unfortunately, the project was not funded for the next thirty years. It was not until the current administration pushed the project forward in 2019 that monies were actually allocated. During that time regular maintenance was not performed

Michael Carrier

in a timely manner. And, we contend, still it has not. ...
But, there is a further glimmer of hope. In May of 2020
substantial work on the new lock in Sault Ste. Marie was
started. It seems that the President has become sensitive to
the problem and has allocated nearly one billion dollars to
build it. If this project is done properly (that is, if the issues
with the dams and locks downstream are adequately dealt
with), our issues with the problem should be resolved.

3) That brings us to the present day disaster. Some time ago
(about three years) it was brought to our attention here at
Crighton, Crighton and Holmes that a number of homeowners who own vacation property along Lake Superior,
and the other Great Lakes, were currently suffering (or
were about to suffer) great loss due to erosion caused by
the incursion of the lakes. Many of these property owners
contacted Crighton, Crighton and Holmes, and asked us
if there was a legitimate/natural reason for their problem,
or if it has been brought about by intentional or careless
behavior associated with the operation of the Great Lakes
shipping industry. And, if anything such as this could be
demonstrated.

Furthermore, if culpability can be determined, could
it be remedied? After over one year of research, we determined that the problem was indeed a direct result of negligent management of regular maintenance of the locks
by the USACE (United States Army Corps of Engineers);
that their failure to dredge the channel on a regular/timely
basis (because it was causing the channel to lose depth)
threatened to force Great Lakes shipping companies to
limit the amount of iron ore they would be permitted to
transport. And, to compensate for their failure to dredge,
they opted to raise the level of the Great Lakes by regulating the height of the dams and gates used to control the

flow of bypass water at the fifteen locks from Sault Ste. Marie, along the Saint Lawrence Seaway through the eastern part of the U.S. and Canada, all the way to the Atlantic Ocean.

We found that the effort to raise the water level in Sault Ste. Marie could not be accomplished simply by raising the level of Lake Superior, because over half of the shipping problem related to shallow channel depth downstream from the lower gates of the Soo Locks. To solve the whole dredging issue, the flow of water throughout the Great Lakes had to be raised as well. That is why we have seen the levels raised in Lakes Huron, Michigan, Erie and Ontario, as well as in Lake Superior. All of the Great Lakes are up two and a half to three feet within the last five years, while the Atlantic Ocean level has barely changed during that same time cycle.

It was at that point that we filed court documents stipulating our demands that the USACE immediately cease and desist their harmful activities that has caused the waters of the Great Lakes to rise, and that the USACE restore and make whole all losses suffered by all of the undersigned property owners and municipalities as a result of its harmful actions.

We can demonstrate just how minimal the impact of a remedy would be on worldwide ocean levels. For instance, if all of the Great Lakes were allowed to go back to pre-tampering levels (that is, if all five Great Lakes were lowered thirty-six inches, back to levels experienced before 2010), it would raise the levels of the Atlantic Ocean less than half the thickness of a potato chip. That is to say, ocean levels would not rise in any significant way (the actual change in ocean levels would be .02427th of an inch.

Rounded off—two one-hundredths of an inch.).

4) If you are interested in signing on to this class action suit, please call us as soon as possible to discuss it. Keep in mind, time is of the essence. We intend to file this lawsuit in the very near future. And, once the suit has been filed, no additional signatories will be permitted.

When he had finished reading the letter he poured himself a second glass of wine. "Might as well give it a try," he said out loud. "They're probably closed by now, but what the hell."

He took an extended sip on his wine, and entered the number.

"Crighton, Crighton and Holmes, Attorneys at Law," the very pleasant female voice on the other end said. "This is the after-hours service. How may I help you?"

"I'm sorry. I didn't realize how late it was. I suppose I should check back in the morning. Right?"

"Are you currently a client of one of the attorneys?"

"Not yet. I was just reading a letter addressed to me by the firm. It's a month—nearly a month—old. It has to do with a class-action suit involving Great Lakes erosion. I should probably call back in the morning."

"I can have our on-call attorney give you a call if you wish. But, if it's not an emergency—it can wait until tomorrow. I know that for a fact. That case is still seeking signatories. I would say to call in the morning. That's what I would recommend. But it is your call."

"That works for me just fine," he said.

"Why don't you give me your name, and I will have one of the attorneys who are working that case give you a call tomorrow."

"My name is Lawrence F. Burns, Esquire. I'm an attorney as well."

"Wonderful. And would the number you called in on be an appropriate phone to call you back on? Or should they use a different number? I see you called in on a Detroit area code."

"Yes. I used to practice in Detroit. I retired. The property that I am calling about is in the Upper Peninsula by Whitefish Point. But I still have a home in the Detroit area."

"Wonderful, Mr. Burns. I'll have someone give you a call in the morning."

"After ten," he said. "I might want to sleep in a bit."

"I'll make a note of that. Thank you very much."

Lawrence Burns finished the second glass of Merlot and poured a third. *I suppose I should nurse this one along a little better than I might,* he thought. *Ten o'clock can come around rather early for me, now that I've retired.*

But, that plan did not work.

Twenty minutes later he drained the first bottle into his glass.

"Shit," he complained. "Can't believe I polished that off so fast. … Oh, hell. They probably won't call me until the afternoon, anyway. I'll be sober by then."

So, he staggered out to the kitchen and scooped up the second bottle. After he had taken three or four steps back toward the large lakeside window he liked to sit by, he remembered that he had forgotten the corkscrew.

"Damn!" he barked.

As he spun around to go back, he lost his balance and tumbled into the bar. He tried to block his fall with his hands, but he missed with his right, and so absorbed the full impact of the bar on the left side of his head. The blow was not a vicious one, but it did knock him out for a few minutes.

When he came to his senses, he lifted himself to his knees and looked around. "What the hell happened?" he asked out loud when he realized that he had been lying in a small puddle of blood. Reaching up to check out his left temple, his finger slid past a matted section of bloodied hair. He immediately realized that there was a decent-sized gash above his left ear.

"Damn! Damn! Damn!" he repeated. "I fell down. But, I don't remember it."

He held on to the bar to steady himself, as he circled around toward the kitchen sink. Yanking off a dishtowel on the way, he turned on the hot and cold water until it reached a cool but not icy temperature. He then moistened the towel and wiped off his face, after which he checked out the towel. *I can't believe I bled like that*, he was thinking.

He rinsed out the towel and repeated the procedure. That time there was not as much blood.

He opened the towel drawer and found a nearly all-white terrycloth dishtowel and pressed it against the gash on his head. After he pulled it off he checked it for blood. "That's better," he muttered, relieved to see that the flow of blood had nearly stopped.

He rinsed out the towel—this time with entirely cold water— and pressed it tightly over his wound.

He walked back to where he had fallen and picked up the bottle of Merlot. "Damn good thing this isn't champagne," he said, "or it'd blow all over hell when I popped the cork."

"Speaking of," he said, "I wonder where the corkscrew is."

Holding the cold compress over his wound, he scoured the

area where he'd fallen, but didn't find what he was looking for. "Where the hell is that stupid thing?" he muttered.

He then pulled the towel off the side of his head and looked at it. It showed almost no blood, so he took it and, using his foot on the towel, he blotted up the puddle of blood from the ceramic tile floor.

He walked back to the cupboard where he'd opened the first bottle. When his eyes fell on the necessary tool he was looking for he laughed at himself and picked it up. And then, standing in the same spot where he'd opened the other bottle, he popped the cork out of the new bottle.

Being more careful this time, he made his way back to his favorite chair and filled up his wine glass.

He didn't remember that he had decided to "nurse" his drinking, but it didn't matter. He took one sip of the wine, and then set the glass back down on the table.

At ten o'clock the next morning his cell phone rang, but he didn't answer. The recorded message that he didn't hear said, "This is Jeffery Reason, from the Law Firm of Crighton, Crighton and Holmes. I'm returning your call from yesterday evening. Mr. Stanley Creighton assigned me to be your contact should you wish to let us represent you in our class action suit against the Federal Government. If you wish to you may give me a call after hearing this message. I will be here until five P.M. Ask for Jeffery Reason. Thanks for reaching out to us. I look forward to meeting you. Have a good day."

One hour and a half later Lawrence Burns' phone rang again. And again Lawrence Burns did not pick it up. The voice said, "This is Attorney Jeffery Reason, from the Law Firm of Crighton, Crighton and Holmes. I'd called you a little earlier. If you receive this message please feel free to give me a ring at your convenience. I'd like to talk to you. Thanks. And have a good day."

Four hours later there was another call coming in from that same 313 area code. "Please be advised that the following is a recorded message. Hello. This is Jeffery Reason calling you with regard to the class-action suit we are entering in vis-à-vis the Federal Government with regard to the erosion issue on the Great Lakes. As of two hours ago this whole matter has entered a new phase. Being closely associated with the Upper Peninsula, no doubt you already know that a short time ago the Soo Locks were viciously attacked by an unknown party. The explosion was so horrific it destroyed both the upper and lower gates of the largest lock, the Poe Lock. Many attribute the attack to terrorism, but none have so far taken credit for it.

As you would surmise, this changes everything with regard to our case. When the locks were bombed, a twenty-two foot wall of water was immediately released, flooding the shoreline from Sugar and Neebish Islands, to all associated waters to the south. It could be days or even weeks before the torrent will markedly subside.

But, for right now, the erosion problems that have recently threatened your property have been postponed or perhaps even alleviated. In any event, we here at Crighton, Crighton and Holmes need some time to assess our options, as well as the options of our clients. We ask that you be patient with us for the next two weeks. At that time we will know better as to how we should proceed in order to best serve our clients. Thank you."

Contrary to what might be expected, Lawrence Burns was not

at all stressed about the destruction of the Soo Locks, nor was he put off by the recorded message left by Jeffery Reason. In fact, none of the numerous negative events that occurred since his retirement fazed him at all.

Three weeks after that fateful day, Lawrence Burns' oldest daughter and her husband, Elizabeth and Brad Romley, drove up from their home in Warren, Michigan, to visit her father. It was fortunate for Lizzy that she took her husband with her for the trip because she not only needed his muscle to force open the front door of her father's house, but she also found his strength useful to catch her when she fainted.

The shock of finding her dad, his body decomposing in his favorite chair, was more than she could bear.

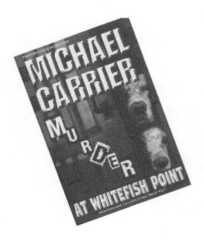

If you find Great Lakes erosion problems interesting, you will especially like *Murder at Whitefish Point. Not only does Jack have to deal with massive beach erosion in this book, but a few people end up getting murdered. That always fans the fire for Jack.*

Chapter 20

The first day of their search started with a cursory visual inspection of the stretch of the Au Sable that ran west to nearby Van Etten Lake. Jack had decided to take a look at it in the unlikely event that the boys might have ventured in that direction. Once convinced that it was the greater likelihood that Legend would have bypassed that opportunity altogether, he set out on the Lake Huron shoreline.

He moved along briskly from a point about two miles north of the Au Sable until he reached the pier/breakwater. Even though he knew starting out that his chances of discovering anything of significance in that section of real estate were slim, he wanted to be thorough. In other words—to leave no stone unturned.

Going ashore so that he could cross over to the south bank of the river, he stopped and talked to several of the people he encountered, asking if they had noticed a group of Boy Scouts fishing in the area. No one recalled having seen anything that resembled what he was asking about. All that they could think about was the "nuclear attack" up north, and how high Lake Huron was getting. "It's been bad for two years now," one man said in answer to Jack's question. "But, the past two days, since the atomic bomb got dropped on us up in Sault Ste. Marie, since that, the lake is just going crazy. I think the world is coming to an end. That's how it looks to me. … What do you think?"

For a moment or two Jack commiserated with him with regard to his distress. But, as soon as he determined that the man had no helpful information to offer, he expeditiously moved on.

Once back on the shore south of the river mouth Jack proceeded in a much more meticulous fashion. For the next six hours he zigzagged back and forth, from the edge of the lake to the sandy sometimes nearly vertical embankment, carefully inspecting every object that caught his eye.

It was a slow, deliberate process. He realized that just because an object might be half buried in the sand did not in any way suggest that it had been in that spot for any significant length of time. *Waves behave in a very strange fashion,* he reasoned, *especially on the Great Lakes. Even in the stillness of a warm summer morning, with the waters gently lapping onto the shore, any object can be buried by several inches of sand by a single wave. And then, once that wave has crawled up the shore face as far as gravity will allow, it turns and retreats to the safety of the lake. And as it washes back, it takes with it more well-washed debris and sand, burying even deeper that newly deposited object. Such is the unpredictable nature of a wave.*

At first he began using his boot to unearth partially obscured objects. If something caught his attention he would hook the sole of his right boot under the piece of paper or cloth, and turn it over. If it continued to look interesting, he would pick it up and examine it more closely.

Over the course of the first eight hours he spent searching on the south side of the river mouth he repeated that procedure close to a hundred times—all without any success. Even though many of the objects he found might have looked interesting, all appeared that they had been in the water for weeks if not longer.

Finally, at 6 P.M., he kicked at a yellow Butterfinger candy bar wrapper. It was partially buried, but barely. The reason Jack's attention was immediately drawn to it was because he knew that both Red and Robby were *very* fond of that brand of candy. Plus, the part of the wrapper that blew in the wind appeared crisp and fresh. While it was not the first candy wrapper that he had come across, nor was it even the first crisp-looking wrapper, as he opened it up with his boot he observed that some of the chocolate on the inside portion was largely intact. "This is pretty damn fresh," he said out loud. "Could have been dropped by anyone, but it's worth hanging on to."

In the back of his mind he was thinking that it really did not seem to fit either of his boys—to carelessly discard litter like that. *But*, he figured, *I'm gonna hang on to this, just in case.* Might be fingerprints on it. Opening a one-quart zipper bag, he picked it up and slid it into the bag and then sealed it. After he had taken off his gloves, he checked his GPS finder, and then penned the numbers on the bag. After he had tucked it safely in the large waterproof canvas bag he was carrying, he continued down the beach. His success, though minor, painted a small but distinct smile on his face. For the first time in the past three hours he felt encouraged. "If I find their prints on that trash I'm gonna have a serious sit-down with them," he said out loud.

Little by little he began losing the sun. So he broke out his Fenix LR40R Rechargeable 12000 Lumen Flashlight. *It works great,* he thought, *but it doesn't take the place of a noonday sun. Gonna have to call it a wrap.*

It was nearly 10 P.M. when he decided to break from his search for the night. "I wonder where the hell Henry is," Jack said. "Thought I'd have heard from him by now." He took out his cell and checked to see if he was hitting a tower. "Cool," he said, seeing that he had three bars.

"Henry, where are you? Think you could pick the old man up?" Henry did not answer, so Jack checked his GPS location finder and copied the coordinates in his log so he would know where to kick off his search the next day. He then shone his Fenix around to capture one last lay of the land. When he did, he spotted a reflection down by, but not in, the water. He walked over and tried to hook his boot onto a small piece of shiny protruding metal, but it did not immediately emerge from the wet sand. He tried again. Still it did not budge. So, he reached down a gloved hand and pulled it out. It was a dog collar. The sharp metal he had tried to use to pull it free was a nametag—half of which was missing. He picked it up and brushed the sand off. On the part of the tag that remained were the letters "DDY."

"Damn!" Jack growled. "That sure as hell looks like Buddy's collar."

Jack spent the next twenty minutes scouring the immediate area looking for relatively fresh dog tracks, but found nothing.

Once satisfied that the collar probably washed ashore at that location, he raised his light closer and more carefully examined the object of his attention.

"Hair," he murmured. "Light golden. This could be Buddy's hair. Sure as hell matches."

He removed another zipper bag and prepared to slide it in. That's when he spotted something that captured his attention. He saw something that looked like a stain under the nametag. He looked more closely. He then carefully removed several strands of the hair and placed them in the zipper bag. After the hair was safely preserved and stored, Jack carefully spun the broken nametag on its rivet until he could get a clearer look at the stain. "That sure as hell looks like blood," he said. "It's been in the water, so most of it's been washed out. But it does look like blood. … Hell, it looks pretty washed out, but maybe there's enough left."

He pulled out his bottle of Luminol, and sprayed it. Almost immediately it turned pale blue. "Damn it!" he barked. "Blood!"

Luminol is a chemical that is employed by most law enforcement agencies during crime scene investigations. When sprayed on a suspicious stain, even if it is not a fresh stain, using a reaction called *chemiluminescence*, it will emit a light blue glow. However, it does not tell the technician whether or not it's human blood—for that, the specimen must be sent to a proper lab so that a procedure such as *The Ouchterlony Test* may be employed.

"Hey, Jack," Henry said. "You just called?"

"Yeah. Wondering if you were in the area."

"Sorry about that," Henry apologized. "Didn't intend to be so late. I assume you're ready. Right?"

"Can't really do it justice once I lose the sun," Jack said. "I'll give you my coordinates. I'll be more precise once I've hit a road. … Try these out: 44.30097 by -83.404196. I can't give you a visual yet, but I'm sure M-23 is right over the hill."

"I'm only a few minutes out."

"What's your 10-20?"

"I'm on M-23 right now. ETA ten minutes, max."

"Terrific," Jack responded. "It might take me that long. Or

maybe a little longer. ... Find anything interesting?"

"Oh yeah," Henry said. "At least I think I might have something. How about you?"

"Possibly," Jack replied. "Can you recall what collar Buddy was wearing?"

"Oh, hell!" Henry answered. "I didn't really check that out. My guess is that it would have been the one he always wears. I know he did have something around his neck—it's got his name and your phone number fastened right to it. Same as always, I think ... Why? What did you find?"

"I found a collar. Part of the nametag is broken off. But, on the part that's still attached, it looks like it might be his name. Phone number is entirely gone."

Jack did not tell Henry right then that he'd found blood on it as well. He decided to save that info for later. He did take a moment to slide the collar into a larger zipper bag and stored it with the other two bags.

"And you," Jack said as he walked. "You suggested that your work proved fruitful. What did you find? I'll put you on speakerphone so I can try to get up this hill and find a road. So, tell me what you came across."

"Well," Henry explained. "It's queerer than all shit. I took some pictures. I can show them to you back in the camper. I don't even know if it belonged to one of the boys, but I found a red cap in a tree. It looked for all the world like the ones the boys were wearing. I can't swear to it, but it sure looked like that to me. I'll show it to you."

"Did you bag it?"

"Oh, yeah. And it won't have any of my DNA on it. ... At least, not on the inside. Sometimes I'll grab the bill on their caps, but that's it. Think you might be able to definitively ID it?"

"I think so," Jack replied. "I don't think there are too many of those caps around with authentic autographs. Roger actually got them signed for the boys."

"No shit!" Henry said. "I didn't know that was real."

"You said you found the cap in a tree?" Jack queried. "The water wasn't that deep, that it would carry anything like that up a tree. The wind might have blown it up there, but it couldn't have washed up a tree. How high up was it?"

"No," Henry replied. "You're right about that. Water could not have produced the scene I found, but neither could the wind. The cap was at least ten feet off the ground. Someone had to have intentionally lodged it up there. For certain. Whoever put it there intended it to be a flag. Something to be found. I think Red or Robby stuck it in a tree, and not too high, specifically because they knew we'd be searching for them, and they wanted us to know where they'd been. It was obviously done on purpose because they cut a hole in the cap, and broke the end of a branch off. And then, they shoved the branch through the hole. They made sure that it couldn't blow off by trimming back a smaller branch on that same limb, and then bent it over and slid the cap over the twig. It was definitely a flag for us to find."

"Just like I taught them to do," Jack said. "Survival 101. ... Anything written on it?"

"You know," Henry said. "I didn't see anything. But I didn't really examine it too closely, either."

"You didn't see any stains on it?" Jack asked. "Like blood?"

Henry did not immediately respond.

Finally, he said, "There is some dirt on the cap. I don't know what it is. I figured you could tell if it's anything important, or if it's just plain old dirt. I really don't know."

Jack could tell by the way Henry stated his case that whatever it was that Henry found on the cap, it meant trouble. Henry just did not want to contribute to his friend's concern. So Jack did not press the issue. *We'll get that all figured out soon enough*, he reasoned.

Neither man spoke for nearly five minutes. And then Jack broke the silence.

"Damn, Henry," he said. "I am not as young as I used to be. That sand hill turned out to be more like a cliff. It took me all that time to get up it. … I'm on a street called Wolverine Road. I think this is M-23 I'm approaching. The sign says N. Huron. But I think it's the same as M-23."

"I can see you," Henry said, flashing his headlights from low beam to high, and then back to low.

Jack turned his flashlight off and waited to be picked up.

"You're one hell of a welcome sight," Jack said as he settled in. "I think we're both going to sleep well tonight."

"Yeah," Henry said, handing Jack the bagged red cap. "Wanna take a look at this and tell me what you think?"

Jack examined it through the bag, but did not open it.

After a minute he said, "That's Red's cap. I'm sure of it."

"Does it have his name on it?"

"Didn't have to. I recognize his printing."

"He wrote on the cap?" Henry asked. "I didn't see anything."

"He printed a message under the inner band. I couldn't really read it through the bag, but I did recognize his hand. We'll check it out in full back at the camper."

Jack had observed the brownish stain on the inside of the cap, but he did not wish to speculate until he was able to test it.

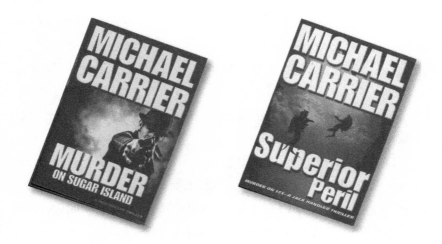

Once you have finished *Sault*, you should consider going back to these two books in order to learn exactly what it is that makes Red and Robby tick. For instance, it is in these two books that you learn the reason why Red can't talk. And how it is that Buddy came to live with the boys.

Chapter 21

U nder any ordinary circumstances, Jack and Henry would have at least considered hitting a restaurant on the way back to the trailer, but not on this night. They had too much to do and they both knew it.

So, immediately upon arriving, Jack removed his three zipper bags and laid them out on the table. Henry tossed his bag containing the red hat beside them on the table.

"What's in that other bag?" Henry asked, sliding the one with the Butterfinger wrapper over a bit so he could get a better look at it. "Where'd that come from?"

"On the shore, not far from the river mouth. Don't know if it means anything, but both of the boys like Butterfinger candy bars. … And it looks pretty fresh. I don't think it was in the water very much, or at all, there's still chocolate stuck to the inside. Had it been there for even a few days, or if it had been in the water, the chocolate would have been washed off. … But, I don't know if they had any Butterfingers on this trip."

"Oh yeah," Henry chimed in. "I do know. They picked some up when I stopped for gas. I noticed that they had bought some candy when we checked out, and they *were* Butterfingers. They each bought two. … You found it on the beach? Why would the boys be on the beach? I can't see them fishing from land at the mouth of the river. In fact, I can't see them littering the beach or the river. Seems out of character for either one of them, don't you think?"

"You're right about all of that," Jack agreed. "But, if one of them didn't like what Legend served up for breakfast, like oatmeal. Neither one of them likes oatmeal. If that were the case, they might have broke out a candy bar on the ride out to the island. And the wrapper might have blown out of the boat and up on the beach. It could have been the wind that deposited it where I found it— considerably away from the water. It might not have even hit the water. ... Sure doesn't look like it did. See, it still has chocolate on it. ... Hell, that's all speculation at this point. I need to see if I can lift some prints. And then we'll know if we've got anything.

"Hand me that hat. I'm going to want to take a closer look at it before we get into the other stuff," Jack said, as he slipped on a pair of latex gloves. He proceeded to stretch out a fresh, clean dishtowel on the counter, and then he opened the bag.

At first he examined the hole that Henry had been talking about.

"That cut is very new," Jack said. "The material has not frayed at all. And almost certainly intentional. I taught the boys to plant something bright, and as high as possible, if they ever needed help in an emergency. And the way you described it, it sounds like that is exactly what they did."

"I've got a picture of it," Henry said, holding his cell up for Jack to see. "When I climbed up that tree to retrieve it. Before I removed it, I shot this."

Jack checked out Henry's picture, but did not comment. He then flipped the hat over, exposing the brown stain on the inside.

"I didn't really notice that stain much before," Henry said, regarding the brown spot. "Do you suppose that's blood?"

"I'll test for blood in just a minute," Jack said. "But let's take a look under the inner band and see if we find anything.

He then carefully lifted the band up and beneath it they found the name *RED* written in black permanent marker.

"Well," Henry declared, "I guess that nails that question. That's a great place to hide a name."

"And, there's more in here," Jack added. "Looks like a short message. I can barely read it, though. Red must have been in a hurry. … Let's see. Looks like it says, 'Flooding. Why? No rain. Got to get off this island.'"

"Damn!" Henry groused. "You gonna check that stain? See if it really is blood? It's pretty dried up. Think you can still tell?"

"Yeah," Jack said as he loosened the nozzle on the Luminol so that he could spray it. "Cut the light for me."

Jack then sprayed the Luminol evenly over the area of the stain on the inside of the cap. Almost immediately the stain began emitting a pale blue glow, thus indicating the presence of blood.

"Shit!" Henry complained.

Jack flipped the cap over and looked at the significantly smaller stain on the outside.

"Doesn't that mean that the blood got there from somebody's—probably *Red's*—head?"

"Would seem likely. But he doesn't write anything about it in his message," Jack said. "And there doesn't appear to be any damage to the outside of the cap where the stain is. So, he either got a knock on his head with a dull object, or he wasn't wearing the cap when the injury took place. Those would be the logical suppositions. And, the former, that actually could be more serious than getting hit with a sharp object, because blunt force resulting in a bloodstain might have done more than just break the skin. Simply don't have enough info to draw a conclusion. … Let's have a look at those *fingerprints*. Let's see if that wrapper was ever touched by one of the boys."

"It's not like this is ever going to prove anything of significance," Jack said as he opened his fingerprint kit. "If it proves positive, it will simply demonstrate that one or both of the boys were on or by the beach by the river mouth. Don't even know if that will be significant. But it's worth checking out."

"What're we gonna do about the cap in the tree?" Henry asked. "That we're quite sure was left by Red. And it tells us that he was on that little island when, or soon after, the explosion."

"It tells us something, alright," Jack agreed. "I just don't know what that is right now. Hard to say how long it would have taken for that twenty-two-foot wall of water to dramatically begin affecting the water levels that far south in Lake Huron. My guess is several hours, at least. We can't think of it like a fast-moving tsunami—not in any way."

"Right," Henry agreed. "It'd behave more like a tidal wave than a tsunami—especially after it'd traveled a couple hundred miles. … Lot of water in Superior, but by the time it'd made it down the St. Mary's River, its force would not be catastrophic. Seems like Legend and the troop would have had time to safely launch for shore."

"We have to assume they did," Jack said. "Between Red, Robby and Legend, we have to think very positively about this. … Still, something else might have come up—unexpectedly. Something that could have changed the dynamic. … That's why we're trying to put the whole matter under a microscope. No way to know what info might become significant in getting to the bottom of it.

"As it stands right now, four bits of evidence stand out in my mind. First, Red's hat in the tree. Why would he do that? What was he worried about? Second, the blood in the hat. I have to think that it's most likely Red's blood. Why is it there? What happened to him? Third, while we can't be positive that the broken collar belonged to Buddy, we have to acknowledge the possibility that it did. If that is the case, why was it broken? And, what is blood doing on it? … This candy wrapper, if it belonged to the boys, might or might not be significant. But, it still represents evidence, and we might be able to learn from it."

"I still have questions about the Coast Guard," Henry said. "Surely they were conducting Search and Rescues on Lake Huron. How could they miss this large a group? Heard anything from Roger on that?"

"Only that they have not yet picked up our group," Jack replied. "We will hear back from Roger the minute he hears anything. But, it's not surprising that they haven't found the boys. Their efforts targeted boaters that were out on the affected waters—the Great Lakes and the rivers feeding them. Right there, that's one hell of a lot of real estate to cover. Plus, you have to assume that our guys would have immediately headed for higher ground as soon as they noticed the waters rising."

"That's why you think there might have been something else happening at the same time?" Henry asked.

"In part. I'm sure we will soon know the whole story. … Perhaps not so soon, but eventually we'll get to the bottom of it all."

While the two were talking, Jack set about dusting the wrappers for fingerprints.

"Looks like we've got something here," he said. "I'm doubting that this litter ever even hit the water. Prints look too crisp. ... But they are pretty small for an adult. We'll see."

He then took a piece of clear Plexiglas and flattened the prints out so that he could capture a good image of them.

"Will your app tell you if it belongs to one of your boys?" Henry asked. "Or will you have to do that visually?"

"I have the boys' prints stored on a separate database. But this app can access about twenty million troublemakers around the world—federal, state, and Interpol. ... These prints obviously belong to a kid, so we will run it through my database first. To see if they belong to Red or Robby."

After about five minutes of searching, Jack announced with a slight sense of approval, "Seems we've got a match here. Red touched this wrapper. ... And, it looks like there is another smaller print. Not Red's or Robby's. Could have been handled at the store. Or, Red could have given it to one of the other boys. ... Critical thing is, we know that Red's candy bar made an appearance at the Au Sable river-mouth recently. We'll log that info for now and see if it comes in handy down the road."

"That blood on Buddy's collar," Henry raised. "Can you tell if it was human or animal?"

"Not here," Jack replied. "I'd have to go to the lab for that. All I can do in the field is to determine whether or not it's blood. Luminol does not discriminate between animal and human. ... And even then, it's still not perfect. Luminol will also react to fecal matter, and urine. But, we can be pretty sure that in this case we're dealing with blood.

"We know that there is a very good chance that it is blood," Jack continued. "Also, we might conclude that there is a reasonable chance that the collar belongs to Buddy—not totally sure about that, either.

"Oh," Jack interrupted himself. "I found some hairs stuck behind that broken name tag. We can't field-test them either, so I didn't pull them out of the bag. But they appear to be from a Golden Retriever. Which further suggests the possibility that we're dealing with Buddy here. … But, I'll admit that there's no solid evidence regarding that.

"Now, the fact that the blood is on the *outside* of the collar, and right next to the sharp metal of the nametag, this suggests that the blood was deposited by a human being. And, more specifically, a human hand that was tightly gripping the collar. So tight, in fact, that the person was exerting enough stress on the collar that he broke the name-tag, and ended up cutting himself on it. … It's even possible that he eventually ended up breaking the collar itself. … Still, that part's all conjecture."

"Damn!" Henry grumbled. "This is getting to sound more and more serious all the time. … You gonna send this stuff to a crime lab for testing?"

"Eventually, maybe. For right now, we're getting enough information to be helpful. That hat, all by itself, is huge. We'll label and log it all. … But, we really don't have time to waste. Forensic testing takes time. That would be more useful in establishing admissibility in a court of law. For us, time's a luxury we just don't have."

"What do we do tomorrow?" Henry asked, his face beginning to exhibit considerable concern.

"They had to have had a fairly large boat," Jack said. "Would be *very* helpful to find it. … I'd like to have you go after that bit of information. I'd start where you found Red's hat—Little Charity

Island. That's about five miles east of Point Lookout. And, maybe two miles or so southwest of the main island—Charity Island."

"Start at Little Charity and search west to Point Lookout?" Henry asked.

"I think so," Jack said. "That boat is not likely to be easily visible, otherwise the Coast Guard would have found it by now. ... It'd sure as hell be nice if we knew what sort of boat Legend was using. Just so we could clue in the Coast Guard on what to look for. Do you recall seeing any boats at the cabin?"

"Nothing large enough. Do you think they rented something?"

"Might have," Jack said. "But it seems like the Coast Guard would have turned up something on it if he had. I had Roger run his name—Legend's, AKA Ted Klanoski—as well as the name of the owner of the cabin, and nothing came up."

"I wasn't aware that you knew the owner," Henry said.

"I don't know him personally. Just have a name. Justin McCarthy—recently deceased. Got the name from Legend when I talked to him in Grand Rapids earlier."

That was virtually the end of the conversation. They each had a bowl of hot soup and a sandwich and turned in. Jack set his alarm for 5:30 a.m., but after a restless night, he was up and cooking breakfast at 5:15. On this new day, wearing a red plaid wool shirt and a pair of Carhartt pants, Jack looked more like a logger than a private security contractor. Henry awoke to the aroma of eggs over easy, bacon, toast, coffee and a couple of flapjacks—generally called a lumberjack breakfast. Both men knew that this day needed to be a big one, and what better way to start a big day than with a "fill you up and give you energy" kind of breakfast.

"Let's run through this again," Jack said as he poured his sec-

8

ond cup of coffee. "I'll pick up where I left off. You can drop me off where you picked me up. And you will head out to Little Charity Island, and start your search there. Hit it heavy between Little Charity to Point Lookout. Search every inch of water. ... Red must have had something in mind when he stuck his cap up that tree.

"Did you tell me which side of Little Charity he hung his hat? Am I correct in thinking it was on the west side of the island?"

"It was. Just about as close to the shore as he could get it. That whole island is only a few hundred feet wide, especially now that the water is up like it is. And the tree he chose to hang the hat was right next to the water."

"Describe to me again about how he attached the cap to the limb," Jack said. "And, in which direction was it facing—you know what I mean. Where did he point the brim? And, is it possible that it could have turned on the limb?"

Henry scrutinized what Jack was asking him, and was careful to answer accurately.

"Interesting that you should ask me that," Henry said. "The cap was slid over the branch to a point just beneath where a smaller limb—more like a twig— had sprouted. He had cut them both off and pulled them both through the hole in the cap.

"But that's where it really got interesting. He pulled the cap down the limb until he was able to lock it over a third little limb. He had also cut that one off. And, he must have measured it so that it would hold the cap in place—that is, in place pointing west out over the lake. It was looking directly at Point Lookout."

"Okay," Jack said. "That could be telling us something. Red appears to have been signaling us that they were heading west toward the shore—toward safety. That's where you should look—

Point Lookout, and, perhaps, south of it a bit."

"Makes sense," Henry said. "But, there's something that I don't get at all."

"What's that?" Jack asked.

"How did that collar get way north of where I found the cap? I mean, if Red and the group were heading west, how did the collar get up where you found it? Doesn't make any sense to me, especially given the prevailing north to south winds. Do you have any theories about that?"

"Not really. I've been wondering about it too. ... When all is said and done, and we're all back on Sugar Island sitting around the fireplace, we'll get it all figured out. But, I'm afraid, until then we're going to just have to plug along until we find the boys—perhaps blindly, at times."

The drive to the drop-off point was uneventful. It was still dark. Not a word passed between the two men while they drove. Henry recalled exactly how to get to where he had picked Jack up, and Jack was deep in thought.

Beating him over the head this morning was the dread of possibly losing the two boys to Lake Huron. But he refused to share his fear with his friend, so he kept silent. Adding to his anxiety was the realization that it had been only a very short time ago that Millie, his very close friend, was murdered. Even though Jack was much older than she, Millie did represent the closest thing in his life to a bona fide lady-friend. While he never discussed the possibilities his subconscious sometimes conjured up, whenever his mind wandered to the roles Millie and her daughter Angel might someday play in his life, without fail one of his favorite scenarios had Millie and Angel moving into the Handler resort on Sugar

Island. *This could actually happen,* he would tell himself. *There is no other man in her life, nor is there another woman in mine—not since Beth was killed. And that was, well, about thirty-five years ago. Could it be?*

At that point he would begin adding up the years that he'd lived alone. Beth, his wife, and the mother of his daughter Kate, had been shot and killed early in their marriage. At the time Jack was a rookie Chicago homicide detective, and Kate was just under two years of age. Jack and Beth were on their way back to their apartment from a "date" when two men approached them. Jack had spotted them walking toward them, but he was too late drawing his weapon. Both Jack and the two men fired numerous rounds before Jack was able to drop them both. The two assailants were both mortally wounded, but Jack was hit as well. The last round fired by the attackers struck Jack, glancing off his head and knocking him unconscious.

But not only had the two men both been fatally wounded, so also had Beth. Two of their rounds struck and knocked her down on the sidewalk. Her crumpled body bled out as she lay next to his unconscious repose. She passed from this world not knowing that her beloved husband was not dead.

Every waking moment over the following thirty-five plus years, Jack was constantly reminded that the fatal rounds fired into the innocent love of his life were actually meant for him. And he never forgave himself.

In fact, it was not until he had met and grown close to Millie that he even entertained the possibility that there might come into his life a woman with whom he would even consider forming any type of close relationship. And now, she too was gone. Worst of all,

Millie had met her end following Jack's directive. *Had it not been for my sending her out East,* he told himself, *she would still be alive. What is it with me? Why do I always have a hand in killing the ones closest to me?*

Henry had no idea as to why Jack had chosen to settle back into himself. But, he knew that if Jack wished to talk to him, he would do it. So, Henry also remained silent until they reached the drop-off point.

As they abruptly stopped moving, Jack turned his head to the window and growled, "Damn it, Henry, I hate being in this position. I hate it with every ounce of passion my anger can muster. ... Why the hell can't life just be simple? Why? And there isn't anyone I can take it out on. Not and feel vindicated. It just must be one of those shit-ass situations that life requires us to deal with."

Henry knew better than to utter a word of consolation. He knew Jack was not ready for that. So, he simply said, "Same thing as yesterday? I find anything interesting I'll call you. You'll do the same. And when you're ready to have me pick you up you'll let me know. Does that plan still work?"

"Yeah," Jack said. "See you tonight."

Just before Jack shut the door, Henry asked, "Hey, I have a question."

Jack stopped and listened.

"This Point Lookout, is there a lighthouse on it?"

"No," Jack replied. "There's actually no lighthouse on the point itself."

"Really? Isn't that a little odd?"

"It is a bit unusual," Jack said. "But there's a good reason. Most of that whole area is littered with rocks—many of them just below the surface of the water. So, there is a lighthouse warning boats and ships to keep their distance, but it is located a few miles out in the lake. It used to be anchored out there like a buoy on a huge shoal. It's called Gravelly Lighthouse."

"A buoy?"

"Not anymore. I'm not exactly sure when they ran electricity to it. But, at least for a time it was lit up using acetylene—like a large lantern. ... The shipping lane runs between the Gravelly Lighthouse and Charity Island. But there're tons of hazards west of the lighthouse—a very large, dangerous shoal."

"Could that have posed a problem for our guys?"

"If they hit it in the right spot, they'd have been okay. But, some of the rocks are just below the surface. I would hate to take anything out there with any significant draft. But, we don't know what they were using—large, small, inflatable. We just don't know."

"Got it," Henry said. "Talk to you later."

Henry was pleased to be on his own this day. While he liked Jack, and had total confidence in his friend's judgment and ability, he could see that Jack was sensing some serious stress. "He needs to be on his own today," he said aloud to himself. "Hell, *I* need to be on my own today."

Henry whipped the Tahoe around and headed over to the dock where he had tied up the Zodiac the previous night. When he went aboard the first thing he did was to check the fuel level. "Great," he said upon seeing that the gauge indicated it had been filled by the manager of the dock as he requested.

"First things first," he said aloud as he made a beeline for Gull Island. The previous day he had asked around on Charity Island as to whether or not his group had spent the day there. Three people had recalled seeing the group and they all indicated that the leader, whom Henry correctly assumed would have been Legend, told them that their intentions were to fish off Gull Island, and maybe Little Charity. Two of those questioned had seen them head toward the little islet. Furthermore, no one that he had talked to remembered the group returning to Charity Island.

While Henry did not expect to find any of the boys on Gull Island, especially since the only evidence he found—namely, Red's cap—was intentionally mounted in the tree on Little Charity Island, still, he decided to take a couple hours and give the little island a thorough once over, which is something he had failed to do on his first visit.

At its widest, the island was only about three hundred feet wide—east to west. Lengthwise, it measured considerably more—probably about eight hundred feet. Running north to south almost through the center of the island was a band of rocks that protruded up out of the sand. Henry had barely noticed them the day before, as he was mostly interested in announcing his presence, and searching for members of the group who might be hunkered down somewhere out there. *That'd be worth checking out more closely*, he reasoned. *If one of the boys wanted to store some gear in a hurry, it would make sense to stick it in the rocks.*

He decided to start that phase of his search on the northernmost part of the island. So, he tied up the Zodiac onto a tree and jumped out of the boat and into the water. "Bet it wasn't this deep when the boys landed," he said to himself.

He had progressed about half the length of the island when he did discover something interesting. Lodged between two of the taller rocks he found a nylon bag. He did not recognize it as belonging to Red or Robby, but it did appear to have been the sort of bag that a teenage boy might have used. At first he could not dislodge it. Finally, after a number of firm tugs, he managed to partially free it. Once he held it in his hands, he opened it and looked inside.

He found in the bag a number of water-soaked items, including a peanut butter sandwich, two candy bars, a zipper bag with a few pretzels, and a pair of fishing gloves. Of all the contents, only the pretzels in the zipper bag appeared dry and intact.

"Whoa!" he exclaimed to himself but aloud. "I'd bet that the water wasn't up to the top of the rock when he first hid that bag."

He stood up straight and looked around. His mind was rushing through various scenarios that could have resulted in the bag having remained on the rock given the fact that there was an obvious onrush of water. *Why is this stupid thing still here?* he wondered. *And why is this all there is? Jack will have some good ideas when I bring this bag back for him to inspect.*

He then grabbed the handle and attempted to remove the bag from the rock, but his first effort failed. Upon further examination he saw that a strap on the bottom of the bag had become securely lodged between two of the larger rocks. "Aha!" he declared. "*That's* why it didn't get swept away. It's all hooked up on the rocks. … I wonder how much other stuff did float off. Maybe even some of those kids. … Damn! This does not give me a very good feeling."

By that time the water had subsided considerably—a foot or more of the tops of the larger rocks were now above the water. Henry was, however, still dealing with a difficult environment to work in. Overall, the lake was still up over two feet. Basically everything on the little islet was flooded over by at least a few inches.

While not making it totally impossible to get around, the excess water was enough to make it difficult to gauge where or if there was a crater deep enough to fall in, or a divot large enough to trip over. So, he proceeded with great caution.

He eventually was able to dislodge the strap that secured the bag. He determined that it was dry enough to transport. Rolling it up somewhat, he tucked it into the canvas bag he had brought with him for that purpose.

There are several possibilities here, he determined. *As the water level rose, the group might have jumped into their boat and escaped. That could have happened. And since the prevailing current in this area is from north to south, it should be a pretty safe assumption that they would have attempted to head back to the cabin soon as it became clear that something unusual was taking place.*

"Legend is a pretty level-headed man, at least when it comes to boating," Henry said to himself. "I have to think he would have quickly concluded the obvious, and high-tailed it to safety."

However, Henry was thinking, *that just did not happen. Had their boat been running properly, then it's a cinch that they would have attempted to return to the safety of the Au Sable River. It must be that they either lost the use of the boat—perhaps it was carried off by the rising waters—or that, for one reason or another, even though they had the use of their boat, for some reason the boat's motor failed.*

"That kind of shit happens all the time on the water," he declared aloud to himself. "Hell, it's happened to me. More than once."

Henry carefully walked the entire surrounding area searching for anything that might provide some clue as to what happened to the group, but was unable to turn up any additional evidence on Gull Island.

He decided to get back to his boat and head in the direction of the lighthouse off Point Lookout. That was, after all, what Jack had suggested.

The slush he had to deal with irritated him. At places the water ran over the top of his knee-high Xtratuf Elites.

Little early in the day for this, he silently thought, *but it's good to get this shitty stuff out of the way.*

Whether he consciously acknowledged it or not, doing this type of work was in his blood—almost as though it was part of his DNA. He was methodical in every aspect of this labor, and intensely tuned in as he turned over each potential clue with care and caution. In his mind, the only acceptable outcome must be success. His ancestors were hunters and fishermen, and he loved the outdoors, even when he had to get his feet wet.

He had moored on the southwest side of the island largely because there were fewer waves crashing in on the rocky shore. And, because he felt it offered a more hospitable place to tie up. As he was unhooking the mooring straps he discovered something he'd missed earlier. Tied directly beneath one of his straps was what remained of a torn strap from an earlier tie-down. It was a little difficult to see because it was connected to the tree at a level that was now below the surface of the water.

"What the hell!" he muttered. "I wonder if this is what happened to the boys."

The frayed end of the torn nylon rope looked to Henry as though it had been broken weeks or months before, and that a makeshift repair had been attempted by simply knotting the rope together above the break. "Damnit all!" he complained again. "That is one screwed-up way to repair a nylon rope. Never works worth a shit."

Any boat of any size would have had two mooring straps, Henry reasoned. *One broke with the rising water, and the second probably just came untied.*

"Bet anything that's what happened," he said aloud to himself.

A hundred thoughts went through Henry's mind at once: *If they didn't have their boat, how the hell did they get off the island? Legend was too smart to have them try to swim in that cold water. One might have spotted the boat and tried to get to it. ... That, too, would be a fatal mistake. The current would have carried it away as fast as a person could possibly swim. Legend wouldn't have allowed that. So, what did they do? ... Did they have two boats? Why didn't the Coast Guard find the boat adrift? Or find the boys? None of this shit makes any sense. ... I'd better get going. Looks like those boys might somehow be out there on the lake. God help them if they are.*

Henry sped up his effort. His first task was to beat it out to Gravelly Shoal Lighthouse. He plugged the name into his GPS but it did not come up. *Maybe I can just find it,* he reasoned. *Jack said it was a couple miles off Point Lookout.*

He knew that the waters were very treacherous for any boats venturing west of the lighthouse, so he determined to center his thoughts on the waters between Charity Island and Gravelly Lighthouse. As he was speeding west he finally was able to find the GPS coordinates for the lighthouse—44.018333,-83.537222.

Soon he spotted the light station. He knew that the name itself, Gravelly Shoal, portended a problem if the warning was not heeded—particularly the *shoal* part. With concentrated caution he slowed as he approached the tiny structure. Looking for any evidence the boys might have left to indicate that they had been there, he slowly circled it.

"Nothing," he growled. "Not one damn thing that I can see."

He called Jack.

"Hey, Jack," Henry said, very glad to have gotten through in this sketchy coverage area. "This is what I found."

He then proceeded to describe the broken rope, and the fishing bag.

"What do you think this is saying?" Jack asked. "What does your gut tell you?"

"It looks to me like the boys spent some significant time on Gull Island. That they tied up their boat on the opposite side from where they were fishing. And that the boat eventually broke loose and drifted off—probably helped along considerably by the rising levels caused by the rush of water. My hunch is that they might have had another boat—perhaps a smaller one without a motor—and that they escaped the flooding on it. There's a lot of assuming going on with that, but it seems feasible."

"So, where would that put them now?"

"I've checked Gravelly Lighthouse. Not much to it. No sign of the boys having been there. If they had—"

"If they had been there," Jack interrupted, "Red and Robby would have figured out a way to leave some sign that they'd been there."

"Exactly," Henry agreed. "And, that's where I'm at right now. It seems to me that had they been through here, not only would they have left some sign at the lighthouse, but they would have made it through to Point Lookout."

"In which case all would be well with them," Jack said. "And they'd be trying to get hold of us. Right?"

"I'm thinking," Henry came back, "that if they were in a row boat on the south side of the island, the current would have carried them toward the thumb—south and east. … Maybe that's where I should move to. What do you think?"

"Do it," Jack replied. "That's a very treacherous stretch of Lake Huron. Can be, anyway. A lot of rocks and little islands there as well—the closer you get to the shore. Especially with the extraordinarily high waters since the lock explosion. I've not found a thing yet today. I'll hurry along and try to make it to Point Lookout."

Henry was encouraged to hear Jack agree with him as to how to proceed. It took him less than twenty minutes to shoot back toward Gull Island and then to return to where he had found the broken mooring rope. He had decided that the way to get the best sense as to the group's direction and speed, would be to return to where the boys had launched, and then to see how the currents would tend to carry him if he were not under power.

If the boys had or found a backup boat, he reasoned, *then they most likely had oars as well. But, they would still want to find the easiest route off the flooding island.*

Just as he had suspected, the lake current began carrying his boat to the southeast. *I wonder if that's the same as the boys experienced,* he questioned himself. *Might have been somewhat influenced more to the south by the rushing waters from the north. Still, I'm going to go with it and see where it takes me. Should not be too far off.*

One of the things that occurred to him was where all the water might go once it hit the end of Saginaw Bay. *There's no way for it to escape down there. The rushing waters would likely raise hell with the Saginaw River, but then bounce back and raise the water level in the bay even higher than Lake Huron to the south. At least down there it would have the north-flowing St. Clair River as an escape hatch.*

Henry checked his compass several times, and then glanced back at Gull Island to confirm his calculations. "Pretty damn close to directly southeast," he said aloud. "Time for me to get a move on."

He then started the motor and shot to the southeast at a forty-knot clip.

He was thankful for the extra windbreaker he had worn, as it turned very chilly when the sun would hide behind the clouds.

His first stop was the narrow strip of land known as "Sand Point." Henry had never been to the peninsula before, but the co-ordinates indicated that was where he was.

No point landing, he determined. *This is altogether too built up. Had the boys touched ground here, they would have found a way to communicate their location.*

And that is what he did. He took a swift run to the northeast end of the real estate, whipped around and proceeded to get as close to shore as he could without running into the occasional large rock.

I don't see anything here, he concluded. *Let's see. Where to now? … What do we have here?* He took a look at his map and read off, "Wild Fowl Bay." Then, looking off to the west, he said, "I guess that would make that flooded out mess *North Island.*"

I'm gonna have to be very careful here, he was thinking. *No way to tell what might be hanging out right beneath the surface. I doubt*

if the boys are anywhere around here or they would have spotted
me. But I've still got to give it a try. Wish to hell I had some kinda
bullhorn.

"Red! Robby! You here?" Henry shouted at the top of his voice.
"Red! Robby!"

Slowly and carefully he made his way around North Island,
shouting loudly the whole time. Finally, satisfied that the boys
were not within earshot, he pulled off and carefully made his way
through and around a labyrinth of small islands that lay just offshore.

"They absolutely could not be here," he said to himself. "If they
were anywhere in this vicinity they would be able to make it to
civilization. This can't be it."

Again he pulled off his search, checked his map, and headed
for the tiny island known as Defoe Island.

"That Defoe Island is totally submerged," he complained to
himself. "Same is true of Long Tree Island. Supposed to be rocks
protruding on both, but I don't see anything. ... This is pretty
damn discouraging. Looks like I misread the situation."

"Jack," he said after ringing his buddy. "I've hit all the small
islands south and east of Gull and Little Charity Islands. Found
nothing. Any suggestions?"

"Shit," Jack moaned. "Nothing comes to mind. What do you
think?"

"Something's up," Henry said. "If they were safe and secure
they'd be calling you, or me. They'd not be leavin' us hanging like
this. ... I have to think that they're stranded somewhere, just not
in this area. And that they have no way to communicate to us.
I can't give up. ... I'm thinking that I should take a more thor-

ough look at the waters surrounding Little Charity. Maybe there's a rock, or something like that—something that they could have latched on to, and are just hanging on for their life."

"Do you have enough fuel?" Jack asked.

"I'm good. I have two extra portable five-gallon fuel tanks, I should definitely be good for the rest of the day."

"Then give it your best shot. If something else comes to mind, feel free to improvise."

Henry slowed to a stop and took out his map again. "I wonder," he said to himself out loud. "I really wonder where they could have gone. … What if I'm misreading this whole thing? What if? … What if they didn't lose the boat? Red left his cap pointing west. What if they managed to head that way, and something happened along the way? It would have happened, most likely, west of Little Charity, and south of the Gravelly Shoal Lighthouse. That's most likely where Red's cap was intended to direct us. If there would have been a change of plans, and if he were able to let us know about it, he would have. … What the hell. I'll give it a try."

Henry spent the next forty-five minutes zigzagging at half speed back and forth, west to east. Each time he would move his search about three hundred feet south. On his first trek he found that he had to take measures to avoid running over a low-floating log in the water. *Probably dislodged from the shore by the rising surge of water,* he reasoned. *I must be very careful. Hitting one of those would tear the bottom right out of my boat.*

His second trip, which was about the length of a football field south of his first, he encountered three similar floating boat-sinkers. "Damn, this shit makes for one *very* dangerous expedition," he spoke quietly to himself. "I wonder if the boys might have struck something like that, at any speed, it would have flipped them over, and probably destroyed the bottom of their boat. Could have even launched some of them into the air. Possibly injured some, or even all of them. ... Or worse. ... If anything like that happened, they would have likely tried to swim into shore. Better make my turns as close to the beach as possible."

Back and forth. Back and forth. Henry was into his seventh round.

"Nothing," he muttered. "Not one damn thing. Not one *damn* thing."

He reached into the breast pocket of his insulated vest and pulled out his cell.

"Jack. Anything new on your end?"

"Nothing," Jack said. "But I did just think of something that might help."

"Yeah? What?"

"That collar I found yesterday," Jack said. "It *couldn't* have been Buddy's."

"Really? You're pretty sure about that?"

"Positive. I played that back in my mind a dozen times. And I'm sure that the last collar that I bought for Buddy had an aluminum nametag. The one on the collar I found was made out of metal, but it was *not* aluminum."

"I never checked out Buddy's collar that closely," Henry said. "So I wouldn't know anything about that. ... I do think that is helpful info for me, given that I am hitting hard the area well south of where you found that collar."

"Where exactly are you concentrating on right now?"

"I'm crisscrossing the stretch of water south of that Point

Lookout lighthouse—Gravelly Lighthouse—virtually east/west. Right now my coordinates are 43.933821, -83.580287. I'm heading almost due west at about six, seven knots."

"And you've not run into anything interesting?"

"Right," Henry replied. "It does appear that the high surge broke a lot of that shit loose from the shore, and it's now just floating around trying to sink boats. ... A lot of significant hazards out here."

"You're thinking that Legend and the boys might have encountered something like that?"

"I'm thinking that it's a real possibility," Henry answered. "They have become a real hazard for me even going really slow. Worth checking out, I think, unless you want me someplace else. What are you thinking?"

"Use your judgment," Jack said. "It's always good. ... If it doesn't turn anything up, when you're satisfied that you've covered the relevant geography, hit me on my cell again. I'll be thinking about our next step."

"Right," Henry said. "I'll do that."

"And the fuel?"

"Still fine. Thanks for the reminder. I'll keep an eye on it."

Henry had called Jack because he felt haunted by the possibility that he was wasting valuable time and resources with what appeared to be a fruitless effort. He wanted to run his plan past Jack to be sure they were on the same page. It helped to have Jack confirm the relevance of his efforts.

I'll make ten more runs at this, he determined. *If I still haven't turned up anything, then I'll rethink its validity. And maybe move on.*

Henry remembered back when he was growing up, his father had taught him so very much about his culture and the heritage of his ancestors. He learned to hunt and fish, trap, and live off the land. When he was twelve, he was part of the Indian Child Welfare Act and was taken away from his family. He, in effect, became a foster child—in much the same fashion as had Jack's two boys. It was probably for that reason that he found it so easy to identify with Red and Robby.

He recalled having been treated well in foster care, but also had many memories of his constantly running away, and going back to his tribe and birth family.

This was one of the reasons the well-being of the group weighed so heavily on him. He was especially concerned about the status of Red and Robby. During the time that he had been associated with Jack, he had grown very close to the boys. They were growing up right before his eyes, and he was relishing his role in their lives. Henry never had siblings that he knew of. In fact, he grew up pretty much on his own. His relationship with women was spotty at best. He did have a daughter, Lily, but she was raised by her mother, for the most part. This meant that Henry never had any real experience with children. So, Jack's two fourteen-year-old foster boys, Red and Robby, were becoming his family as well. And now they were missing. Henry's stomach churned in anguish as he continued his search.

He was just completing his seventh westward run since talking to Jack. "Three more trips," he said aloud to himself in the grumpiest of tones. "Three more times and I'm going to call this shit done."

He pulled in very close to shore again, and looped around to head back east.

Impatience had gripped him two circuits earlier, and he increased his speed to nearly ten knots. *I need to get this over with and move on,* he reasoned. *I'm never going to find them out here. Time to come up with a better plan.*

Even though he wanted to get through the additional ten laps he'd promised Jack, he fought back the urge to increase his speed again. He timed his eastward runs. He gave it fifteen minutes, and held his course to east by southeast. He calculated that by so doing he would be covering close to two and a half miles to the east, and the same to the west on his returns. The angles he was cutting was beginning to amount to significantly more than one hundred yards to the south with each run.

"What should I try next?" he asked himself silently. "Where the hell could those boys be?"

Just as he reached the end of the fifteen-minute limit on his ninth lap he heard something that got his attention. Immediately he cut his motor off and listened intently. For over a minute he remained silently drifting. His boat did a three-hundred-degree turn in the slightly choppy water, and still nothing happened—he neither saw nor heard a thing.

"I wonder what the hell *that* was all about," he growled. "Must be I'm getting tired. I'm beginning to hear shit that just ain't there."

He leaned over to restart the motor.

"I've got to get this over," he said silently to himself. "I'll finish this run, and one more. And then move on. ... To where? I'll be damned if I know. ... Those stupid-assed kids! ... Jack's to blame! Jack should *never* have agreed to let them go fishing with that asshole lunatic Legend. What was Jack thinkin'? Wasn't necessary.

Jack's usually more careful than that. … I'm sure he feels like shit too. *Damn* it all!"

But just as he was about to crank the motor, he heard something again. He stood up straight and looked around carefully, but still didn't see anything.

"Sounded like it was coming from the south," he muttered, squinting his eyes as he surveyed the surface of the lake. "But I don't see a damn thing."

And then he heard it again. "What the hell's a dog doing out in the middle of Lake Huron!" Henry bayed in his most booming voice.

Chapter 22

"M r. Legend," Billy pleaded in a whiny voice, "I'm really sorry—"

"The name is Legend," Ted Klonski interrupted. "Or Ted. The only *Mister* in my world is my father, and he's no longer with us, God rest his soul. So, just call me Legend or Ted—not Mister. ... Now, what is it you wanted?"

"Legend," Billy said in his still most irritating tone, "I'm really sorry about hurting Red's head. Do you think he hates me now?"

Red and Robby were sitting toward the front of the wooden-hulled twenty-six-foot skiff that Legend had borrowed for his fishing trip with his group of scouts. Even though their backs were to Legend and Billy, both boys could hear Billy's irritating moaning over the boat's two hundred ten horsepower inboard diesel. Without turning his head, Robby glanced out of the corner of his eye to see Red's reaction. Red picked up on Robby's response but he did not overtly react. He merely raised his eyebrows and smiled.

Earlier that day Billy Christopher, who at twelve years of age was the youngest and by far the smallest of the boys in the group, had managed to rip a small gash in Red's scalp with a fishhook. Legend had been helping the more inexperienced of the boys learn to cast. Of all the boys on the trip, Billy best fell into that category. Twice earlier, Red had heard Billy's small mouth bass lure whiz past his ear. Both times he moved. The second time he removed his cap because he feared the newbie fisherman would hook his cap and cast it irretrievably into the lake. Jack had just brought the caps home for the boys from a recent DC trip, and Red did not want to gamble with losing his. Robby had spotted him when he bared his head and he teased him about it: "Hope Legend packed some first aid stuff—I think you might be needing it," he said to his friend.

Both boys chuckled about it.

But, just as Robby had predicted, less than five minutes after Red had tucked his prized red cap under his shirt, Billy's errant cast slid his minnow-shaped swim bait across the top of Red's head, with one of the hooks ripping his scalp open with a narrow slit. When it happened, Red bleated with a sound of terror that only his poorly developed voice box could possibly generate.

Robby turned to see what had happened. He found it amusing.

Billy and Legend did not think it was so funny. Legend took the fishing rod away from his shocked and now weeping student and laid it in the sand beside the boy—careful, of course, to place the reel safely into his tackle bag.

"You'd better sit tight for a bit and let me bandage up your victim," Legend said to the boy. "And stop crying. Everyone knows you didn't mean to do that. It was an accident. And accidents happen to all of us. … Actually, it was more *my* fault than yours. I should have seen this coming. Don't worry about it. I promise you that Red'll be fine. And he doesn't hold a grudge. Don't worry."

"Let me take a look at that nick," Legend said as he made his way over to where Red was fishing. Then, noticing that Red was not wearing his red cap, he said, "What happened to the cap? Did it end up in the lake?"

Grudgingly Red pulled it out from inside his shirt and showed it to him.

"Good," Legend said. "I'm glad you didn't lose that cap. I know how much it means to you. ... Here, let me take a look at the damage."

"Oh," Legend said, "that ain't nothin' to worry about. Just a little scratch. Hang in here for a minute and I'll grab something to put on it. It's not much. Barely even bleedin' anymore. I'll be right back."

As soon as Legend walked away, Red got up and went to where Billy was sitting. He placed his hand on Billy's shoulder. When Billy looked up at him through his red, teary eyes, Red offered his best smile and tapped the novice young fisherman on the head.

By that time Robby had joined them.

"What Red is getting at," Robby explained, "is that he knows this stuff happens. Don't worry about it. Red's gonna be fine. It's all part of fishin'. Accidents happen to everyone. Don't worry or feel bad. Okay? You're probably goin' to pull out the biggest fish in all of Lake Huron. Just don't give up."

Billy nodded his head slowly and wiped his runny nose with the sleeve of his shirt. "I'm really, really sorry," he said. "This is the first time I've ever been fishing. Are you really gonna be okay?"

Red nodded his head and smiled.

"It'll all be just fine," Robby said. "In fact, Red has done the same thing himself, when he was learning to fish. He got a hook caught in my shoulder once. And boy, did he feel bad about that. Just like you feel right now. So don't worry about it. We've all been there. And Red is tough. He'll be just fine. I promise you that it ain't nothin' to worry about. ... After Legend pours some stinging, painful alcohol on his head. He loves that part too."

Red tossed out his best smirk in Robby's direction. His reaction was prompted partly because he realized that Robby was telling Billy about an event that never occurred—Red had never caught Robby with a fishhook. And the last thing Red wanted was to have burning alcohol poured into his wound.

Red was relieved to see Legend walking up with a dark brown plastic bottle and some gauze. He knew that hydrogen peroxide would not sting.

"Dang," Robby said to Legend. "Don't you have any alcohol? Red prefers alcohol when he gets a cut."

Red balled up his right fist and stuck it in his friend's face.

"No," Legend said, trying to console Billy one more time. "Red's a big boy. He understands how things like that can happen, and I promise, he doesn't bear grudges."

"Right, Red?" Legend said, looking toward the front of the boat.

Red heard him. He turned and smiled. And then he signaled a thumbs-up.

Twenty seconds later the boat lurched up and to the port side. The boat had struck a water-soaked tree trunk. It was one of many that had been wrenched from the shore and washed out into the lake by the surging waters.

At the time of the accident, James Christopher was piloting the boat. James, at sixteen, was the oldest boy in the group, and was Billy's older brother. Legend had given him that job only a few minutes earlier on the basis of his age and experience. James's father was a professional seaman, having served for decades on

Great Lakes' ore carriers. While James could read the chart and knew how to avoid the dangers posed by large rocks, he was not adequately prepared to watch out for special threats, such as newly arrived floating trees. The problem with them was that, if they were old and sufficiently waterlogged, they had a tendency to hover right at water level. So, if the sea was calm, these naturally evolving torpedoes posed an immense hazard to a small moving boat—particularly one with an aging wood hull.

Even though the twenty-six-footer received substantial below-water damage, its momentum carried it entirely over the log and on to the other side. Unfortunately, even though the hole in the hull would have been small enough to have limited the intake of water long enough for them to have made it to shore, when the boat passed over the rotten wood, it had slowed to the point that its forward motion had virtually stopped just as the propeller passed over the log. Therefore, the propeller guard failed to prevent the damage it was designed to deal with, thus causing half of the propeller to break off.

"What the hell just happened!" Legend shouted as he scrambled to take control of the boat.

"I don't know!" James said, sounding panicked. "Felt like I hit something, but there wasn't anything there … not that I could see."

He immediately slid the throttle back because there was a loud vibrating noise coming from below.

"The prop's broken!" Legend shouted. "I think we're in big trouble. Shut the motor off and don't touch anything until I check it out."

He then ducked down below to check for damage.

Less than a minute later he came back up and announced,

"We're taking on water, and the prop is busted. We're gonna have to get off. … What have we got for a life raft here? Is it big enough for all of us? Maybe there's a couple. Shouldn't need more than that. Just see what we got and what it's rated for."

Robby and Red had already checked it out that morning, so Robby said, "We checked it out before we pulled out. It's good for twelve hundred pounds. And there's eight life jackets, too. So we should be fine. … How far from shore are we, anyway?"

"Not that far," Legend said. "Looks like it would be about a mile. No storms coming, so we should be fine. … Take your time. Do not panic. No need to rush. At the rate the water's coming in, we should be good for an hour, at least."

"Can we stick something in the hole from down below?" Robby asked.

"Can't get at it," Legend answered. "If we had power, we'd see what we could do. But, the way it is, plugging up the hole would serve only to delay the inevitable. … Just keep in mind that we have plenty of time. So do not panic."

"Are we gonna take our fishing gear with us?" Robby asked.

"No," Legend replied. "We'll take only the lifejackets. Once we get on land, we might be able to have somebody bring me back out, and I can gather up our gear. Or, maybe we will be able to tow the boat in to shore, too. All that's possible. But, for now, our only concern is to get all of us on dry land."

"Let's break out that boat and get it blown up."

James, Robby and Red set the inflatable in the water, tied it up to the side of the sinking twenty-six-footer, and triggered the inflators.

Legend passed around the lifejackets and showed each of the

boys how to strap them on. "Important to do this right," he said, as he cinched up the one he was using to demonstrate. "Once each of you get yours on, I'll check it to be sure you've got it right. Can't have any of you slip out and drown. … And, remember that the water is going to be *very* cold. None of you would survive very long in it. Especially without a proper lifejacket."

But before the boys had begun putting on their lifejackets, Red pointed to the north and made his patented guttural growl.

And almost immediately Robby said, "I hear a boat out there, and I think it's headed our way. Can you see it?"

Legend and all the boys turned toward the north, and finally Legend said, "You're right. It's a boat. And it is headed this way, I think. Not totally sure about that. But I think it is."

All eight of them stood transfixed as they stared out to the north.

"Yes!" Legend said excitedly after over a minute. "It looks to be a large boat, and it is coming in our direction."

"Do you think they see us?" Robby asked.

"Don't know that," Legend said. "But it's a *big* boat. It could be the Coast Guard."

They all watched intently, as the object on the horizon grew larger and louder.

"It's not the Coast Guard," Legend announced as it approached and began to slow down. "But, it is plenty large enough to squeeze all of us on it. Looks like we won't be needing that lifeboat after all."

A large sincere smile crept across and lodged on Legend's face.

"Hold on now," he said to the boys. "We can't just assume any-thing yet. They have to give us permission to board their boat. I'm sure they'll be good with it, but we have to get permission before we do anything."

The large boat slowed to a crawl until it had approached to within a few yards. It was not a Coast Guard boat. But, as Legend had suggested, it was big. It turned out to be an eighty-foot Viking Convertible. A man, who appeared to be the owner or the captain of the boat, walked out on the aft deck, which was just about at the same level as where Legend and the boys were standing.

"We're having some trouble here," Legend told him. "We hit a floater and seriously damaged our boat. It broke our prop and we're taking water. Do you think you could transport the boys and me to land? There are eight of us in total—seven Boy Scouts and me. And, of course, one Golden Retriever—Buddy is his name. Think you have room for all of us?"

"Sure," the man said. "What's your name and where are you from?"

"My name is Ted Klanoski, and we are from Grand Rapids. At least most of us are. Two of the boys are from the Upper Peninsula. Do you think you might be able to tow the boat to shore? Before it goes down. If not, could we bring some of our stuff on *your* boat? We do have some fishing gear on it we'd like to save, if you can help us."

"You say your name is Ted Klanoski, and you're from Grand Rapids?" the man asked. "And what are you doing over here?"

"Doing some fishing. We're staying at a cabin up the Au Sable River. We were fishing off one of the islands, Gull Island, and we got caught up in that surge of water. What's that all about? The surge of water. It seemed pretty weird to me."

The man did not answer Legend's question. Instead he asked

to be excused for a minute, and he disappeared into the cabin of the boat. There he made a call to New York to talk to his boss.

It was five minutes later before he returned. And when he did, he walked up to the boat's railing carrying his right hand behind him as though trying to hide something.

"Mr. Klanoski," he said to Legend. "Would you mind stepping a little closer? I would like to have my friend snap a picture of you. Would that be okay with you?"

Legend looked confused.

"I don't mind having you shoot a picture of me," he said, taking a step toward the other boat and turning his body slightly until he was facing the visitors. "There, is that what you're looking for? … I would like to get these boys off this boat while it is still afloat. Are you going to be able to help us, do you think?"

"We'll help you," he said. "But I just need to be sure about who I'm dealing with. There are a number of drug dealers running shit into Canada. Just need to be sure you're not one of those fellows."

The man then handed his cell phone to his friend and asked him to shoot a picture of Legend. Afterwards, he told his friend to do an identity check using facial recognition.

Only a minute or two later the friend said, "That's him. We've got a match."

"Good," the captain said as he placed his right hand behind himself again. But this time, when he brought his hand around it was squeezing a short-barreled blackened-steel nine millimeter semiautomatic pistol.

In the same motion as he used to retrieve the firearm from behind him, he pointed at Legend's chest and he fired. The bullet struck Legend on his left side just below the collarbone.

Even as the boat was first pulling up, both Red and Robby were beginning to suspect something was amiss. Unlike most fourteen-year-old boys, they had witnessed the darker side of humanity in action.

Legend was in shock. Because that first round was a little off, it not only did not kill Legend, it did not even knock him off his feet.

"Why the hell did you do that?" he asked as he instinctively tossed his hand over the entry wound in his upper chest. "What's goin' on here?"

The captain took aim and fired again. This time the round missed Legend altogether. So, he fired again, and again—a total of four shots.

By then Robby and Red were shouting for the boys to jump into the water.

Only the first round struck Legend, but it did rip a vicious hole through his shoulder, tearing apart a good-sized blood vein on its voyage. Legend turned and shouted for all the boys to jump overboard as well.

Buddy, who had begun barking even before the first shot had been fired, had now taken a position at the railing of the sinking boat. He looked as if he was trying to get at the shooter, but the distance between the boats was too great for him to jump.

The captain pointed the pistol and tried to shoot Buddy, but it appeared as though sufficient moisture had accumulated on the rounds in the magazine, or possibly on the slide itself, to render the firearm useless for further action.

By that time all the boys and Legend had dived into the water and were beginning to swim south, away from both boats. Buddy, heeding Red's command, then quickly followed them into the water.

Fortunately, most of the boys knew how to swim at least a little. Only Billy could not swim. However he, along with a few of the other boys, had already put on their lifejackets, and were thereby staying afloat.

"What shall we do?" the captain's friend asked. "Some of them are wearing lifejackets. They're going to get away."

"How *far* they're gonna get's the question," the captain replied. "That water is freezing. Their muscles are going to give in to the cold, and they're all going to drown. ... Hook on to their boat, and we'll tow it out of reach, and scuttle it. They'll all be dead within the hour. ... Let's just grab the boat and get the hell outta here. We've accomplished our mission."

The captain's friend did as ordered, and tied the damaged boat to the fifty-footer.

"How about that inflatable life raft?" he asked the captain. "What shall I do with it?"

The captain thought about it for a few seconds, and then said, "First, drain the air out of it. And then unhook it. Set it adrift. ... But, don't just pull the plug. Use your knife. Don't want those damn kids to be able to come back and blow it up with their mouths.'"

Chapter 23

The sound of a barking dog reinvigorated Henry. In fact, it was the first actual "sign of life" he had observed since his search had begun. Even though he was fully aware that the dog he heard barking might not have anything to do with Buddy, the barking was coming from a real dog, and Buddy was definitely one of the *people* he was trying to find.

He heard it again. It sounded to him as though it was coming from the east, and maybe a little south. He checked his compass, restarted the motor, and then turned his boat to that direction.

For the next minute he listened intently, but heard nothing over the sound of the boat's motor. So he turned the motor off again and just listened. But he heard nothing. He waited another couple of minutes, and still nothing. Finally, he cupped his hands to direct his voice, and he shouted as loudly as he could: "Buddy! Buddy! Good boy. Can you hear me?"

Nothing. He repeated his effort. But, again, there was no barking.

"I know damn well I heard a dog barking!" He protested. "I did *not* imagine it. I'm positive. I heard a dog."

Knowing that it is difficult to determine with any accuracy the direction a noise is coming from, especially when you are out on a large body of water with no distinct points of reference, he was hesitant to continue his search until he had heard the barking again. "What if I'm misreading this, and head off in the wrong direction?" he asked himself. "I could lose it for good."

So, again he cupped his hands around his mouth and shouted in the direction he presumed the original sound to be coming from. And then he waited again.

"Damn it all, Buddy," he said angrily to himself. "Just bark back, will you?"

He waited nearly a minute. Still no return. So he again checked his compass and again shouted as loudly as he could. But, he stopped after only one round. He thought he heard something. But it didn't sound like a dog. Instead, it was a strange, unintelligible noise.

"What the hell!" he grumbled to himself. "What the living hell was that?"

"Red!" he said through his cupped hands. "Is that you?"

And then Henry listened. He had been listening for the barking of a dog, but what he had just heard sounded nothing like that.

Could it be Red? he wondered. *Or my desperate imagination? What the hell would they be doing in the water anyway? They've got a boat. My mind could just be playing tricks on me.*

He waited. But there was no response. He continued to repeat his pleas to the broad horizon.

A breeze was picking up.

"I can't stay here all day playing stupid games with myself," he complained aloud.

Just then his phone rang.

"Jack. Can you hear me?"

But there was no answer.

He looked at his cell and saw that his battery was dead. "Too long with no towers," he said to himself. "It took all my battery."

As quickly as he could he rummaged through his vest's inner pocket until he found his battery cell charger and plugged it into his cell. He gave it a minute to charge up a little, and then looked to see if he was reaching a tower. It was bouncing from one bar to none.

"What the hell else can go wrong?" he asked himself in frustration.

He held his cell above his head and searched for a tower, but he could not consistently hit a single bar. Finally, he could not hit a tower at all. "This is not going to work," Henry mumbled to himself.

Henry wanted to talk to Jack to get his advice, but he soon became convinced that it was useless to keep trying to reach out to his friend. At last he gave up and stuffed his cell back into his pocket.

After another round of shouting, Henry gave his cell one more chance, but still he could hit no tower.

"Jack," Henry said into his cell. "I've got a question for you."

Henry had not actually reached anyone on his cell, and certainly not his friend. But out of his desperation he decided that he knew Jack well enough that he would have nothing to lose by feigning a two-way conversation.

"What're you finding?" Jack asked.

"I'm still out on the lake," Henry replied. "I thought I heard a dog barking, but it stopped. I've been shouting out, but I've not got anything back for a while. Can't be sure what I heard the first time, or if I imagined it. Just don't know."

"Can you tell the direction of the barking?" Jack asked.

"Can't be sure. Thought I could, but it stopped."

"Are you within sight of land?" Jack asked.

"No. I can't see land from here."

"Then something's out there, Henry. Go for it," Jack said.

"If I start up the motor I won't hear a thing, even if they're out there."

"Get the coordinates for where you're at right now. And determine as close as you can those for where you were when you last heard the barking, so you've got something to work from, and then develop a grid and work it. Time is running out, if those boys have been in the water for any length of time. … If what you heard is really Buddy, then our boys will be there too, so you've got to hit it hard. No time to waste."

"And if it wasn't Buddy? What if my mind is playing tricks on me?"

"Same thing," Jack snapped. "What's there to lose?"

Henry's make-believe conversation with his boss galvanized his resolve. Immediately he logged his location at the time. It was 43.85361,-83.673670.

He took a look at his compass and logged that the last time he heard anything he estimated he was five hundred feet west and ninety feet north.

"That damn wind's picking up," he growled out loud. "Must be between seven and ten knots, with gusts. … That won't be helping matters either."

And then something akin to panic hit him. *Now I'm setting up another grid,* he was thinking. *That's what I was doing before—running a damn grid. And where'd it get me? Nowhere! Those boys are still out there freezin' their asses off. … I'm gonna be out here until I run out of fuel, and then what do I do?*

Thankfully, Henry had his faux conversation to fall back on. "Jack gave me this job—gave me these orders—to establish a grid and search it. I'll faithfully execute the orders he gave me. And I'll do it to the absolute best of my ability."

That was the end of his second-guessing himself.

He started up the motor and pointed the boat almost directly east. He tried to keep the speed at about three knots per hour. He ran it for five minutes and then shut it off again. He listened to the lake. The wind was creating small waves, and they were tossing his boat around like a bobber in the rapids. It was difficult to keep his bearings, so he frequently referred to his compass.

After a minute or so, he pointed his face to the east, cupped his hands around his mouth, and shouted, "Red, Robby, Buddy. Can anybody hear me? Buddy."

He had shouted so many times over the past forty-five minutes that his throat was growing sore from it. Still, he repeated his efforts three more times. But no one responded.

What am I going to do if—when—I find them? They're gonna need a hospital. Will the kids even still be alive? If that was Red who yelled out, why didn't he keep doing it? So I could find them. What do I do then? I could sure use the Coast Guard to help in this. He checked his phone, still no cell towers.

He knew he was out of radio range, but he tried it anyway. Nothing.

Henry made three more five-minute runs to the east, and then he was faced with a decision: should he take his search to the north or the south? Since the wind was blowing out of the northwest, he determined that it would make sense to take his search south a hundred yards. So that's what he did.

At first he thought of moving it south by a few hundred yards, because it seemed likely that if he passed within that distance of the boys they would have heard him shouting. However, he questioned whether or not any of the group would still be able to respond even if they did hear him. *I have to be close enough to them so that I can actually see them—and that would be no more than a hundred yards—especially with the way the waves are building. ... If it ended up that I passed them by and didn't know it, I could never live with myself.*

He was only about fifteen minutes into his run when he spotted something bright colored floating in the water. When he first saw it, it was directly ahead of him, but by the time he reached the object, it had drifted slightly off to the port side of his boat. He slowed and turned over toward it. He knew immediately what it was, and what it might mean. It was an empty lifejacket.

He retrieved it and quickly tossed it on the bottom of his boat. He cut the motor off. And just like he had done dozens of times earlier, Henry cupped his cold trembling hands around his mouth and screamed, "Buddy. Hey, Buddy. Good boy. Can you hear me? Buddy. Red. Robby. Answer me."

He turned his body ninety degrees and repeated his plea. After he had finished the cycle, he began to repeat it. And then he heard something sounding like Red again.

"Red. Red. Do you hear me?"

Again he heard what sounded like the raspy, indecipherable articulations that Red was known to utter.

This time was different from before, because Henry was able to get a more definite fix on the direction from which it was coming. He quickly checked his compass and made a mental note of the direction the sounds came from. "South by southwest," he said loudly. He then restarted the boat and turned it toward what he felt should be the source of the sounds he had heard.

And then he spotted them by the bright orange of their life-jackets. He could not tell how many were there, but there appeared to be a bunch of them, all clustered together. Redheads, brown-haired teenagers, and blonds, but none of them were moving as he approached. He did not recognize either of the first two that he pulled into the boat. They appeared to be teenage boys, but neither of them were moving. They both appeared to be unconscious, or dead.

The third boy he did recognize. It was Robby. But he didn't move either.

"There should be a total of seven boys," he said silently to himself. "Should be three more boys and then Legend and Buddy. Don't see the other boys, or Buddy. And I don't see Legend."

Henry took his jacket off, opened it wide, and lay it over the four boys who were lying motionless on the bottom of his boat.

He then stood erect and shouted again: "Red. Red. Where *are* you?"

And he heard it again—the patented noises owned by Red. After Red voiced his response, Buddy whined. And Henry heard that as well.

"Oh my God!" Henry shouted. "Red and Buddy are still alive." No longer could he hold back his emotions. Tears began streaming down his face faster than he could wipe them off.

The waves had gotten larger. That was why he had been unable to spot the other group right away. He started the boat and turned it toward the sounds made by Buddy and Red. As he pulled closer he could see that there were several young bodies stretched out inside a partially inflated bright yellow and orange life raft, along with that of an adult. He then spotted Red's mop of curly red hair, but he was not in the raft. Red had tied himself to the raft, but he didn't get in it. Buddy was also in the water with Red. As far as Henry could tell, only Buddy and Red remained conscious.

Henry began grabbing the boys from the raft one at a time and laying their still bodies with the other boys. The third boy moved slightly as he dragged him into the boat. After he had pulled all the boys from the raft into his boat, Henry untied the rope that secured Red to the raft and pulled him in, giving him a big hug as he did it.

Red smiled.

Buddy had already begun trying to claw his way up and into the boat, so Henry took hold of his collar and right paw and pulled him in.

That left Legend. As soon as Henry grabbed the unconscious leader he noticed that there was a wound in his left shoulder.

"What the hell happened to you?" he asked, but received no answer.

Henry did a quick head count to be sure that he had all eight of them, plus Buddy. He then opened a waterproof bag that he had brought with him, and pulled out a dozen thermal blankets and two large weighted waterproof blankets. He retrieved his jacket and put it on, and then covered all nine of the victims with the space-age thermal blankets, followed by weighted blankets.

Still, none of the victims had spoken. But Henry did observe that at least some of the boys were still alive. Legend had not yet moved.

"What to do?" Henry silently asked himself. "Hospital ASAP!"

He took one quick look around to see if he might have missed anything. The only thing he might have some interest in saving was the raft Legend and three of the boys were on, so he grabbed it quickly and tossed it into the back of his boat. When he did, he heard something hard strike a thermos of hot coffee he had brought with him.

"What the hell was that?" he asked himself out loud.

And then, surprise, surprise. One of the second group of boys spoke up. He had heard Henry ask the question, and he had the answer. "It's a pocket knife," the boy said. "One of the bad guys dropped it in the raft when he was cutting a hole in it."

Henry had no idea which one of the boys had spoken up, only that it was not Red or Robby.

Chapter 24

H enry considered stopping off at Charity Island and seeking help, but thought better of it. Instead, he decided to head directly south toward Bay City. He was somewhat familiar with that city—at least, he knew Bay City had a good hospital, the McLaren Bay Region Hospital and that was what he needed right now. He checked his map and determined that it would take him over half an hour to reach the mouth of the Saginaw River, but he knew that was the right move.

One after another he heard the boys complain about how cold they were. But he still had not detected Robby's voice. Nor had he heard anything out of Legend.

"One nice thing about the cold lake water," Henry said to himself, "it can dramatically slow down the loss of blood."

While Henry had no idea as to the damage the bullet might have done to his friend, he was hoping for the best.

After about ten minutes, Buddy crawled out from beneath the blankets and walked over to the pilot's wheel. Henry looked down and saw Buddy shaking the water off and wagging his tail with great enthusiasm. Henry reached down and petted the happy dog on the head, and then he took Buddy's head between both of his hands and planted a big kiss on the dog's icy cold nose.

Buddy did not know how to handle that. The first thing he did was sneeze, and then he licked his nose. And then he sneezed again.

"Never been kissed like that before, have you, Buddy," Henry said with a chuckle.

And then it happened. A voice very familiar to Henry spoke up from the big pile of little people. "Oh, Henry," Robby moaned. "You *kissed* Buddy? That's disgusting. Ough. Really disgusting. But I would like to have a picture of that. Big, tough Henry Chuchip Kalyesveh, kissing a dog. ... Where'd you kiss him, anyway? On the mouth? I'm never gonna let you forget that."

And then Henry could detect Red laughing out loud. And that was all it took. Henry again burst into tears—more violent than before. And, this time they were not to be controlled—not even by big, tough Henry Chuchip Kalyesveh.

Henry was now within the range of a cell tower, and he wanted to call Jack to give him the good news. But, to do that would require him to get control of himself. So, he again wiped his tears away with his sleeve, blew his nose on a towel he always kept handy, and then called his boss.

Chapter 25

Henry's first attempt to reach Jack did not go through. *Must be he's busy on the beach, and out of range,* Henry concluded, *I'll leave a message.*

"Jack. I've got the whole group in my boat. Headed for Bay City hospital. Red and Robby are talking. Most of the rest are not, at least not at this point. They were all in the water. Legend too. And he has a gunshot wound. Know nothing about what happened yet. I'll check back with you after all are admitted. … Oh, yes, Buddy is *talking* too."

Henry's next call went to the Bay County Sheriff's Department: "Hello. My name is Chuchip Kalyesveh—

"Could you spell that please?" the dispatcher interrupted.

"That's C-H-U-C-H-I-P. Last name is Kalyesveh. That's K-A-L-Y-E-S-V-E-H. I'm coming into your city by boat. Not sure where I should dock up. I've got eight injured—possibly some very seriously. Seven Boy Scouts. All of them are suffering from severe exposure. They were in the water—Saginaw Bay—for several hours. Some are unresponsive. And, I have one, an adult, suffering from a gunshot wound. He, too, is totally unresponsive."

"How did that all happen?"

"Don't know much. All I know for sure is that I need several ambulances down at wherever you tell me to dock. I might have some dead kids here, so can we get on this quickly?"

"What is your location right now?"

"Just entering the mouth of the Saginaw River. Coming in off the Bay. Can you please get those ambulances down to the water now? ... And tell me where I should dock. Give me an address or a location, and I'll plug it into my direction finder. Look, lady, these kids are in bad shape. I need ambulances! ASAP!"

"I'm sending a patrol car down there right now. He will have his strobes on. He will be on the west side of the channel. Pull up there. I will also dispatch as many emergency vehicles as possible."

"I need four."

"I'll have four. Stay on the line, Mister Kalasaba."

"Yes, ma'am."

A few minutes passed, and then the dispatcher came back on the phone. "The chief wants you to pull into the Coast Guard Station. It's about one mile in from the Bay, and it's on the *east* side of the channel. I've got two units there right now. Watch for the strobes. And, the ambulances are on the way as well. Some might already be there."

"Yes, ma'am."

Just then Henry saw that he had a call coming in from Jack, so he took the call.

"Henry," Jack said. "You found them?"

"Got them all," Henry replied. "But I'm not sure about their conditions. They were in the water for who knows how long. All I can say is that both of our boys are cracking jokes, and Buddy seems okay too. But, as for some of the other boys—I don't know anything. Some are moving around a little. One of them has me worried. The little fellow. I think they called him Billy. But only one of the other boys, aside from Robby, has so far spoken. ... Legend, as I said in the message, might be in very serious condition. In fact, he might not have made it. Somehow he took a round to his left shoulder. He has at least one gunshot wound. Don't know anything beyond that. He hasn't moved since I pulled him out."

"You don't know how that happened?" Jack asked.

"I made a beeline from where I found them to here. I'm just pulling up to the Coast Guard Station here in Bay City. They're supposed to have ambulances waiting. ... How far out are you?"

"It could take me over an hour to get there," Jack said. "Maybe much longer. Got to get a ride to where you parked the Tahoe. Not sure how Uber works down here. ... If you get a chance, find out from Robby who it was that shot Legend. Okay? The sheriff might not let you talk to them separately—not until his people have debriefed them. But, if the situations allows, find out what you can about that before the law gets involved. And maybe how they ended up in the water. My hunch is that the two matters are related."

"You mean," Henry asked, "Whoever shot Legend might be the one who put them all in the water? That seems likely, alright."

"As long as my boys are conscious, we'll be able to get some helpful information out of them. Just see what you can find out. ... And, keep in mind, you will be a suspect before this whole thing gets sorted out. So, watch what you say to the cops. My guess is that they will have the FBI involved as soon as possible. I will get hold of my attorney on the way over, and have him meet us at the hospital. ... And, when you get a chance, begin logging, via voice mail, or however you think, log everything you can remember.

Make sure it's accurate. Hang on to it until you've talked to the lawyer. I've seen cases like this go south in a hurry. So, be careful."

Henry felt his cell vibrate.

"Got another call coming in," he said to Jack. "It's the Sheriff Department. Better take that call."

"Hello, this is Henry … Chuchip Kalyesveh. Sorry about getting disconnected. I had to talk to the foster father of two of the boys."

"I asked you to stay on this line. Please do that. Okay? Stay on this call until you talk to one of my officers. Are you at the Coast Guard Station yet?"

"I am just pulling in right now. … I see the strobes. … And there are ambulances there already. I thank you very much for that."

"Stay on this phone until I say otherwise. Do you understand?"

"Yes, ma'am. Not a problem. I'll stay on with you as long as you wish."

"Uncle Henry," Robby said, sticking his head out from beneath the blankets. "Where are we? And have you talked to Uncle Jack yet?"

"We are in Bay City. Just pulling into a dock at the Coast Guard Station. We've got help waiting for us."

"Legend got shot in the shoulder. Did you know that?"

"Yes, I saw the wound when I pulled him into the boat. How long ago did that happen? And do you think he bled a lot? What do you remember about that?"

"Almost a day ago. Or longer. We spent the night in the water. Is everyone okay?"

"Don't know yet. How about you? Are you okay?"

"I still can't feel my fingers or toes. But I'm starting to feel better. I think I blacked out for some of that time. I have never been that cold in all my life. I think Red's okay, too. But, I don't know about some of the others. And Buddy, he doing okay? If it weren't for him, we'd all be dead. He saved our lives. ... But, I still can't believe you kissed him. He can't believe it either. Where'd you kiss him, anyway?"

From Deadwood to Deep State is the longest to date of
all the books in the Jack Handler Saga. The story is set in several locations,
including Sugar Island and Newberry in Michigan's Upper Peninsula,
as well as at several other sites such as Washington D.C. and Singapore. Both
Secret Service Special Agent Roger Minsk and Former President Bob Fulbright
play powerful parts in the story.

Chapter 26

R oger," Jack said to his friend. "Henry just called me. He's found the boys."

Jack was still an hour out of Bay City's McLaren Bay Hospital, but he wanted to let Roger know that Henry had located and rescued all the parties involved with the boys' fishing trip on Lake Huron. "But all is not entirely well," Jack told him, "Legend, the man we'd talked about over a few beers in New York—he was shot and seriously wounded while fishing."

"Shot!" Roger bellowed. "That's bullshit! You're putting me on. Right? I thought you told me that this was your kids' *fishing* trip? What the hell were they trying to do? Follow in their old man's footsteps? ... But, your boys are both okay. Right?"

"I don't have definitive information on that yet," Jack replied.

"You're quite sure that Legend took a slug?"

"Right," Jack said. "Henry took a look at the wound when he pulled him out of the water."

"Jack," Roger said. "I think you can understand that you're going to have to be on your own with this. At least for the short term. I've already got a lot of *explaining* to do with regard to the mess we just stirred up in New York. As you know, that Emma babe was *very* closely associated with Allison. Well, she's, Allison, that is, she's called me in twice to see what I might have heard about that *Strip Club Incident*. That's how she refers to it. Of course, I'm pleading total ignorance on the entire matter. But, I'm not sure she's buying my story. I don't know what she's up to right now, but she is on the move. … And she has made it a point to be sure that my guys are not around to protect her. So, keep your eyes open over there in Michigan."

It was Roger's job to head up the Secret Service detail responsible for protecting Allison Fulbright. And now Roger was concerned that, for some reason known only to her, she had separated herself from the Secret Service.

"That's strange alright," Jack said. "I'll relay that message to Henry when I see him. We'll want to be watching each other's backs. … Well, Roger, if the situation changes at my end I'll let you know. And if you hear anything new about Allison's mischiefs, I'm sure you'll be in contact with me."

"Absolutely," Roger said. "And if I can help you from here, don't hesitate to rattle my cage."

"Will do, my friend. Talk to you later. … Whoa, Roger. I just had an idea. … Are you still there?"

"Yeah, Jack. What can I do for you?"

"I need you to do a favor for me."

* * *

"Tell me again," Sheriff Glock said to Henry, "What exactly were you doing when you ran across this group of young fishermen?"

Before entering the hospital's coffee shop—which is where the sheriff had chosen to conduct his interviews—he had asked Henry to place all the contents of his pockets into a plastic zipper bag. The sheriff then passed the bag over to one of his deputies, and told him to label it, log the contents, and then to "be sure to check everything for gunshot residue before you're done."

Henry had already twice exhaustively explained to the sheriff what his role had been in the effort to locate the boys and their leader. He was sure that he had told the same story both times, but he suspected that the sheriff was just trying to trip him up. And he understood why. Legend, AKA Theodore Klanoski, had suffered a very serious, life-threatening gunshot wound to his shoulder—one from which the doctors were saying that he might not survive. So, at the very least, the sheriff was looking to charge someone with assault with the intent to kill. Since Henry was apparently the only adult around, and since he might have had the opportunity, he was Sheriff Glock's first choice as a suspect.

Besides that, he had just received Henry's rap sheet, and was disconcerted when he read that Chuchip Kalyesveh, AKA *Henry* Kalyesveh, had already done hard time for second-degree manslaughter. The sheriff had not yet slapped handcuffs on him, but Henry could sense that moment coming. Nevertheless, Henry dutifully repeated his story to the sheriff for a third time.

"Mr. Kalyesveh," the sheriff said, "what type of handgun do you own?'

"None, sir. That would be a violation. You see, sir, I am on probation for a crime of violence, and I will probably never be permitted to carry a weapon of any sort. So, no, I do not own a handgun. Or *any* gun, of any type, for that matter."

Henry sought to make strong eye contact with the sheriff, but his effort was rejected.

"How do you know this man? The man with the bullet hole in his shoulder? This Ted Klanoski? How, and how well, do you know him?"

"I met him only once before. When I dropped my friend's two boys off so they could go camping and fishing with Legend's scouting group. Just talked to him once, and that was only for a short time."

"Had you intended to shoot him at *that* time, or did you *always* plan to do it later, like when you met him in the middle of Lake Huron?"

"I didn't shoot him *ever*. And I certainly never considered it. He is a good friend of *my* good friend, Jack Handler. I was just trying to do everyone a favor by dropping off his two boys at Legend's, Ted's, fishing cabin. And then that explosion happened up north—in Sault Ste. Marie. Jack tried to call the boys on their cells, but could not get through to them. So, he and I hurried over there to personally search for the group. ... You know, you could ask Jack's two boys about that, Robby and Red, or any of the other boys, for that matter. One or more of them can probably describe the shooter. I'd have to think that some of them would have seen the whole thing go down."

"I will do that when I'm ready to," the sheriff said. "Right now I'm talking to you, and I expect you to answer all my questions, and to do it thoroughly and honestly. Or you can accompany me down to my office. Do you understand what I am saying?"

"Absolutely, sheriff," Henry answered. "No problem."

Henry needed a break. "Sheriff," he said, turning his eyes over to the coffee machine, "Would you excuse me for a minute? I'd like to get a cup of coffee."

"That's fine," Sheriff Glock said. "Do what you need to do and then come right back."

Henry stood up and walked over to the coffee dispenser and poured himself a cup of their very black, pretty bad—but highly caffeinated—coffee. Henry and the sheriff were the only two sitting in the small hospital coffee shop at that time. Henry did not mention it, but he suspected that the sheriff had commandeered the facility for his use, as there were no other people in it.

Henry really needed that hot cup of nervous energy. He was still chilled, physically tired, and totally stressed out from all the pressure. Soft, comfortable chairs in blues and greens ringed the perimeter, yet the sheriff chose for them the hard plastic chairs that surrounded the Formica tables in sets of four. Henry stood still and silent as he downed the first half of his cup. His eyes stared at the bubbling salt-water fish tank that was mounted on the wall—fixated but not focused. He needed to warm up, contact Jack, check on Legend and the boys, and to solve the shooting. His mind was racing and his body was exhausted. But, the fact that the sheriff needed his question answered brought him back to his present reality.

"Now, tell me again, what was Mr. Klanoski doing when he was shot? What do you know about that?"

"I don't know anything about it," Henry replied. "I didn't see it go down. Red, Robby, and at least some of the rest of the boys, they were there—not me. I don't think they know *why* he was shot. But you could ask them."

"I'm not talking to them right now," the sheriff growled, "I'm asking *you*. What was Mr. Klanoski doing when he was shot? What have you heard?"

"Don't have any idea. I wasn't there."

"Then who shot him, if *you* didn't?"

"Don't have any idea about that, either."

Sheriff Glock said nothing for nearly a minute. He just stood motionless in front of the seated Henry. He was staring at Henry's nose but saying nothing. He then looked down at his cell phone, and then back at Henry.

Finally, he spoke. "I have you living on Sugar Island. That's in Michigan's Upper Peninsula. Right?"

"Yes."

"Why do you live there? In the Upper Peninsula. Do you have family up there?"

"I work up there. On Sugar Island. I help my friend, Jack Handler. I help manage his resort."

"Really? That's all very interesting. But my information is that you were recently traveling in New York. Does your boss own another resort out East? What were you doing there—in New York?"

For a moment, Henry was at a loss for the right words to say. *If I say the wrong thing here, I could create all sorts of problems for Jack,* he was thinking. *Or, I could create big problems for myself. Shit! This is not very much fun. What the hell should I say?*

While Henry was weighing his next words, Sheriff Glock's phone vibrated. He looked at it and said, "This is Sheriff Glock. Who the hell are you?"

"My name is Special Agent Roger Minsk. I'm in charge of the New York office of the Secret Service. I understand that one of my good friends, Mr. Chuchip Kalyesveh, AKA Henry, has just saved the lives of a group of boys—young fishermen. That group is headed up by another friend, Mr. Theodore Klanoski—AKA Legend. Do you know where he is right now? Mr. Kalyesveh? I need to talk to him if I could. Can you locate him for me?"

"Well, yes, I'm talking to him right now. Here, I'll loan him my phone."

"Roger," Henry said. "We found the boys. All seven of them.

Not sure about their condition. But we got them all."

"*We* found the boys," Roger said. "Who's the *we*? Who was helping you?"

"Jack's helping. He was searching the shore, I was assigned to search the big lake."

"Then, *you* found the boys. Jack told me that you found them. I wanted to thank you for all your good efforts on their behalf. Congratulations."

Roger was talking loud, hoping that the sheriff could hear him.

"Well," Henry said. "I found them out in the lake. No land around. They had a life raft, but the fellows who shot Legend, I assume it was them, apparently they tried and failed to totally destroy it. Looked to me like they cut and drained out the air on the main flotation pouch, but missed the floor. The raft had an inflatable floor. Wasn't enough to support the group, but the kids put Legend on it. He was the guy who took the bullet. And then I'm guessing they alternated—the boys alternated—crawling up on the raft when they had to. Anyway, at least Jack's boys made it through. Pretty sure they're okay. I don't know about Legend, or the rest of the boys. We'll just have to hope for the best."

"Is the sheriff giving you a hard time?"

"I don't know about that."

"Give his phone back. Let me talk to him. Tell him Special Agent Minsk wants to talk to him."

"Yes, sir," Henry said as he proffered the sheriff's phone back to him.

"I think Special Agent Minsk wants to talk to you."

Almost immediately after receiving his phone, the sheriff turned and walked away.

Five minutes later Sheriff Glock walked back into the room.

"Here you go," he said to Henry as he handed him the plastic zipper bag containing his cell phone, wallet, loose change and keys. "We've got the info we were after. You can have your personal items back. Would you like to visit the boys in their rooms? The leader, the adult male, he's still being attended to. Surgeon wants to work on his shoulder. But he said they'd have to get his body temperature up before they can tend to the wound. They've got him hooked up to an IV. … The doctor said his body temperature was down below seventy degrees. That's pretty cold—almost fatal. Still might be fatal. The doc couldn't say. If he makes it, you will have saved his life."

"How about the boys? They're going to be okay? Right?" Henry asked.

"None of them were as bad off as the adult, but I don't have a lot of information. One of your boys is talking—Robby. He seems to be doing well. You can see him, if you wish. Nurses tell me that he's asking for you. I'd like to go with you to talk to him, because he is a minor. I need to ask him some questions. With your help, I could do that."

"Jack will be here at any time. I'd like you to wait until he gets here to talk to his boys. He's their legal guardian—I'm just a family friend. He should be here when you talk to them. But, if it's okay, I would still like to see them."

"No problem," the sheriff replied as he turned to walk away. "Go for it. Go talk to your little friends. Knock yourself out."

The sheriff was not happy about his Henry interview. As he hurriedly walked through the small doorway he almost knocked over a cart of meds being pushed by a tiny blonde RN. She had seen him coming and managed to stop and back up in time to prevent the collision. She groaned and rolled her eyes as the sheriff crowded past her, all the while calling out for his deputy.

Henry, who had witnessed the near miss, said to himself, "Too bad that the sheriff got so bent out of shape like that, but I know better than to stick my neck into a noose. He'll get over it when Jack gets here."

The room, with curtains pulled together tightly, was dark and quiet. Two stationary mounds under the white blankets on two hospital beds revealed the still sleeping bodies of the Handler boys. Even though he did not make a noise, both boys began stirring when Henry entered their room.

"Uncle Henry," Robby said from his pillow.

"Hey, Rob. You starting to get warmed up yet?"

"No. I've never been so cold. … You seen Buddy?"

"Buddy?" Henry said. "No. That's a good question. Maybe the sheriff's got him. I'll find out in a minute. How are you guys doing?"

"We're both doing okay. Just real cold. The nurses come in every few minutes and switch our blankets with hot ones. I'm starting to feel my fingers and toes."

"How about you, Red?" Henry asked, turning to the other bed. "You good?"

Red stuck his hand out from beneath the blankets and gave Henry a smile and a shaky thumbs-up. And then quickly pulled his hand back under the warm covers.

"Good," Henry said. "Very good. I'll be right back. I'm going to check with the sheriff about Buddy."

Henry headed directly for the nurses' station, figuring that they would most likely be able to direct him. But he was pleased to find Sheriff Glock standing at the station and talking with the nurses. He turned to Henry as he walked up.

"The boys doin' okay?" he asked.

"Seem to be," he replied. "But they wanted to know about Buddy, their Golden Retriever. He was with us when I pulled up to the dock. I didn't see what happened to him. Do you know?"

"Yeah," the sheriff said. "You don't remember? The dog jumped off your boat as you pulled in. Hopped right up on that dock. He hit the ground running and then took off like a bat outta hell. Just like that Meatloaf song. He ran like a crazy animal right past my deputies. Never saw anything like it. Deputy Edwards figured he was just really cold, and he wanted to run to get his blood pumpin'. Maybe warm him up. I watched him myself. He ran to the end of the dock, and then just kept on going. I watched him. He was still going full speed until he hit Weadock Street. I couldn't see him after that."

"Where was I when all this was happening?" Henry asked.

"You were taking care of the boys. Trying to talk to them. Keepin' them wrapped up in those shiny blankets."

"So, I've lost Buddy?" Henry asked. "I've got to find him. Could you have one of your men drop me off back at the dock? I've got to see what's up with the dog. He means everything to those boys."

"You can go back there, but you can't touch that boat, or anything on it. I've still got a unit or two there. That's evidence in a crime. That whole dock is tied off. Will be for a few days."

"That's fine," Henry said. "I don't need anything on the boat. I just need to find Buddy. ... I'll tell the boys where I'm going, and then come back here?"

"Just go straight out to the patrol cars. I'll send a deputy out there. He can drop you off. But remember—do not even try to approach the boat. It will not work out well for you if you make *any* attempt to do that. Understood?"

"No problem."

Henry did as he said, then ran back to the boys' room and let them know he was going out to locate Buddy.

"Then, Buddy's really gone!?" Robby said as he sat up in bed. "Where is he?"

"The sheriff said he went tearing off when we pulled into the Coast Guard dock," Henry said. "From that point he lost him. So I don't know. I'll let you know as soon as I find him."

Both boys threw off their blankets and jumped out of bed. They were sockless and wearing white cotton hospital gowns with a faint blue pattern running throughout.

"We're goin' with you," Robby said.

"No!" Henry barked. "You've got no clothes. And we don't know how it's going to turn out for Legend. He'll be fine, I think, but the sheriff wants to talk to him about the man that shot him. And he's not going to let you go anywhere until he talks to you. Did you guys see the shooter?"

"Yeah," Robby said. "We sure did."

"What'd he look like? Can you describe him?"

"He looked pretty average," Robby said. "Probably about fifty years old—maybe a little younger than that."

Robby looked over at Red to see if he agreed, and Red nodded his head in enthusiastic assent.

"Not as big as you. Was wearing white pants and a bright red jacket. I think he had a white shirt under the jacket. I think it was a pullover jacket. And he wore a white captain's hat."

Red then offered his distinct signal for attention. "Uhhh." And he pointed to the back of his own right hand. And then he looked over at Robby to have him explain what he was wishing to express.

Robby knew immediately the thought he was transmitting.

"Oh! Right!" Robby said. "He had a tattoo of a spider in his web on the back of his right hand. We saw that very clear. That's the hand he used to hold the gun."

"Really," Henry said. "What do you suppose he went—170, 180?"

"I don't know," Robby said. "It all seemed to happen fast. What do you think, Red? Maybe 180?"

Red nodded in agreement.

"Oh yeah," Henry said as he turned to leave. "He had a boat, Can you describe it?"

"It was a pretty big boat," Robby said. "White—but I guess they're all white. It looked to be *very* long."

Red made a small noise and held up seven fingers.

Robby saw him and said, "You think it was seventy?"

Red nodded and pointed up.

"Seventy feet. Maybe longer." Robby said. "Right, it probably was closer to eighty feet. We were looking at the back of it. But it was pretty big. Eighty feet sounds about right. But I really couldn't tell."

"That's huge for the Great Lakes," Henry said. "Be tough to find any marina big enough to accommodate a boat that size. They'd have to have a railed gangway for something that big. ... Whatever became of the boat you guys were using?" Henry asked.

"They tied a line on it and towed it away. Don't know where, or what happened to it after that. At least *I* don't know where they were heading. Do you, Red?"

Red shook his head.

"The gun the shooter was using jammed up on him. Red thought that the ammunition might have gotten wet. We couldn't tell. He managed to get four rounds off, and then it just misfired. It looked like a smaller semi-automatic."

"What color was it?"

"Black. Red thought that it should have been stainless steel, if it's gonna be carried on a boat. I don't know. Maybe Legend just got lucky that it jammed."

"Good info," Henry said. "I'm going to take off now and see if I can find Buddy. ... Hey, the boat you guys were on ... the one Legend was using ... what can you tell me about it? It was still afloat when they towed it off. Right? Tell me what it looked like."

"It was taking water," Robby said. "But it was not sinking—at least, not right away. The prop was broken, and the hull was damaged. We hit a sunken log, or tree. Don't remember the name of it, but it was an old wooden-hulled boat. Not big like the other boat. I think it was about twenty-five foot long."

"What color?" Henry asked. "White?"

"White, mostly. Had some varnished wood on it. But, it was mostly white, and quite old."

"Okay, thanks," Henry said. "Remember, your Uncle Jack should get here at any time. I'll catch you guys later. Remember, don't talk to *anyone* until you first talk to your Uncle Jack about it—not even to the sheriff."

Henry then hurried out to the waiting patrol car. But, instead of having the deputy drop him off at the boat dock, he asked to be driven to the nearest car rental shop. There he picked up a silver Jeep Cherokee.

Henry's first stop was out on the Coast Guard dock, where the deputies were guarding his leased Zodiac.

He pulled up to the police line, rolled down his window, and called out, "Buddy. Hey, Buddy. You here?"

Nothing.

He made virtually the same call again. And then waited.

Again, nothing.

"Can I be of help to you?" a deputy said, stepping out of his car which was parked inside the tape.

"No. I'm fine. I'm just looking for our dog. A Golden Retriever. He answers to the name of Buddy. That's my boat over there behind the line. I thought he might have run back to it. But, that apparently is not the case. Have you seen a dog matching that description hanging around here?"

Henry observed that the water was lapping over the dock at the Coast Guard Station. *That would make it very difficult to easily tie up a large boat here*, he reasoned. *Probably just about like this at all the docks and marinas.*

"I remember you," the deputy said. "You're the guy who brought the boys in from the lake. I was here when the ambulances took them in to the hospital. I saw you. ... And, I saw the dog, too. But not since he ran off. I seen him jump onto the dock and take off. That's the last I seen him."

By that time the deputy had walked over to Henry's Jeep. Henry wrote his phone number down on a piece of paper and handed it to him.

"If you see Buddy around here, or anywhere, would you please give me a call?" Henry asked. "The boys really want to get their dog back."

"Sure. Be happy to. I'll keep my eyes peeled for their dog. ... How they doin', anyway?"

"Okay, as far as I know," Henry said. "Thanks for your help. See ya later."

"See ya," the deputy responded.

"Where could he be?" Henry asked himself as he turned the Jeep around. "I wonder ... I wonder if he might have gone off looking for the boat the shooter was in. Sounds like somethin' he'd do. Or, maybe the boat that was sinking. Hell, I might as well look around for them too. They just might be here in Bay City."

* * *

"Uncle Jack!" Robby shouted as Jack walked into their hospital room. Red had heard Jack talking down the hall and was already sitting up in bed. Sheriff Glock was practically stepping on the backs of Jack's heels.

"Guys," Jack said as he walked in the door. "My God, you two look mighty good to me. And, for what all you've been through. You look better than I expected—given all this shit you've had to put up with. ... You feeling okay?"

Robby looked over at a smiling Red and said, "Yeah, you could say that we're feeling pretty good. Now that we've warmed up a bit. It was really cold out there. And wet. Never been so miserable. Do you know how Legend's doin'? And the rest of the boys? We haven't seen any of them since we got here."

"How about it, sheriff?" Jack asked. "Any word on the rest of the crew?"

"The adult," the sheriff replied, "Theodore, I guess you call him

Legend. Well, the adult just got out of surgery. He's doing better. Received three units of blood since he came in. But the doctor told me that they got him all sewed up, and cleaned up. And that he should soon be waking up. This is, you know, an ongoing investigation of an attempted homicide. So that's all I can tell you. When he's able, I'm gonna need to talk to him first."

"How about the rest of the boys? I think there's five of them," Jack asked. "They doing okay as well?"

"We do have five more boys," Sheriff Glock said, "in addition to these two. Now, I'm not supposed to be telling you this, but the doctor tells me that four of them are suffering from exposure, but those four are going to be fine. Not sure about one of them, though. The youngest one. A kid named Billy. The doc says that he still has not responded, but that he did say he was *hopeful* about him as well."

"Sheriff," the nurse in charge said, sticking her head in at the door. "You asked me to look you up when Mr. Klanoski was able to talk. He's still a little out of it, but he is quite lucid. The doctor says that you may go in and talk to him now if you wish."

"Thanks," Sheriff Glock said. "Jack, you're welcome to see Mr. Klanoski when you're finished here. But right now, I need to talk to him first."

"Good. I'll come over after I'm done with my boys."

Jack then walked fully into the room and stood between the two of them.

"I understand Legend took a bullet to the chest. Did you guys see that?"

"Yes," Robby said. "Actually more to his shoulder, than to the chest."

"How many times was he hit?"

"Just that once. The shooter tried to shoot him three more times, but he missed. And then his gun misfired."

"Really? What was he using?"

"Smaller semiautomatic. Red thinks his ammo might have gotten wet, or something."

"He didn't hurt any of you kids?"

"Nope," Robby said. "He had his guy cut our life raft. And then he towed the boat away. The fishing boat. The one that was taking on water. It sure felt like he was trying to kill us and make it look like an accident. Like shooting Legend didn't look like an accident. The rest of us, we should probably all be dead. They tried to ruin the raft. His guy pulled a knife out and cut a hole in our life raft. Drained the air out. But he missed cutting the bottom of it. That was full of air too. That mistake saved our lives. We took turns. We boys took turns on it. Legend was out of it, so he stayed on what was left of the raft. We were all getting pretty cold, but he was *totally* unconscious. The whole time. Glad Henry got there when he did. Don't know how much longer we could have held out."

"Can you identify the shooter?"

"We gave all that information to Henry. I think he's out looking for him right now. *And* Buddy. He's looking for Buddy, too. The guy was pretty average looking. About your height, but a little skinnier. And he had this tattoo on his shooting hand. A spider on a web, on the back of it—between his thumb and his index finger. No beard. Regular dark hair. Pretty average looking—maybe fortyish, or a little older. Wearing white pants, red jacket, and a white yacht-captain's hat."

"Was his shooting hand his right or left?"

"Right hand."

"His boat?" Jack asked, "What can you tell me about that?"

"We talked about that with Henry. We decided that it was probably an eighty-footer, or thereabouts. Not like anything we'd typically see fishing on the St. Mary's by our house. It was huge by that standard."

"Good sized boat," Jack said.

"Yup. It was white. And it was set up for fishing. We think it was a Viking—a Sport Fisher, or a Convertible."

"And *your* boat?"

"Twenty-six foot, white, mostly, with a wooden hull. Was taking water. We hit a log—broke the prop. They—the guys that shot Legend—they hooked onto it and towed it away."

"Okay, fellows," Jack said. "I'm going to go see Legend now. And then I'm going to see if I can find Henry."

Just before Jack said his goodbyes, Red sent him a signal that he was not yet done "talking."

Immediately Robby knew what Red was thinking, and he said, "Uncle Jack. Can we talk to the sheriff or should we keep our lips buttoned?"

Jack thought about it, and said, "You can tell him what you told me, but nothing else. Do not ramble on. Okay?"

Jack gave each of the boys a kiss on the head, and a hug.

"You guys try to stay out of trouble for a while. I'm going to go see how Legend's doing."

Neither of the boys said another word as Jack left their room.

Ginger, one of the very sweet nurses, came in with a freshly heated blanket for each of the boys. "Lunch is on the way," she announced to near applause.

As Jack walked out in the hall he could hear Legend's grating voice from two rooms away, and so he followed the sounds. When Legend's eyes discovered him, he got even louder.

"Why the hell did that guy shoot me?" Legend fired off at Jack. "I never, ever saw that guy before. And all he wanted to do was to kill me. And he should have. He's just a bad shot. Missed three times. The sheriff tells me that the boys are all okay. Is that right? Or is he just trying to ease my mind? Are they okay? All of them? Please, tell me the truth."

It was becoming obvious to Jack that Legend's anesthetic was wearing off.

"Legend, I just talked to Red and Robby, my boys, and they are fine. And, the sheriff tells me that he thinks all but one of the other boys are doing okay. And now I see that you are awake and alert. So that all sounds like good news to me."

"Which of the boys isn't faring so well?" Legend asked.

"He said that the little one, Billy, wasn't responding as well as the others, but that the doctor was still hopeful."

"Billy, huh," Legend moaned. "I could have guessed that. He's the baby. The youngest. He just turned twelve. That poor little blue-eyed towhead. Damn! He's gonna be okay. Right? Billy's gonna get better, isn't he? … Damn!"

"I would think so," Jack said, trying to encourage his friend. "Like the sheriff is saying, the doctor thinks everything's going to be fine with the boy."

Legend accepted Jack's positive words, and turned his attention back to himself.

"Why did that guy try to kill me?" he asked. "I never saw him before in my life. Never!"

"Not sure about that yet," Jack said. "But we're looking into it. The only really important thing is that, as far as I know, my boys and you, and all the others are doing well. So, don't worry. Relax and get better."

"I'm not worried about myself. I'm just mad."

"Yeah, I get it," Jack said, trying to console his friend. "But it's not going to do any good to be mad or worried."

"How about Lindsay?" Legend said. "She's got to be worried sick. Could you call her and tell her we're all okay? Don't mention Billy. Not yet."

"I've already been texting her," Jack said. "And that's basically what I said. She's on her way from Grand Rapids as we speak."

"What was that water surge all about? I have some theories about that, too. … About what caused it. Did someone take out the Soo Locks? Must have. That's the only thing that could have made that kind of a crazy rise in the water level. That fast. There was no rain. And no earthquake. So, someone must have blown up the Soo Locks. Right?"

"Can't fool you, can I?" Jack replied with a big smile. "There was an explosion up there—a really big explosion. It totally took out the two largest locks. That sent a twenty-two-foot surge of water down into the lower Great Lakes. Most of it headed into Lake Huron, I'd guess. … But what gets me is why that fellow shot you and tried to kill the boys. Any ideas about that?"

"Actually," Legend said, "I can see why they tried to kill me, at least I have some ideas. I've been writing letters for the past several months. One big law firm really was taking my theory seriously. A firm called Crighton, Crighton and Holmes. Big-shot firm. I think that *the powers that be* got scared about all the shit that was coming their way, and blew the damn locks up—destroying the evidence. And, they wanted to shut *me* up, and so they shot me."

Jack feigned a smile. He was growing a little tired of Legend's motor mouth. For a moment he was thinking that just maybe the shooter might have missed a great opportunity, but then he put that thought out of his mind.

* * *

Henry covered the east side of the channel quite thoroughly, but did not find anything out of the ordinary. So he proceeded down to the Harry S. Truman Parkway and crossed over the Saginaw River.

He pulled up a Google Map on his cell phone and surveyed the area.

He determined that the people he was looking for were most likely somewhere in the general area, probably still on their big boat. *Shouldn't be too hard to spot that monster,* he reasoned, *a boat that size. At eighty feet, there won't be many like that around except for freighters and bulk carriers. … And Buddy might be looking for it too.*

He intended to access every street and private drive from the Saginaw Valley Naval Ship Museum to the bay. But, he didn't get far. He had driven down Tieman Road only a short distance when he came upon an access road that appeared to lead toward the river. So he headed down it. In less than a quarter mile he noticed off to the left there was a little private drive with a gate that looked to have been recently compromised. So, he drove in to investigate.

He quickly found himself at a docking area large enough to accommodate the off-loading of huge one-thousand-foot Great Lakes aggregate carriers. *This place ought to suit their needs just fine,* he reasoned. *If it can handle a thousand-footer, it could easily handle their eighty-foot Viking.*

And, sure enough, there in the docking area, he spotted a large fishing boat. It immediately got his attention because the mooring lines appeared awkwardly tied off because the securing posts were so far apart. "This is clearly not set up to accommodate fishing boats," he said to himself. "Not even big ones like this."

He drove up to within ninety feet of the boat and prepared to get out of the Jeep.

"Damn," he said to himself. "Some sort of weapon would sure as hell come in handy right about now." Of course, as an ex-convict, he knew that he could not carry any weapon in the State of Michigan.

He sat there long enough to come up with a basic plan. "The best approach just might be to play dumb," he said to himself. "These guys shouldn't have any idea who I am or what I'm after. … So, here goes."

As soon as his feet hit the gravel he started yelling, "Hey, anybody around?"

He knew people were on the boat because he could see some movement on the deck and in the illuminated cabin.

"Hey. Can somebody please help me? I'm lost."

Still, no one responded.

He walked up a little closer, and stopped.

"Hey. Excuse me. I need some help out here. Please. Can somebody help me?"

The boat he was shouting to was on the north side of the docking area, as was he. On the south side of the one-hundred-foot wide anchorage was a flatbed trailer hooked up to a Peterbilt 579.

Loaded on the trailer was what looked like a good-sized wood-en-hulled boat. He could not tell much about the sort of vessel it might have been because it was almost totally wrapped up under a blue nylon tarp. But, he thought that it looked to be about the right size and type to be the boat Legend and the boys had used.

He considered stepping back into his Jeep and pulling up closer to the boat dock, but thought better of it. Instead, since he had not gotten a response, he walked closer.

"Hey. Anybody here?" he shouted as he walked.

Finally, Captain Greg and his assistant stepped out of the cabin and promptly hit Henry with a blinding LED floodlight. "Who the hell are you?" Captain Greg shouted. "And why are you making such a big fuss out here? Just turn your ass around and get the hell outta here? This is *private* property—and you're trespassing."

What Henry did not yet know was that only a few minutes earlier, the crew of the boat had *entertained* another visitor—a very persistent Golden Retriever.

* * *

In Allison's mind, life seemed good, and celebrating was most certainly called for.

But then this strange, unhappy dog showed up—a Golden Retriever. He parked himself beside their boat and he just would not stop barking. Allison heard the incessant woofing and howling, and so she took a peek out of the cabin window. While she did not actually recognize Buddy, she did remember that Jack Handler's boys had a Golden Retriever. Feeling a surge of anger and frustration, Allison impatiently slid the curtains closed and returned to her glass of 2006 Moet Chandon Dom Pérignon.

While he was dealing with the barking dog, out of the corner of his eye Captain Greg had noticed Allison observing what was going on through the window, and that exacerbated his frustration. He grew more and more annoyed by the situation. While, unlike Allison, he *did* recognize Buddy, he could not even hazard a wild guess as to how the boys' dog managed to survive the ordeal, and then be able to find him. That dilemma compounded his annoyance.

Finally, he realized that no matter how hard he might try to talk Buddy down, the dog would have none of it. And so, he panicked and pumped two rounds into the poor barking animal.

Initially, Allison had remained at the window to observe the activity outside through a small slit in the curtain. But just before the shots were fired she had walked over to the bar to top off her glass and was trying to explain to Maximilian what was going on outside with the barking dog. And then the blasts from the pistol rang out.

Maximilian, who had been intrigued by Captain Greg's impressive collection of vintage portolan charts from every corner of the world, now had his attention drawn to all the distracting activity taking place just off their rear deck. The thirty-five-year-old well-dressed heir to the Hungarian billionaire Alexander Sipos' fortune exuded confidence and determination, as had his father before him. And, just as his father had done, Maximilian conducted all of his international affairs as the *de facto* leader of the American Deep State establishment.

The piercing shock wave generated by the 10mm rounds nearly caused Allison to drop her glass. She jumped up and ran to the window in order to see what could possibly have precipitated the firing of a weapon. When she saw the Golden Retriever lying on his side and quivering, she realized what Captain Greg had done. Angrily, she bolted out of the cabin door to confront him.

"Greg," she yelled loudly, while stabbing her index finger into the air barely an inch from the captain's nose. "What the hell was *that* all about? *Why* in hell did you shoot that poor dog? That's insane!"

Captain Greg did not have an answer for her. He knew that shooting the dog was wrong, and that the noise of his gunshots could easily attract unwanted attention. He knew he had made a huge mistake, but he also realized that there was really nothing he could do about it at that point. So he simply did not respond to her diatribe.

This whole week was supposed to have been one of celebration. That's how she'd planned it. And that's how it was promised to her. What would she be celebrating? For one thing, if all worked as planned, Jack Handler, her nemesis for decades, would be terminated by Emma. And Allison had a lot of confidence in Emma's abilities because for years she had served as Allison's preferred "gun for hire."

Allison's second reason for celebration was also to be delivered by Emma's professional hand. Along with killing Jack, Emma was similarly contracted to terminate the two men who earlier had killed Jack's friend Millie. Allison was so upset at the sloppy manner in which that hit had gone down that she had begun to refer to those two men as the "loose-end killers." She felt strongly that they needed to go. And, in Allison's opinion, no one was more capable of handling that sort of job than Emma.

After the triple hit, Deep State rogue FBI embeds were then supposed to whisk Emma away from the scene and out of the country.

That was the plan. And, to all appearances, that's exactly how the whole matter went down. As far as Allison knew, fatal rounds had been fired into each of the loose-end killers of Millie, and two more into Jack Handler. And then, only a day ago, Allison had received a phone call from Emma.

"All three targets had been successfully terminated," Emma told her. "And I am just about to set down in Budapest."

* * *

Allison continued scolding Captain Greg for his carelessness in the shooting of the dog. Her yelling did not let up until he spotted a pair of headlights pulling into the Aggregates Loading Dock. She had caught his change of focus, and along with him, glued her eyes on the approaching vehicle.

At that very moment, Maximilian exited through the cabin door and was walking over to where Allison and Captain Greg had been sparring.

Noticing that they were staring at the vehicle headed their way, he said, "What's going on out here? And who's that driving up?"

But, before Captain Greg could begin to explain, Allison firmly grabbed Maximilian by the arm and said, "Let's get inside. We can't afford to be seen here."

Captain Greg and his aide slid into the cabin right behind them.

Initially, the captain was content with observing the vehicle's approach through the curtained window. But, when Henry did not turn around and leave, Captain Greg and his assistant stepped back out onto the deck and directed a large spotlight on Henry as he approached.

Allison closed the door on the cabin behind the captain, and killed the main cabin lights. Maximilian took a seat at the galley table and poured himself another glass of Dom Pérignon. As Henry continued walking toward the boat, Allison could not believe her eyes. So, she pulled the curtain wide open to get a better look.

"Well I be damned!" she growled in Maximilian's direction. She then pulled the curtain closed and turned away. "I *know* that bastard. That's Handler's friend—Henry, Henry … something. What the hell is *he* doing here?!"

"Are you sure?" Maximilian asked. While he had never met Jack, he'd heard Allison talk about him.

* * *

So, that's where Henry found himself. Standing much too close to the boat, unarmed, and about to be faced off against a man who had a very bad attitude.

Captain Greg did not allow any time for Henry to respond before he let loose with another threat. "I'll tell you one last time, my friend. Turn your ass around and get moving."

"I'm sorry," Henry said. "I was just looking for the Coast Guard Station. I guess this wouldn't be it, would it?"

"The Coast Guard is north of here," Captain Greg said. "Almost to the bay, and on the *opposite* side of the river. You're nowhere near it. Now, turn your ass around and get movin'!"

When the man yelling at him pointed toward the Coast Guard Station, Henry spotted something terribly alarming in the illumination of the bright LED floodlight. On the captain's right hand was a dark-ink tattoo of a spider stretched out on his web.

Henry immediately knew what that meant: "This is the man

who shot Legend."

"Damn it all," Henry said in his most apologetic tone, realizing that he had to get out of there as soon as possible. "I am *really* sorry. I hate it when people do this to me. So sorry. So very sorry. My mistake. I'll just get the hell off your property and be on my way. I sincerely apologize for any inconvenience."

Henry was just about half way to his truck when, in the beam of the bright LED floodlight, he spotted Buddy lying off to the side of the path. It was obvious from the blood on the gravel where Buddy was lying that he'd been injured. The sight so shocked Henry that he could not help himself. "Buddy!" Henry yelled as he rushed to his beloved friend's side and knelt down to check his condition. "My God. Buddy. You've been shot!"

That's all it took. Henry was so disconcerted that he did not observe what was happening on the boat behind him. He did not notice that the man with the tattoo was drawing down on him with a Glock 29 10mm Semi-automatic. Using a laser site, Captain Greg let loose three rapid rounds. The first struck Henry in the back just below his collarbone. The second shot grazed his skull. The third missed him altogether.

Even though the third round had missed, the first two had done enough damage to put Henry down and out of commission. He was seriously injured by the first shot, which was through and through, and he was knocked totally unconscious by the second. Blood was profusely pouring out of his back.

The two men on the boat talked briefly, and then using a cell, Captain Greg called the driver of the truck across the water. "What are you waiting for?" he barked. "You need to get the hell outta here right now!"

Immediately the huge Peterbilt 579 diesel cranked over and ground into gear. As soon as they witnessed the truck pulling out, Captain Greg's assistant untied the mooring lines, while the captain darted back into the cabin and immediately started the motor on their 80.6 foot Viking Convertible. Within seconds they had pulled away and were heading down the channel.

All the commotion of the shooting had awakened the seriously wounded Buddy from his injury-induced stupor. Immediately recognizing the man lying beside him, he instinctively began whining and licking his friend's badly bleeding shoulder wound.

As Henry lay there helplessly unconscious on the cold, dark gravel, his phone began to ring.

Had he been conscious, Henry would not only have been able to alert Jack to his condition, but he would also have recognized the familiar female voice which was cursing out the shooter from inside the boat. ... And, he would have been able to have Jack intercept the big boat as it made its way down the Saginaw River toward a Lake Huron rendezvous with an unmarked floatplane.

* * *

"Let's run through what just happened," Allison commanded Captain Greg in her patented ego-crushing tone. "I want you to explain this to me. Do you have *any* idea who that was that you just shot? ... I want to know just what the hell's going on here. ... I knew that man! The asshole you just shot was Jack Handler's right hand man. ... You idiot! Handler doesn't take a piss without him. What the hell was *he* doing here? ... Step on the gas and get this piece of shit the hell out of here! ... If that guy is poking around here now, others can't be far behind!"

"But the bodies," Captain Greg protested. "The man and the

dog. We can't just leave them lying there. We've got to get rid of them."

"You pathetic imbecile!" Allison snapped. "What the hell are you gonna do with them? You gonna pull them onto your boat? … You stupid fool. You'll do no such thing as long as I'm here. The *only* thing we can do right now is to get the hell out of here as fast as we can."

"Right," Captain Greg compliantly responded.

He reluctantly held the throttle back so as not to exceed the "No Wake Zone" speed. But, as soon as he had cleared the mouth of the Saginaw River, he turned the wheel to head out on a due-north course, and then nailed it to just under forty knots,

Fifteen minutes later a single engine Cessna 208 Caravan Floatplane buzzed the Viking—no lights and no markings were visible on it. On Allison's orders, the captain cut the power to a dead stop. The plane pierced the dark cerulean sky again, circled, and then set down beside the boat.

"I need you or your boy to run us out to the plane," Allison said tersely.

Captain Greg was still shaking from his last war of words with her. "Run them over there," he told his aide as he pointed toward the plane.

Not one word was spoken as Allison and Maximilian departed Captain Greg's boat and boarded the floatplane. After they were safely onboard, the aide shoved off and powered back over to the Viking.

"What did she say to you?" the captain asked as he helped his aide board his boat.

"Not one damn word," was the answer. "Neither one of them

opened their mouths."

The plane quickly took off and disappeared into the south-eastern sky. Captain Greg, happy to have her gone, hit the throttle again and continued north.

But, he had made it only about one mile when an incredible explosion ripped the Viking to pieces. Both men were instantly killed, and what was left of the eighty-foot Viking Convertible was set afire in Lake Huron.

* * *

"Henry," Jack said, leaving a message on his friend's phone. "I've got your location—or at least the location of your phone. I'll be there in fifteen minutes. If you hear this message before I get there, call me back."

Jack followed the GPS coordinates to Henry's phone. He was a little concerned to drive up on a vehicle parked out in the middle of the expansive vacuum of the aggregate loading area.

"Engine off, but lights on," he said to himself as he pulled up beside Henry's rental Jeep. Leaving his lights on, he jumped out to inspect.

"Henry," he said, peering into the open door. "Where the hell are you?"

He did not recognize the vehicle, but he knew for sure that it had been driven by Henry when he spotted Henry's leather work gloves on the front passenger seat.

"Henry!" Jack shouted again—this time louder.

Still no answer from his friend.

However, while he didn't hear anything that sounded remotely like Henry, he did hear something that did sound familiar. It reminded him of one of Buddy's barks, but very weak.

Jack bolted on foot in the direction of the sound.

"Oh my God!" he yelled as he came upon the severely wounded Buddy lying next to Henry. Jack could tell immediately that Henry was also in very bad shape—probably kept alive only because Buddy had been licking his bleeding back. Jack understood that K-9s instinctively know that by licking an open wound they can sterilize it and mitigate the flow of blood.

Jack dropped to his knees beside Buddy. "Hang in there, brave warrior," Jack said as he embraced Buddy's head.

He then turned his attention to Henry. He leaned over his friend's motionless body and felt his neck to check for a pulse. Jack then sprang to his feet, grabbed his phone, and dialed 911.

"Central Dispatch, what is the nature of your emergency?" said the female dispatcher.

"My name is Jack Handler. I need an ambulance down here by the river. West side. At the Aggregates Loading Docks. Look for two vehicles, both with lights on. I actually need *two* ambulances. I have *two* injured friends here. Both shot. One severely injured in both legs. He's stunned and down, but not dead.

"The second looks like he was shot twice—one round struck him in the upper back. A through and through. And a second round creased his skull. He's not responding. But both are still alive. The one with the hole in his back has a pulse, but it is weak. Please hurry!"

Jack considered requesting the sheriff, but thought better. *I need ambulances right away. I'm sure she'll notify the sheriff. He'd want to be on scene if shootings are involved.*

Ninety minutes later Jack walked into Red's and Robby's room at McLaren Bay Region Hospital. He was carrying Buddy like a baby, with splints on both front legs. They extended from just below his chest to his paws.

When Jack plopped Buddy—tail wagging and head on a swivel—down on Red's bed, the mop-haired fourteen-year-old let out a bleat such as had not been heard in Michigan since the Wolverines won the Rose Bowl in 1997. Robby hopped over from his bed and jumped up to join the reunion.

"Buddy! Where have you been?" Red asked with his eyes.

"Uncle Jack, "Robby said. "What happened to Buddy?"

"That, my boys, is a long story. And we'll just have to wait until Henry is in a mood to tell us. Right now he's getting patched up."

"What?" Robby asked. "What happened to Henry? Is he okay?"

"He's fine. Or, he's going to be fine."

"But, do we know what happened to Buddy?" Robby implored again. "Why's he got these big bandages on his legs?"

Both boys were staring at Jack.

"I honestly don't know what happened," Jack said. "And Buddy isn't talking. But, I think it's safe to say that both Henry and Buddy are going to be fine. That I can confidently say. ... But, both of them were shot. Why, or by who, I don't know. When Henry comes around, we'll be able to find out more about it then."

Jack looked around the room until he spotted an empty soup bowl on the stand beside Robby's bed. He quickly retrieved it and went into the bathroom. A few seconds later he emerged after having filled the bowl with water. He set it down on Red's bed for Buddy.

The smiles and laughter lasted until a nurse walked in.

"Hold everything," she said. "You can't have animals in the hospital! It is in total violation of our policy! You'll have to remove

3

4

that dog immediately. … I mean it. The sheriff is still in the hospital. I can go get him if you don't believe me."

Jack had already filled the bowl with water a second time, and he set it in front of the very thirsty Golden Retriever.

"No problem, ma'am," he said, apologizing. "The boys and I were just leaving. Grab your stuff, boys. I brought you some dry clothes in that bag in the closet. Just get changed. Toss your wet stuff in the bag, and we'll be on our way. I got a room for the night, and the sheriff's permission to take you two with me."

"Nurse Karen," Jack said, reading her name-tag. "I want to thank you for all your wonderful help tonight. You and your co-workers have been a huge blessing to our whole group."

Nurse Karen was taken aback by Jack's praise. She smiled and nodded, but did not say a word.

"Now, I know you can't take these from me," Jack said as he pulled two one-hundred-dollar bills from his wallet. "But, I'm going to drop them off with your boss. Then, when we all get out of your hair, you guys can order pizza, or something."

Nurse Karen smiled and gave him a hug. "Thank you, Mr. Handler. The whole staff here all just loves your boys."

"And so do I," he said as he started to pick Buddy up.

"… And, I am *so* sorry, Mr. Handler, about that one boy—the tiny one. There just wasn't any—"

"Yes," Jack said, cutting her off mid-sentence. Then turning his back on Buddy and his boys he gave Nurse Karen big eyes and raised eyebrows. He then held his index finger over his lips. She got the message.

* * *

Sullen would be the best word to describe the cloud trapped

inside that Cessna 208 Caravan Float Plane cruising at just under 300 km/h ten thousand feet above Pennsylvania that night. Neither Allison Fulbright nor Maximilian Sipos had much at all to say—at least not to each other. Both had sunk deep into their own world of thought.

Finally, Allison spoke.

"Max. Are you awake?"

He had been sitting with his head back.

"I'm awake," he said. "Just resting my eyes."

"Check your settings," Allison said. "Be sure your headset is switched to *privacy*."

"It is," he said after visually inspecting the jack.

"What do your friends, the bankers, what do they have in mind for the locks?" she asked. "It's safe to say that there'll be no swift recovery for the U.S. without the ability to ship iron ore. And that's where they are. No iron ore, no steel production. What are they going to do? Your banker friends?"

"Hard to say," he said after taking a few moments to weigh his words. "Pretty safe to say that they're going to start off by waiting. Probably waiting for a long time."

"Why's that?"

"Until the price is right. … You do know what's going to take place here in the States. Right?"

"It's going to be a difficult period of time," Allison said.

"*Much* more than difficult," Maximilian replied with a slight chuckle in his voice. "No steel production means a 1930s style depression. We'll—*they* will—be able to buy up businesses, and U.S. patents, and rights to manufacture, for virtually nothing."

Allison caught the Freudian slip, and she smiled.

* * *

It took the four of them, Jack, Buddy, Red and Robby, less than a minute to get packed up and to leave the room. And, one minute later, Red was downstairs holding the door open for Jack and his *baby*.

The next morning, after a big breakfast, and after they had returned to their room, Jack explained to his two boys that their young friend, little Billy Christopher, didn't make it. Red and Robby burst into tears. … And Buddy, it was almost as though he understood Jack's devastating words, and Buddy cried.

For the longest time that morning the mood among the Handlers was thick and sad. Though they weren't discussing it, both of the boys blamed themselves for the loss of their friend, Billy. "What could we have done differently," they wondered, "so that Billy could have done better and lived? Why did he have to die?"

Just then Jack's phone rang.

"Kate, where are you?" Jack excitedly asked.

"At the front desk," she said. "I finally found you."

"And just at the right time," Jack said. "Get up here now. I've got two … three kids who are very eager to see you."

Both Red and Robby had heard the exchange, and their countenance lit up like a ray of sunshine as they wiped away their tears.

* * *

"Who's going to rebuild the locks?" Allison asked Maximilian as they were preparing to land after the second leg of their journey. "Any ideas about that? Someone's got to sink the investment in it. It will have to be done ASAP. Is that not true?"

"It'll have to be done, alright. But what's your president going to do? He can only print so much money. Especially after the dollar ceases to be the world standard. When that happens, he loses the ability to indiscriminately run his presses at the Federal Reserve."

"So," she said, "you didn't exactly answer my question. "Who's going to build the new lock assembly? Will it be called the 'Maximilian Locks'? … Or, since it's going to be an *international* project, might you call it the 'Sipos Seaway'?"

He laughed out loud at her last question, but did not otherwise respond—at least not immediately. Finally, after nearly a minute, he said, "I think maybe we'll call it the 'John Galt Canal.' What do you think of that?"

He then switched his headset to *passive noise reduction*, and again laid his head back. But his smile remained.

Allison thought about what he had just said. The deeper his words sunk in, the more she realized that they didn't make any sense to her.

"Who the hell is *John Galt*? Anyway." She asked herself. She shot a sharp glare in his direction, but it missed.

* * *

Legend Presents Some of His Thoughts on Great Lakes Erosion

First of all, I want to thank Michael for letting me include these notes at the end of his book. He doesn't like to get engaged in controversy, so it was not easy to convince him to let me state my case.

My concern is not that homes, streets and other property is being damaged, my gripe is that all my fishing spots are getting messed up. And none of it is necessary. When the powers that be decided to raise the level of the Great Lakes in order to pad their bottom line on the cheap, they screwed up the whole ecosystem of the Great Lakes area. By raising the water level of the Great Lakes, they've not only changed the very nature of the Great Lakes themselves, but they've effectively built "water dams" across the rivers downstream from the inland lakes, because they all eventually drain into a Great Lake. This careless act dramatically changes inland lakes as well as the big ones. To think otherwise is to believe it is possible to set up a designated defecation section in a swimming pool.

I contend that they had no right to tamper with a whole ecosystem simply so that they can cheaply float larger and fuller vessels from Duluth to points south and east.

The facts remain: Lake Superior starts out six hundred feet higher than the Atlantic Ocean, and each of the other Great Lakes, to one degree or another, come in lower than Lake Superior. The only thing that prevents Lake Superior from assuming the same level as Lakes Huron, Michigan and Erie are the locks at Sault Ste. Marie. Like all locks, the Sault (Soo) Locks are nothing more than an adjustable set of dams holding back water. In the case of the Soo Locks, it constrains the flow of twenty-one feet of water—remove it, as did the "bad guys" in Michael's book, and Lake Superior would immediately drop considerably. Then take out the Welland Canal Locks east of Lake Erie, and those lakes would drop a tremendous amount—Lake Superior possibly as much as thirty feet.

And then open the locks east of Lake Ontario and it would bring all five of the lakes down to their natural levels.

All I'm saying here is that water levels in the Great Lakes are entirely arbitrary. Absolutely nothing about these levels can possibly be dictated by rainfall for a time period lasting longer than a week. Any argument to the contrary regarding this fact is either totally dishonest or just stupid (pardon my use of that word, Michael prefers *ignorant*).

Now, please understand that I'm not advocating that anyone revert to TNT or RDX (as was the case in Michael's book). But it seems to me that for the powers that be to increase the levels of the lakes simply to avoid the cost of dredging is an unconscionably greedy and callous thing to do. And that is exactly what they've done. All they would have to do to return to previous levels would be to adjust the locks slightly.

The current administration obviously sees the problem and has already agreed to fund the new lock at Sault Ste. Marie. That having been decided, the US Army Corps of Engineers, in cooperation with their counterparts in Canada, should immediately drop the water levels by adjusting the various locks (as outlined above), and then set about dredging the channel in order to accommodate the larger ore carriers. It is just wrong for those responsible to play God with the Great Lakes ecosystem for their own profits.

As an interesting aside here, if the Poe Lock were to be destroyed (as was portrayed in Michael's book), it's quite possible that the rapid rush of twenty-two feet of Lake Superior water would do a large part of the necessary dredging simply by moving the buildup downstream all the way to Lake Huron. As an alternative method, both the upper and lower gates of Poe Lock could be opened for two whole days. … Just saying, if they don't want to spend the money, that would be another way to "dredge" it. But what do I know—I'm just a fisherman.

I was just amazed to learn from scientists that they could demonstrate how minimal the impact of a remedy would be on worldwide ocean levels. For instance, if all of the Great Lakes were allowed to go back to pre-tampering levels (that is, if all five Great Lakes were lowered thirty-six inches, back to levels experienced before 2010), it would raise the level of the Atlantic Ocean less than half the thickness of a potato chip. That is to say, ocean levels would not rise in any significant way (the actual change in the level of the ocean would be .02427th of an inch. Rounded off—two one-hundredths of an inch!).

Again, Michael, I want to thank you for allowing me the use of this podium from which to state my argument; and for giving me your permission to include with this note a copy of the proposed class-action document drafted by the fictitious law firm of Crighton, Crighton and Holmes, Attorneys at Law:

Press Release—Notice of Class Action

What this note is designed to do is to serve not so much as a warning of the plight about which you might already be aware, but to inform you that you do have a solid and reliable recourse. What this class action case maintains is that you are not battling Mother Nature. We contend the evidence shows that because of the vociferous greed of some very wealthy businessmen, and of their even more greedy investors, necessary funding was blocked, causing the USACE to neglect their duty to properly maintain the Great Lakes locks and dams. We believe we can definitively show that the USACE are the ones responsible for the destruction of hundreds of private and public beaches, of hundreds if not thousands of homes, of dozen of streets and roads, along the shores all of the Great Lakes, and their callous actions threaten to decimate thousands of more homes. Following is the history surrounding this problem—how we hold that this problem began, and why it persists:

1)   Back in 1986 preliminary plans and authorization were made to build a new "Super Lock" where the dormant Davis and Sabin Locks lay. Three of the arguments proposed prompting the project were:

A—The Poe Lock (the only lock large enough to handle the newer one-thousand foot ore carriers) occasionally has to be closed for repairs. Usually those repairs can be made when the locks are closed for the winter. But, were the lock to go down between March 25 and January 15, it would basically shut down the nation's ability to produce steel, thus creating a national security emergency. The United States Department of Homeland Security estimated that a six-month closure to the Poe Lock during shipping season could cost the U.S. $1.1 trillion and the loss of over 10 million jobs. A new Super Lock would prevent that loss.

B—A second larger lock would streamline navigation, and thereby encourage the growth of the Great Lakes shipping industry.

C—It was estimated that the new lock would directly produce over 1000 new jobs.

2)   The Regan Administration, who approved the construction of the Super Lock in 1986, left the design and implementation of the new lock in the hands of the USACE. Those planning the Upper Peninsula project believed that the new lock would be constructed in the imminent future. However, the project was not formally funded at that time, and it was even further stalled by subsequent administrations. Therefore, we contend, necessary maintenance efforts on the existing locks and the downstream channel (such as dredging) were not performed in a timely fashion. This meant that the channel east and south of the existing locks grew more and more shallow due to the buildup of normal-use debris carried downstream by the swift flow of water through the bottom gate. Unfortunately, due to this procrastination, necessary regular maintenance was inap-

propriately postponed in anticipation of the construction of the new lock. The reasoning: We contend that it was determined that since the construction of a new lock would require massive dredging, significant savings could be achieved by combining the projects—regular maintenance and the construction of the new lock. Unfortunately, the project was not funded for the next thirty years. It was not until current leadership pushed the project forward in 2019 that monies were actually allocated. During that time regular maintenance was not performed in a timely manner. And, we contend, still it has not.

3) That brings us to the present day disaster. Some time ago (about three years) it was brought to our attention here at Crighton, Crighton and Holmes that thousands of property owners along Lake Superior, and the other Great Lakes, were currently suffering (or were about to suffer) great loss due to erosion caused by the incursion of the lakes. Many of these property owners contacted Crighton, Crighton and Holmes, and asked us if there was a legitimate/natural reason for their problem, or if it has been brought about by intentional or careless behavior associated with the operation of the Great Lakes shipping industry. And, if anything such as this could be demonstrated.

Furthermore, if culpability can be determined and attached to a third party (such as USACE), could it be remedied? After over one year of research, we determined that the problem was a direct result of negligent management of regular maintenance of the locks by the USACE; that their failure to dredge the channel on a regular/timely basis (because it was causing the channel to lose depth) threatened to force Great Lakes shipping companies to limit the amount of iron ore they would be permitted to transport. And, to compensate for their failure to dredge, they opted to raise the level of the Great Lakes by regulating the height of the dams used to control the flow of bypass water at the fifteen locks from Sault Ste. Marie, along the Saint Lawrence Seaway through the eastern part of the U.S. and Canada, all the way to the Atlantic Ocean.

We found that the effort to raise the water level in Sault Ste. Marie could not be accomplished simply by raising the level of Lake Superior, because over half of the shipping problem related to shallow channel depth downstream from the lower gates of the Soo Locks. To solve the whole dredging issue, the flow of water throughout the Great Lakes had to be raised as well. That is why we have seen the levels raised in Lakes Huron, Michigan, Erie and Ontario. All of the Great Lakes are up two to three feet within the last five years, while the Atlantic Ocean level has not measurably changed during that same time cycle. It was at that point that we filed court documents stipulating our demands that the USACE immediately cease and desist their harmful activities that has caused the waters of the Great Lakes to rise, and that the USACE restore and make whole all losses suffered by the undersigned property owners and municipalities as a result of its harmful actions. We must convince the USACE that we are totally convinced that they must, to this end, immediately take action, and to immediately exert maximum influence upon the International Lake Superior Board of Control.

(The views expressed above (in Ted Klanoski's "Thoughts") are not necessarily the views of the author or publisher of this book.)

Check out the U.P. Reader

In my opinion, there is no more intriguing place on planet earth than Michigan's Upper Peninsula. From its unique physical attributes to its amazingly diverse, tough-spirited population, the UP provides the perfect backdrop for the adventures of Jack, Kate, Red, Robby and Henry. If you would like to learn more about the UP, Check out the *U.P. Reader.* This is a collection of writings from the Upper Peninsula Publishers and Authors Association. Writer, Photographer and Videographer, Mikel Classen, is the managing editor for this fine publication (http://upreader.org).

* * *

Cast of Main Characters in the "Getting to Know Jack" Series

(Characters are listed in a quasi-chronological order.)

This book, *Sault,* is the fourteenth book in the Jack Handler Saga, and the seventh (and last) book in the second Jack Handler series—*Jack's Justice. Ghosts of Cherry Street—and the Cumberbatch Oubliette, Assault on Sugar Island, Dog Fight, Murder at Whitefish Point, Superior Shoal and From Deadwood to Deep State* were the earlier books in this series.

While many of the characters encountered in this book have already made appearances in one or more of the previous Jack Handler books, if you want a deeper understanding how a character thinks, you can refer to *The Cast* to answer additional backstory questions.

Main characters include:

Jack Handler:

Jack is a good man, in his way. While it is true that he occasionally kills people, it can be argued that most (if not all) of his targets needed killing. Occasionally a somewhat sympathetic figure comes between Jack and his goal. When that happens, Jack's goal comes first. I think the word that best sums up Jack's persona might be "expeditor." He is outcome driven—he makes things turn out the way he wants them to turn out.

For instance, if you were a single mom and a bully were stealing your kid's lunch money, you could send "Uncle Jack" to school with little Billy. Uncle Jack would have a "talk" with the teachers and the principal. With Jack's help, the problem would be solved. But I would not recommend that you ask him how he accomplished it. You might not like what he tells you—if he even responds.

Jack is faithful to his friends and a great father to his daughter. He is also a dangerous and tenacious adversary when situations require it.

Jack Handler began his career as a law enforcement officer. He married a beautiful woman (Beth) of Greek descent while working as a police officer in Chicago. She was a concert violinist and the love of his life. If you were to ask Jack about it, he would quickly tell you he married above himself. So, when bullets intended for him killed her, he admittedly grew bitter. Kate, their daughter, was just learning to walk when her mother was gunned down.

As a single father, Jack soon found that he needed to make more money than his job as a police officer paid. So he went back to college and obtained a degree in criminal justice. Soon he was promoted to the level of sergeant in the Chicago Police Homicide Division.

With the help of a friend, he then discovered that there was much more money to be earned in the private sector. At first he began moonlighting on private security jobs. Immediate success led him to take an early retirement and obtain his private investigator license.

Because of his special talents (obtained as a former army ranger) and his intense dedication to problem solving, Jack's services became highly sought after. While he did take on some of the more sketchy clients, he never accepted a project simply on the basis of financial gain—he always sought out the moral high ground. Unfortunately, sometimes that moral high ground morphed into quicksand.

Jack is now pushing sixty (from the downward side) and he has all the physical ailments common to a man of that age. While it is true that he remains in amazing physical condition, of late he has begun to sense his limitations.

His biggest concern recently has been an impending IRS audit. While he isn't totally confident that it will turn out okay, he remains optimistic.

His problems stem from the purchase of half-interest in a bar in Chicago two decades earlier. His partner was one of his oldest and most trusted friends—Conrad (Connie) O'Donnell.

The principal reason he considered the investment in the first place was to create a cover for his private security business.

Many, if not most, of his clients insisted on paying him in cash or with some other untraceable commodity. At first he tried getting rid of the cash by paying all of his bills with it. But even though he meticulously avoided credit cards and checks, the cash continued to accumulate.

It wasn't that he was in any sense averse to paying his fair share of taxes. The problem was that if he did deposit the cash into a checking account, and subsequently included it in his filings, he would then at some point be required to explain where it had come from.

He needed an acceptable method of laundering, and his buddy's bar seemed perfect.

But it did not work out exactly as planned. Four years ago the IRS decided to audit the bar, which consequently exposed his records to scrutiny.

Jack consulted with one of his old customers, a disbarred attorney/CPA, to see if this shady character could get the books straightened out enough for Jack to survive the audit and avoid federal prison.

The accountant knew exactly how Jack earned his money and that the sale of a few bottles of Jack Daniels had little to do with it.

Even though his business partner and the CPA talked a good game about legitimacy, Jack still agonized when thoughts of the audit stormed through his mind. This problem was further complicated when Conrad was murdered in what was thought a botched robbery. Connie's lazy son, Conrad Jr., inherited his father's share of the bar.

A year earlier Jack had been convicted and sentenced for attacking a veteran detective, Calvin Brandt. The day that his conviction was overturned, an attempt was made on his life inside a federal prison camp (*Assualt on Sugar Island*). He believed at the time, and still does, that Calvin Brandt had been responsible for contracting the Aryan Alliance to carry out the hit.

Fortunately for Jack, Chuchip (Henry) Kalyesveh a Native American of the Hopi tribe, who was also an inmate at the prison camp, came to his rescue.

Kate Handler:

Kate, Jack's daughter and a New York homicide detective, is introduced early and appears often in this series. Kate is beautiful. She has her mother's olive complexion and green eyes. Her trim five-foot-eight frame, with her long auburn hair falling nicely on her broad shoulders, would seem more at home on the runway than in an interrogation room. But Kate is a seasoned New York homicide detective. In fact, she is thought by many to be on the fast track to the top—thanks, in part, to the unwavering support of her soon-to-retire boss, Captain Spencer.

Of course, her career was not hindered by her background in law. Graduating Summa Cum Laude from Notre Dame at the age of twenty-one, she went on to Notre Dame Law School. She passed the Illinois Bar Exam immediately upon receiving her JD, and accepted a position at one of Chicago's most prestigious criminal law firms. While her future looked bright as a courtroom attorney, she hated defending "sleazebags."

One Saturday morning she called her father and invited him to meet her at what she knew to be the coffee house he most fancied. It was there, over a couple espressos, that she asked him what he thought about her taking a position with the New York Police Department. She was shocked when he immediately gave his blessing. "Kitty," he said, "you're a smart girl. I totally trust your judgment. You have to go where your heart leads. Just promise me one thing. Guarantee me that you will put me up whenever I want to visit. After all, you are my favorite daughter."

To this Kate replied with a chuckle, "Dad, I'm your only daughter. And you will always be welcome."

In *Murder on Sugar Island (Sugar)*, Jack and Kate team up to solve the murder of Alex Garos, Jack's brother-in-law. This book takes place on Sugar Island, which is located in the northern part of Michigan's Upper Peninsula (just east of Sault Ste. Marie, MI).

Because Kate was Garos's only blood relative living in the United States, he named her in his will to inherit all of his estate. This included one of the most prestigious pieces of real estate on the island—the Sugar Island Resort.

Reg:

In *Jack and the New York Death Mask (Death Mask)*, Jack is recruited by his best friend, Reg (Reginald Black), to do a job without either man having any knowledge as to what that job might entail. Jack, out of loyalty to his friend, accepted the offer. The contract was ostensibly to assassinate a sitting president. However, instead of assisting the plot, Jack and Reg worked to thwart it. Most of this story takes place in New York City, but there are scenes in DC, Chicago, and Upstate New York. Reg is frequently mentioned throughout the series, as are Pam Black and Allison Fulbright. Pam Black is Reg's wife (he was shot at the end of *Death Mask*), and Allison is a former first lady. It was Allison who contracted Reg and Jack to assassinate the sitting president.

Allison:

Allison is a former first lady (with presidential aspirations of her own), and Jack's primary antagonist throughout the series. Usually she fears him enough not to do him or his family physical harm, but she and Jack are not friends. She seems to poke her nose into Jack's business just enough to be a major annoyance.

On a few occasions, however, Allison's anger at Jack reaches a boiling point, and she strikes out against him. To this date, she has been unsuccessful.

Over a year ago Allison suffered a severely debilitating stroke, so her current activities have been dramatically limited, a situation which has provided Jack a bit of a reprieve in his having to worry about what she might be up to vis-à-vis his well-being.

Roger Minsk:

Roger is a member of the Secret Service, and a very good friend to Jack. Roger is also friendly with Bob Fulbright, Allison's husband, and a former president.

Red:

This main character is introduced in *Sugar*. Red is a redheaded fourteen-year-old boy who, besides being orphaned, cannot speak. It turned out that Red was actually the love child of Alex (Jack's brother-in-law) and his office manager. So, Alex not only leaves his Sugar Island resort to Kate, he also leaves his Sugar Island son for her to care for.

Red has a number of outstanding characteristics, first and foremost among them, his innate ability to take care of himself in all situations. When his mother and her husband were killed in a fire, Red chose to live on his own instead of submitting to placement in foster care.

During the warmer months, he lived in a hut he had pieced together from parts of abandoned homes, barns, and cottages, and he worked at Garos's resort on Sugar Island. In the winter, he would take up residence in empty fishing cottages along the river.

Red's second outstanding characteristic is his loyalty. When put to the test, Red would rather sacrifice his life than see his friends hurt. In *Sugar*, Red works together with Jack and Kate to solve the mystery behind the killing of Jack's brother-in-law (and Red's biological father), Alex Garos.

The third thing about Red that makes him stand out is his inability to speak. As the result of a traumatic event in his life, his voice box was damaged, resulting in his disability. Before Jack and Kate entered his life, Red communicated only through an improvised sign system and various grunts.

When Kate introduced him to a cell phone and texting, Red's life changed dramatically.

Robby:

Robby is Red's best friend. When his parents are murdered, Robby moves into the Handler home and becomes a "brother" to Red. Robby and Red are now virtually inseparable.

Buddy:

Buddy is Red's golden retriever.

Bill Green:

One other character of significance introduced in *Sugar* is Bill Green, the knowledgeable police officer who first appears in Joey's coffee shop. He also assumes a major role in subsequent books of the series, after he becomes sheriff of Chippewa County.

Captain Spencer:

Captain Spencer is Kate's boss in New York. The captain has been planning his retirement for a long time, but has not yet been able to pull the trigger. Kate is his protégée, and he almost seems to fear leaving the department until her career is fully developed.

Paul Martin and Jill Talbot:

Two new characters do emerge in *Sugar Island Girl, Missing in Paris (Missing)*. They are Paul Martin and Jill Talbot. They do not appear in subsequent stories.

Legend:

Legend is one of the main characters in the sixth book of the series, *Wealthy Street Murders (Wealthy)*. In this story, Jack and

Kate work with Red, Robby, and Legend to solve a series of murders. Wrapped up in a rug and left for dead at the end of *Wealthy*, with Buddy's help he lives to play an important role in *Ghosts*.

Mrs. Fletcher:

Mrs. Fletcher, one of the caretakers at Kate's resort on Sugar Island, progressively plays a more prominent role as an occasional care-provider for the two boys. And, of course, she becomes embroiled in the intrigue.

Unfortunately, Fletcher and her husband are murdered in an earlier segment of this series: *Dogfight*.

Sheriff Griffen:

The sheriff first appears in *Murders in Strangmoor Bog (Strangmoor)*. He is sheriff of Schoolcraft County, which includes Strangmoor Bog, and Seney Wildlife Preserve.

Angel and her mother Millie:

In *Strangmoor*, the seventh and last book in the "Getting to know Jack" series, two new main characters are introduced: Angel and Millie Star.

Angel, a precocious fun-loving redhead (with a penchant for quick thinking and the use of big words), immediately melts the hearts of Red and Robby and becomes an integral part of the Handler saga. In *Deadwood*, everything changed for Millie and Angel.

Lindsay Hildebrandt and Calvin Brandt:

These two significant new characters are introduced in *Ghosts of Cherry Street (and the Cumberbatch Oubliette)*. Lindsay, a rookie detective in the Grand Rapids Police Department, quickly becomes a special person in Jack's life. If you were to ask her if she is dating Jack, Lindsay (who is about two decades younger than Jack) would immediately inform you that people their age don't *date*. But she does admit that they are good friends and occasionally see each other socially.

They have in common the fact that they both lost their spouses in a violent fashion. Lindsay's husband, also a Grand Rapids detective, was shot and killed several years earlier. This crime has not yet been solved.

Calvin Brandt, a veteran Grand Rapids detective, does not get along with anyone. And that is especially true of Jack Handler. Jack would be the first to admit that he was not an innocent party with regard to this ongoing conflict.

Chuchip Kalyesveh:

Chuchip generally goes by the name of Henry because he has found most people butcher his Native American first name.

Jack first met Henry in a federal prison camp where both were serving time. They became good friends when Henry saved Jack's life by beating up four other inmates who had been contracted to kill him. Jack says he has never met another man as physically imposing as his friend Henry.

Now that both are free men, Henry works for Jack at the Sugar Island Resort. And, sometimes, he partners with Jack (unofficially, of course) to help out with some of his tougher private security cases. And, of course, he has absorbed more than a couple rounds intended for Jack. Expect to learn more about Henry as subsequent Jack Handler books roll off the press.

Emma:

Emma (Legs) is a very attractive thirty-something-ish contract killer. Prior to this book, Emma makes her first powerful appearance in *Dogfight*. Expect to see her again.

* * *

Here are the Amazon links to my previous books in the Jack Handler Saga:

Getting to Know Jack Series

Jack and the New York Death Mask: http://amzn.to/MVpAEd

Murder on Sugar Island: http://amzn.to/1u66DBG

Superior Peril: http://amzn.to/LAQnEU

Superior Intrigue: http://amzn.to/1jvjNSi

Sugar Island Girl Missing in Paris: http://amzn.to/1g5c66e

Wealthy Street Murders: http://amzn.to/1mb6NQy

Murders in Strangmoor Bog: http://amzn.to/1IEUPxX

Jack's Justice Series

Ghosts of Cherry Street: http://amzn.to/2n3lrRf

Assault on Sugar Island: http://amzn.to/2n3vcyL

Dogfight: http://amzn.to/2F7OkoM

Murder at Whitefish Point: http://amzn.to/2CxlAmC

Super Shoal: https://amzn.to/2Vd6jCP

Deadwood to Deep State: https://amzn.to/3bSjwba

Sault   (TBD)

Jack Unleashed (Upcoming Series)
To China with Love (Late 2020)